PRISONER 441

By

Geoff Leather

This novel is entirely a work of fiction

The names, characters and incidents portrayed in it are the work of the author's imagination. Any resemblance to actual persons, living or dead, events or localities is entirely coincidental.

A catalogue copy of this book is available from the British Library

ISBN:978-1-9163494-2-1

The criminal mind is challenging. The lessons from history are rarely learned. I love the combination of them.

I grew up in Devon and went on to University in Cardiff and Bristol College of Law. I have a Law degree and a Diploma in Forensic Science and Profiling.

Academically, Criminal Law is a fascinating subject, but its practice never appealed to me, although I spent many an hour listening avidly to my colleagues in that field when I was a practicing lawyer. Some of those revelations appear now and again when I am writing.

Geoff Leather 2020

PRISONER 441

Chapter 1

Belmarsh Prison South East London

The heavy glass wood framed door swung open to the sound of the buzzer. Dr Solomon Isaacs took one step forward and passed through. He hesitated uncertain how he was meant to feel. He shifted his feet and looked back as the door closed and up at the coat of arms above the words H M Belmarsh Prison with the morning sun glinting of the freshly painted lettering. To his right the smell of mown grass lingered in the air. To his left through the ground floor window of the purple brick pentagon tower he saw the library warden tip his forehead in what looked to Solomon like a gesture of good luck. He smiled weakly back. Gone was the deep brown hair that once graced his head, now all that was left under his hat was a shiny top surrounded by carefully manicured fine grey hair. His brown, almost black, eyes were still as bright as the day he started his sentence belying the aging skin around them. He took a

1

deep breath of the first moments of his freedom and started to walk towards the carpark and then onto the main road that led past the Crown Court at Woolwich.

Solomon had been one of the early Category A prisoners transferred when the prison opened in April 1991. It had been life with a recommendation of a minimum of thirty-five without remission. There was nobody there to welcome him. He didn't expect anyone. He had had only one visitor for the last ten years but that was his choice. As far as the prison staff and governor were concerned, Solomon Isaacs' was the model prisoner. Intelligent, very intelligent, compliant, co-operating and never caused any trouble. In fact, he had tended those unable to cope with incarceration and through an understanding of the human condition guide them back to living for another day. He treated infections with simple organic remedies, surprising the medics in the hospital wing. They all said it was a sad day as he reached the term of his term.

The warden needn't have been so generous as Solomon was not exactly without resources but now waiting by the bus stop fingering his transport pass given by the warden together with one hundred and fifty pounds that he had taken from his wallet, Solomon smiled to himself.

He was aware of the tall man in a long black raincoat who had followed him from the carpark, watching. Solomon would recognise this face again. He had learned all those years ago as a persecuted Jew in Nazi Germany to notice everything and be careful, very careful. The tall man was oblivious to Solomon's observation.

Solomon was clutching his only possession, his shabby leather case.

No-one knew anything about 'Stealing the Staircase to Heaven'. To them it was his favourite book when working in the prison library. He read it over and over again. Whenever he was asked about its fascination, he merely commented that even though it was not well written or by a well-known author, it soothed his nerves and took his imagination away from Belmarsh. What no-one could possibly have known was that the simple story with its simple words became a work of code. Each letter, each word, each chapter, the page number, Solomon Isaacs' had translated so that he alone had memorised everything and now he had his life story tucked under his arm for the world to read for better or for worse.

Chapter 2

Jonny Wightman left school as soon as he could. He wanted to be a newspaperman. From an early age he'd read avidly devouring stories his contemporaries couldn't be bothered with, as they ran out of the classroom as soon as they could, chasing each other aimlessly around the playground. His teachers implored him to stay on at school. Mrs Richards, the English teacher, had told him he could enter any University he wanted to. 'You don't get straight 'As' by being an idiot, Jonny,' she implored. Jonny had made up his mind, he wanted to leave school now. Clearly, she wasn't going to change his mind so finally, she told him a friend of hers could take him under his wing and teach him the trade.

It was the 31 August 1956 when Jonny entered the offices of the Northfield Times. He was greeted by Rosa. She was seated behind a shiny red Remington typewriter and stood grinning at him as she held out her hand.

'Welcome, Mr. Wightman."

Jonny hesitated. He'd never been addressed as 'Mister' before. It sounded grand. He stretched over the desk and took her hand.

'He's waiting in his office', she said pointing to the door to her left. 'Always keeps it shut. Hiding most of the time, from me!' She laughed.

Jonny knocked and entered. Sam Thomas surveyed this young lad. Tall, still a bit thin but time would take care of that. He had an air of determination hidden behind the youthful face that had hardly needed a razor.

'Hear you're a bright lad, Jonny. Gloria, Mrs Richards to you, told me she couldn't persuade you to stay on and go to College. Well, stay close to me and we'll see what we can make of you, my lad.' He said a little condescendingly.

Jonny smiled not quite knowing how to respond, finally he said, 'I'm here to learn, Mr. Thomas, but I'll do anything.'

'Good,' said Sam, 'because you'll be learning to make good tea and coffee. So, you're the official teaboy from now on and the most important job after that is the waste paper bins, nothing goes out of here that is legible, apart from The Times.' Sam laughed again at his own joke. 'Understood, can't have people reading the news out of our dustbins.'

Jonny had thought he could learn more in the years others spent at college or university. He was now beginning to wonder if he had been a little hasty.

'Oh, by the way, that's your desk. You're to sit in with me, listen and hopefully learn,' quipped Sam again.

In the cramped space of the Northfield Times offices, he had Sam Thomas to work off. Sam had been an old newspaper hack for more years than he wanted to remember. He was the archetypal late forties chain smoking local know all. Even the police bobbies needed his ear when investigations into some minor misdemeanour were giving their station boss grief.

Jonny shadowed Sam gaining in confidence that one day he would have his piece on the front page for his mum and dad to tell their friends 'That's our Jonny, you know'. Proudly.

That break came unexpectedly, as these things do, a year and a half later when Sam was suffering from a bout of influenza. Jonny was sitting behind Sam's large oak desk which was normally covered with cigarette ash, papers, hand written notes and stained tea cups. Today, the picture of Sam's organised chaos had gone and the desk was clear and clean.

No one was manning the front desk when Mrs Osborne from 16 Florence Grove walked in. She was shaking and Jonny needed her to calm down. Jonny by then made the best tea in Northfield and handed her a cup. She cradled it in her hands allowing the warmth to penetrate her red woollen gloves. The story that Mrs Osborne told Jonny that morning would propel him to a major newspaper in London within twelve months.

Chapter 3

Northfield Times Southampton 1957

What Mrs Osborne of 16 Florence Grove told Jonny Wightman was unbelievable. He listened to her story that rambled all over the place between dabbing tears and sips of tea. Jonny watched her as she heaved her large torso from one cheek to another clearly uncomfortable sitting in Sam's interview chair. Sam had told him that he'd lowered the front legs a little so that people would feel the strain of leaning forward after ten minutes and get to the 'bloody point', as he told Jonny. Mrs Osborne had reached that point now and started talking very quickly.

'It's not that I don't believe you, but we have to be certain from this side of the desk. We don't want to be in trouble in the courts or with an Official Secrets Act violation, now do we Mrs Osborne?' said Jonny with authority gained from listening to Sam Thomas.

'Look, I have these papers.'

Mrs Osborne put down her cup, wrenched the gloves from her hand and dipped into her voluminous faux leather bag. She handed Jonny a large envelope. On the outside was a hand-written note. "Don't go to the police. Suggest a newspaper." She handed them to Jonny. He scanned them, his eyes darting to and fro and up and down. They appeared to contain a detailed copy of an experiment that her son had been subjected to. He put down the first two pages. The next contained what for Mrs Osborne would have been a harrowing description of her son's death. Jonny looked up at Mrs Osborne as he finished reading her son's last minutes on this earth. The rest was his military record then the autopsy report.

'These are all on official Porton Down letter heading,' announced Jonny incredulously. 'How did you come by these? I can't make out the signatures, totally indecipherable,' he said holding several sheets closer to the light.

'They were hand delivered yesterday whilst I was out walking my dog, Domino. He's black and white reminded me of the game we used to play as kids, you know.'

Jonny sat back in Sam's chair and folded his hands behind his head. He looked at Mrs Osborne. She was staring at his desk, there was a sadness all over her face. Jonny could read the pleading, he had to help this poor lady.

'Look, Mrs Osborne, there's a lot here for me to read more carefully and think about, can you leave them with me. I promise, I mean, promise that I will get back to you as soon as I can. I will put them over there. You'll not hear from me for a while. I'm going to have to check some things out. You know, verify.' Jonny pointed over his shoulder to the large green heavy looking object that graced the corner of Sam Thomas' office. 'They'll be safe there.'

'All I want is to know why my son died,' she blinked away some more tears. He was a gallant boy always willing to try his best. This shouldn't have happened to him. Please help me?'

'I will, but in return, you have to promise me not to talk to anyone about this.' He paused, 'save Domino, of course,' said Jonny with a smile. She laughed for the first time that day. He rose and took Mrs Osborne's arm and sympathetically guided her out of the building, promising again that he would do his best for her son.

Jonny sat back with a steaming cup of black coffee laced with too much sugar. He read the papers for a third time. Each time with a different thought in mind. He needed to make many more enquiries and they had to be discrete but effective. Eventually, he'd find the right angle to present the facts without laying his provincial paper open to being a victim of a gagging order or closure through legal or non-legal means.

Chapter 4

Southampton 1957

Jonny picked up the sheaf of copied papers he had obtained from the central library. Written by some chap that he had never heard of, Professor Edwin Carstairs and started to read. After a while he stretched back in his chair, musing, 'This is what I wanted. The thrill of a story, discovery, piecing together, looking beyond what is simple to see in front me. This is the investigative journalism, I want.' He read on.

During the final stages of the Second World War, the top officials, political and military, from the Britain, America and Russian were keen to find and keep the secrets of German technological advances for themselves. The Germans discovered a new nerve gas they called, Tabun, which was toxic to humans but also another gas, Sarin, even more toxic.

Jonny took a sip of his cold coffee and read on.

The Government had established Porton Down during the First World War to provide a proper scientific basis for the British use of chemical warfare, in response to the earlier German gas attacks in 1915. Work started in March 1916, at the time, only a few cottages and farm buildings were scattered on the downs at Porton and Idmiston in the beautiful Wiltshire countryside.

It was originally opened as the Royal Engineers Experimental Station. The laboratory's remit was to conduct research and development into chemical weapons agents such as chlorine, mustard gas and phosgene used in retaliation by the British armed forces in the First World War. By 1918, the original two huts had grown into a large hutted camp with 50 officers and 1,100 other ranks.

'This is fascinating stuff,' Jonny said to himself and read on. He knew nothing of this, even though it was going on just down the A3 road from his hometown.

By 1926, the chemical defence aspects of Air Raid Precautions (ARP) for the civilian population was added to the Station's responsibilities. By 1938, with the worsening political situation in Europe, the Government authorised offensive chemical warfare research and development and the production of stocks of chemical warfare agents by the chemical industry. Britain had ratified the 1925 Geneva Protocol in 1930 with reservations. The Protocol permitted the use of chemical warfare agents only in retaliation.

'So, Porton was and still is at the forefront of producing highly toxic lethal chemical weapons.' He looked at the papers from Mrs Osborne. 'Someone needed to know what they could do to humans.'

'How much of this is in the public domain?' he said out loud.

'What did you say?' shouted his secretary, Rose, from the front office.

'Nothing. Well, actually, how much do you know about chemical weapons?' Rose was now standing in the open doorway looking blank. Jonny continued.

'How much is out there in writing and where do we look.'

As usual when you asked Rose a question the blank stare had actually set the wheels in motion as if you'd put a penny in the slot and pressed the button. Seconds later came the winning result.

'What about one of the scientists at the University. They're meant to know. Aren't they?'

'Great idea. Bless you, Rose. Can you find someone who would be willing to speak to me?'

Two days later, Jonny walked into The Red Lion public house just off Marine Parade near the University. Dr Paul Bartlett PhD MSc, researcher in Chemistry at Southampton University, was already nursing a pint of beer and assumed that the tall lanky young man with fair hair and open shirt walking towards him was Jonny Wightman. He stood and they shook hands.

'I've taken the liberty of getting you a pint. Please sit down, Mr Wightman. Your secretary told me how to recognise you. All she said was tall, very. Well I am here to listen to the questions, so….'

'Information within the public domain about chemical weapons research,' Jonny plunged in.

'Interesting, but why me?'

'I learnt from reading your University profile that your father had been a victim of the first chlorine gas attack by German forces that took place on 2 January 1915.It must have been an awful shock. Sorry.'

'One hundred and forty English officers were killed including my father. It was barbaric. It was that event that had prompted me to become a chemist and antiwar campaigner,' said Dr Bartlett with the force of sadness in his eyes.

Jonny waited until Dr Bartlett recovered.

'I am on your side, Dr Bartlett. What I want is your knowledge and your considered opinion as an expert. 'Sources in the field', as they say. Can we agree that?'

'Yes, of course.'

'OK. What's still going on here in Britain? Do you know or are we into the realms of secrecy?'

'Bit of both, Jonny. Most of it is shrouded in the Official Secrets Act, but there are some published articles within the circles I move academically, mostly about what happened after Germany surrendered in 1945.'

'I've seen a few, but they were in very general terms.'

'Well, you'll know that our experts swarmed over there to confiscate paperwork on biochemical warfare amongst other things. Most of our men came from Porton Down where they were carrying out their own research. What they discovered was that the Nazi's had poured millions of Deutschmarks into nerve gas research and were way ahead of what we were doing here.

'I am sorry to say, but they had human volunteers by the thousands in concentration camps all over Germany and Eastern Europe. That is why they were so advanced. The data from the experiments was meticulously documented and the Germans were able to move forward rapidly. We had no way of obtaining the same data.'

'Well on that count alone, I am grateful,' said Jonny. Dr Bartlett nodded his agreement.

'But what these experts saw, gave them. How should I put it? Food for thought.'

'You mean that they too had to find a way to carry out biological and chemical on humans instead of animals.'

'That's exactly what I mean. You must remember, Jonny, we were in a new world order in the late 1940s and early 1950s. The research and development at Porton Down were aimed at providing Britain with the means to arm itself with a modern nerve agent-based capability and to develop specific means of defence against these agents. In the end, these aims came to nothing on the offensive side because of the decision to abandon any sort of British chemical warfare capability.'

'So, are you telling me that that type of research stopped altogether?'

'Oh no. We knew others were still secretly developing offensive chemical capability, so we concentrated on the defensive side. There were years of difficult work ahead to develop the means of rapid detection and identification, decontamination, and more effective ways of protecting humans against nerve agents that are capable of exerting effects through the skin, the eyes and respiratory tracts.'

Dr Bartlett sat back and took a long sip of his beer. Jonny hesitated then asked the question he really wanted Dr Bartlett to answer.

'Have you ever been able to verify that servicemen have been subjected to live experiments to further the effectiveness of this defensive capability?'

'No, but I am certain it happens. There are a lot of young military personnel stationed at Porton Down and the turnover is large. Some say that up to now some 15,000 servicemen have passed through the establishment.'

'Gracious, that's quite a few potential volunteers. Would they really understand what they are volunteering for, in your opinion, after all, most were National Service conscripts?'

'I doubt it. Think about it. Not even the scientists knew. If they did, why experiment? They can give a scientifically calculated guess, but that's all. There're bound to be risks, but I would be doubtful if they had to give each volunteer a medical prognosis. This is a secret establishment. I doubt, also, if Government Ministers know the whole truth of what goes on.'

'So, would it surprise you, if there were deaths during experiments at Porton?'

'Not in the least. They are dealing with very dangerous and toxic chemicals.'

Chapter 5

Solomon Isaacs' Apartment London

The tall man in a long black raincoat had been replaced by a young woman dressed in a floral skirt that hung beneath her brown woollen coat. He'd seen her linger outside the office equipment megastore looking somewhat forlorn as he worked his way through the list of items he required to be delivered to 22A Belvoir Mansions Belvoir Square Finsbury Park. He knew Mrs Green would be in to take the delivery, she always was in the morning. The Warden had let him speak to her, in privacy, days before his release so he'd not feel so alone out there.

The tail from where she had stationed herself, whoever she was, could have no idea what Solomon was ordering. At the cash desk he pocketed the smaller items and waited for the man to check the next morning delivery date for the larger items. No, he didn't want "set up" advice or extended insurance warranties.

As he set out to walk to his new home, the woman was replaced by two men. This time dressed to blend in this most of the pedestrians walking the street, one with a woollen black hoodie. Solomon was not as nimble as he used to be, but had been used to shrugging off tails in his home town of Munich way back. You never forget those life and death precautions. He entered the

Red Lion public house and ordered a coffee and lingered by the bar.

'See that guy with the hoodie.' The barman looked at the door onto the street. 'He and his mate are following me. I am afraid something bad might happen to me when if I leave through the front door.'

The barman looked at Solomon. He'd seen enough street crime and took the bait. He leaned in closer to Solomon as he took a cloth as if the clean the bar.

'Out the back, across the yard, there's a locked gate. Here's the key, I'll follow after you and relock it. Turn left and follow the path. Good luck, my friend.'

Certain that he'd shaken his tail, Solomon relaxed for the first time in hours. His mind was travelling back and forth trying to figure out who had authorised the tail and why. Nothing was ever what it seemed. He'd been through too much not to be concerned, not about his physical safety even though he was an old man, he wanted some time to be free again, to complete his story, his conscience of guilt.

The key to his basement apartment was just as Mrs Green had explained. He entered 10A Belvoir Mansions in the attached block next to where Mrs Green lived but separated with different entrances.

Two days later unseen by prying eyes, Mrs Green took delivery as agreed of the packages from the megastore. Over the fence dividing the two apartments at the back of Belvoir Mansions, Mrs Green handed them the Solomon.

'What are you going to be up to, Solomon. Not a terrorist, are we? Your lease says no explosive materials,' she said with a big smile.

17

'It's a computer and all the bits. It will keep me quiet for years.'

'Rather you than me. I prefer the television, myself.' Her broad London accent coming to the fore.

Inside, Solomon unpacked the printer and set it on the edge of his desk connecting the cables to his computer. Even though he'd been away from the world for some considerable time, working in the prison library had enabled him to keep pace with developments in computer technology if only how to use the machines, not mend them. His desk overlooked a small park enclosed by black rusting railings with a small gate. He was given a key by his landlady and when the sun was shining or he needed to rest his eyes, he'd wander up the stone steps from the basement flat to sit a while on one of the wooden seats, his eyes taking in a very different world than the one he'd left behind all those years ago. He'd deliberately rented a basement flat. Anything else would be too much of a shock, when he'd been used to a cell with a window out of reach perched high on a wall as company, a basement felt secure for the moment.

This morning was going to be the start. He opened "Stealing the Staircase" and started to type, translating each letter, punctuation mark, number as he'd remembered them and gradually the page formed. After several hours had passed without noticing, Solomon was well into the first part of his story. He sat back and stretched his arms above his head flexing his fingers, staring out of the sitting room window in front of him. Momentarily, a shadow in front silhouetted against the sun hovered and disappeared. Had they found him again and his hideaway? Was it the same man that had followed him from Belmarsh or one of the two he'd lost in the Red Lion? It certainly wasn't the woman. Was he being paranoid? He dismissed the thought, for the moment.

Each morning, as he set his coffee on the side of his desk, he'd looked at the book and then his printed paper stacked by the side of it. Yesterday, the mid-point was reached. A kind of boredom had set in. Whilst he was in Belmarsh, it had been exciting each day as every word and thought was new. There was also the element risk, breaking the rules without being caught. He needed a break, and in any case, it was a dull day outside with the threat of rain in the air.

Well hidden under a slightly too large raincoat, he walked into the post office and bought a roll of brown tape and two large sheets of brown paper and enquired about guaranteed signed delivery. Not satisfied that the manuscript would be in safe hands with the Post Office, he was directed by the kind lady behind the counter with an overpowering voice to the offices of a courier service further down the street.

Clutching his bag with his recent purchases, he exited the post office. The man that was in the adjoining queue abruptly left just as his counter became free and followed Solomon into the street. He knew that whatever Solomon was engaged in, it was something highly confidential that he'd have to report to his boss at Scotland Yard, London's headquarters of the Metropolitan Police Service responsible for policing most of London but for the moment it was "observe only" order.

'OK, keep your eye on the old man. Let me know anything unusual. Jones will join you in rotation. No need to say, but stay out of sight. He maybe old but remember he was once a prodigious brain and has a lot of history. Anything suspicious….'

What was the old man up to? Inspector Vernon Smith tilted back his chair and looked out of the window watching the rain touch the glass and run down in rivulets disappearing beyond the frame, lost in his own thoughts. He needed to see the contents of the parcel. He was sure Solomon Isaacs was too intelligent to use a delivery service for transporting whatever it was in that parcel. He stood and began to realise that his surveillance team had been less than honest about their tracking. Did Solomon Isaacs know someone, somewhere wanted to know what he was doing? Had his early surveillance been too sloppy?

They'd lost him once and it was only by pulling a massive favour that his contact in Belmarsh Prison revealed Solomon' address. They'd glimpsed his computer from a walk past. He'd been sitting there for days after that, but what had he been doing before they re-established contact.

From the time Solomon had ditched his tails, he been working on several strategies and now he had the answer. Once the first draft of the manuscript was complete, he printed it out in full ready for editing by hand. In the meantime, he searched the internet. "Stealing the Staircase to Heaven" had been out of print for years. He wasn't surprised. Who would want to buy a mediocre adventure story like that? He had only one option, but it would cost and take time.

Mrs Wendy Green had grown into quite a friend as time had passed and was only happy to help. Solomon had been very generous with his small gifts of her favourite tipple, a fortified wine named Dubonnet. Not the sort of drink held by most alcohol outlets. She knew lots of people and he knew she'd do her best for him if he ever asked.

'Wendy, I wonder if you can find someone to do me a favour,' he said one early evening as they were chatting in her lounge.

'What is it Solomon? I could do it for you.'

'I have a book.'

'So that's what you've been hiding away from me.'

'Yes. I want you to deliver it to my editor in person in Fleet Street. Could you do that?'

'Yes, of course but why can't you do it? Take the no.41 bus or a taxi. It's that easy.'

'It's not that easy. I don't want anyone to know about the book quite yet. There's a lot of people still alive that may not be altogether happy to read about themselves and my editor has told me to be very careful, hence the subterfuge, Wendy.'

'I'm not going to get into any trouble, Solomon, am I?'

'No, no, of course not. What day do you usually go to the chiropodist, Wednesday, isn't?' Wendy nodded. 'Good, take the taxi as usual but this time take another afterwards. Here I'll pay.' He handed her two twenty-pound notes.

'That's far too much.'

'No, it isn't. The taxi will have to wait for you outside. I will need you to make sure it is given only to this person, no-one else. Not a receptionist. No-one else.' Solomon handed her the details of the recipient. 'I'll give you the package on Wednesday morning, over the fence.'

Solomon returned to the computer and started to scan the pages of "Stealing the Staircase to Heaven" into the computer from the original book he'd taken from Belmarsh. It was a long and laborious job. The assistant in the technical department of the computer megastore, for half an hour's tuition, had taken him through the process of converting the page scans into a printable *word* format. When he'd finished, Solomon wrapped it in brown paper and put it with the one for Wendy on the shelf ready for Wednesday.

**

Police Sargent Warren flashed his badge.

'The old man that just left a parcel for delivery, I need the destination address and recipient.'

The surprised man did as he was told and retrieved the package and swivelled it face the policeman who noted down the details with a surprised look on his face.

'Is that the scheduled time of arrival? Thanks. Forget this, young man. Never happened.'

His boss listened carefully to Sargent Warren with incredulity pervading his face.

Temporarily lost for words, he stuttered. 'Grrrab it when it arrives and bring it to me immediately,' he shouted.

Solomon smiled to himself that evening when Mrs Green arrive home and gave him the receipt that Jonny Wightman had signed and knowing that the second parcel with the typed version of the *Stealing the Staircase to Heaven* would have arrived and, he hoped, would now be the subject of shaking heads and a great deal of embarrassment, somewhere in the police headquarters and give them a reminder that they weren't dealing with an idiot.

He poured her another Dubonnet, as she described her most exciting day in years.

'To us, a great team, cheers.'

Chapter 6

Southampton England 1961

Jonny Wightman now needed someone close to Government who could answer a few more questions. It was now clear to Jonny that the papers Mrs Osborne had brought to him were likely to be authentic.

He'd ring Sam at home, he'd have a few contacts.

'How are you feeling, Sam? Any better?'

'No, not really. Goes on forever, one day, I feel better and get up, then the next, I'm bad again. Anyway, what do you want, Jonny?

'Actually, I need an introduction to one of political contacts, MP or someone close to Westminster.'

'What on earth for, you digging up dirt?'

'No. I need some historical information about Bio-ethics?'

'Bio-ethics. What the hell are you doing, Jonny?'

'Look, Sam, I'll let you know all when I am certain that we have a story. Anyway, can you help me, Sam, or not? I'm just doing some research for an article I think we could use when we are short of news. Something our educated readers might appreciate,' he lied, trying to put Sam's suspicious mind at rest.

'We don't have any educated readers, Jonny, but I admire your sentiment. Speak to our local MP, Roger Gainsforth. He's a dear chap, bit old now but used to be attached to the Director of Public Prosecutions

(DPP) office some years back. Ex- barrister. Hang on.' Jonny waited as he heard Sam rifling through some papers. 'Take down this number and mention me.'

'Thanks, Sam. See you soon. No, sorry, don't want your 'flu in the office. Speak soon.'

Jonny rang Roger Gainsforth and arranged to see him after his weekly surgery for his constituents held at the Civic Centre down the road from Jonny's flat. The MP had typically asked for a list of questions before hand which Jonny had provided.

The day had been a shocker, rain and more rain. By the time Jonny reached the Civic Centre despite it being only a short walk, he was drenched and his umbrella had seen better days having been turned inside out several times by the gusting wind. He shook it out and palmed the excess water from his coat and waited outside the MP's office, watching a straggle of local people coming and going at regular intervals. Some smiling, others shaking their heads in disappointment. Eventually, Roger Gainsforth emerged, carrying his briefcase and coat. It was clear in his face and demeanour that he didn't want any more aggrieved locals pestering him about such trivial matters which they could, with a modicum of sense, solve themselves.

'I'm getting too old for this malarkey. Don't you quote me, Jonny. May I call you, Jonny?'

'I most certainly, Sir.' Jonny would have doffed his cap if he had one.

'Good. Let's get to the Golden Hind over the road. They have quiet little corner and a very good beef pie.'

Jonny followed in Roger Gainsforth's wake as he strode across the road, expecting the cars to make way for his bulk, for he was now a portly white-haired man in his early 60s. Once inside they settled into a booth well clear of the bar and the tobacco smoke that hung in the air swirling as the door opened and shut at the other end of the public house.

'Well, Jonny, you've come to the right chap. Interesting set of questions. I spoke to Sam and he told me about this ambitious young man he was mentoring. Happy to help, but not as an official source, you understand.'

'I don't intend to quote you at all. I just need to understand attitudes and the application of the law in reality and, of course, your expert opinion.' Jonny hesitated and just to emphasize to point, added 'but certainly not to quote.'

Roger and Jonny sat silently as they tucked into the beef pies.

'Your right, Sir, they are good,' said Jonny scooping the last morsel onto his fork.

'OK, let me start at the beginning. You asked about 'Informed Consent'. You may already know that in the past, not all experiments on humans required consent. The subjects were volunteers. You know the phrase, *deemed consent*.'

Jonny nodded.

'What about the law? Didn't it say anything?'

'Not really. To avoid litigation, most physicians usually obtained consent after they had explained the nature of the operation. If I remember correctly the principle was enshrined in English law in the 1830s but I have to check the case law to be certain.'

'Did things change after the gas attacks in the First World War?'

'Yes. The British military, after that war, vowed that such events would not happen again and that they find ways to combat the situation. I was still a barrister in the 1930s and in our London Chambers, we had a man, Sir Norman Gibbs, who was asked by the British Medical Council (BMC) to advise them on the ethics of human experimentation. After you rang me, I looked up some papers I had come across during my time with the DPP. They are in the public domain. Here read this.'

Jonny took the hand-written note and read aloud what Gibbs had said.

I am of the opinion that the consent of a person on whom the experiment is made would afford a complete answer to any claim for damages ....I assume that the nature of the risk would be explained....and that the experiment would be conducted with all due care and all precautions suggested by medical science would be taken....'

Jonny handed the note back to Roger Gainsforth.

'No. you keep it. After this, things got a little bit more difficult. Well, this was fine for the 1930s but after the next war, with all the atrocities and the discovery of new nerve gases.'

'Like Sarin, that the Germans had tested in the concentration camps.'

'Yes. That was one thing but don't forget, Jonny, there was another threat. The one from Russia, the Cold War and nuclear proliferation.'

'So are you telling me that the Nuremberg Code was going to be ignored in the interest of self-preservation of Britain and the rest of the free world.'

'Ignored is too strong a word, Jonny. I'd use the words "economically varied", if you get my drift. The Nuremberg Code is a set of research ethical principles for human experimentation as a result of the trials at the end of the Second World War. On August 20, 1947, the judges delivered their verdict in the "Doctors' Trial" against Karl Brandt and 22 others. These trials focused on doctors involved in the human experiments in concentration camps. No. The aim of the Code was to find a balance, between, on the one side, the right of the individual to choose whatever he or she wanted and, on the other, the need to benefit the human race by pushing the boundaries through experimentation.'

'A good code for barbarians but unnecessary for ordinary physician-scientists,' quipped Jonny with a degree of journalistic scepticism.

'Maybe, Jonny, maybe. But I have an open mind on the subject. The BMC have always been committed to upholding the highest moral and ethical standards, as good as if not better than those recognised internationally.'

'But what about Porton Down, was that establishment committed to the Nuremberg Code?'

'Of course, they were ordered by the Government to adhere to the principles.'

'That's interesting, Sir, because I wonder whether what you said about Informed Consent applies to those in the services, Army, Navy or Air Force in the same way as it would to you or me. I'd worry now with National Service for all fit young men for several years.'

'You may have a point. It is a huge reservoir of potential volunteers.'

'Do you think these young kids in uniform would be able to resist the pressure from senior officers?'

'Possibly not, although our Government made it quite clear publicly, last year, that what you're suggesting would be unacceptable.'

'Did you know that most of the volunteers at Porton Down are conscript servicemen.'

Roger Gainsforth nodded in agreement, so Jonny continued. 'Does that mean, in your opinion, changes in procedures in obtaining Informed Consent, Sir?'

'Jonny, times are difficult internationally. There needs to be an equilibrium between East and West. You must come across it all the time, reading newspapers from all over. I would imagine that sometimes the normal strictures of the Nuremberg Code may become blurred. That's my guess after sixty years of living and observing the human condition when the pressure is on, as it is at the moment, but I have no evidence.'

'When you say 'blurred', are we back to Informed Consent.'

'Yes, I suppose we are.'

'So, what we may see is that volunteers may be told exactly or in general terms what the experiment procedure is, thus complying with the Code but from then on, it was up to the volunteer to ask for information thus shifting the responsibility from scientists and that is a breach of the Code, is it not?'

'Roger Gainsforth MP, nodding said, 'you may believe that, but you cannot expect me to comment, Jonny.'

'I take that as a 'yes', said Jonny smiling.

Chapter 7

Jonny Wightman returned home that night after his meeting with Roger Gainsforth and opened Mrs Osborne's file he'd collected from the office safe. The details of his first meeting with Mrs Osborne and the family background would be added later. He set the typewriter in front of him and started writing.

In early 1953, scientists at the Biochemical Warfare establishment at Porton Down in Wiltshire had been working on a nerve agent called Sarin for some years after they had discovered that the Germans had been developing various nerve agents before and during World War Two.

Leading Able Seaman Osborne, a National Service conscript, together with several other volunteers were given respirators and entered an experiment chamber at 10 am with cloth tied to his forearm impregnated with pure Sarin at a dose over ten times that previously recommended. The experiment was meant to last thirty minutes. After twenty minutes, Osborne had said he felt pretty queer. The observers took him from the chamber and walked him to a bench nearby. He was sweating profusely. Within two minutes he was put in an ambulance complaining that he couldn't hear and then became unconscious. Two injections of atropine sulphate intravenously and intramuscularly were administered. In the medical centre, he was given oxygen but started gasping for breath. By eleven o'clock he was dead.

Mrs Osborne has asked that her son's death be the subject of a full and urgent open enquiry. We, at the Northfield Times, ask whether the Ministry of Defence and the Government to state precisely why it was necessary to use the level of dosage in this experiment, whether he did truly 'volunteer' to take part in the experiment that killed him and were the international terms of the Nuremberg Code complied with and produce evidence in support.

'Sam, surprised to see you. I was just about to ring you. Here, I'll be back soon. Some case in the Magistrates Court about a series of house breaks. Probably drug money wanted. Keeps the readers informed. Whilst I'm gone, Sam, read this. Easy first day, there's tea in the pot. I'll get Rosa to pour some.'

With that, Jonny put his story in front of Sam and closed the door.

'Rosa. Leave him in peace for a while. He's got some reading to do,' as he hesitated by the front door.

'You've given him the Osborne story. What's he going to say, Jonny? It will frighten the life out of him. It did me when I copy typed it for you.'

'Just keep him quiet. OK.'

The revelations published in the Northfield Times propelled Jonny Wightman from provincial obscurity to national recognition as the story was syndicated nationally and then internationally. He was a fearful opponent in the eyes of some and a sought after commodity in eyes of others. Within a year he'd

32

accepted a post in Fleet Street with a national newspaper and said goodbye to Sam. He was 21 years old.

Chapter 8

Jonny had been head of a team of investigative journalists at the "Journal" as it was known in Fleet Street for several years. His motto 'check the facts twice and check again'. As Sam had suspected, the years had filled Jonny out a little. Long gone was the two-piece dark grey suit and tie. For years, he'd dressed in casual trousers and open neck shirt. Winter saw the addition of various monochrome waistcoats. To gain a little age he'd grown a beard when he first joined the Fleet Street mob but now all that was left was a greying moustache and goatee underneath. He thought it made him a little more authoritative especially as his hair was what June called 'heather brindle'.

June shouted through to his office, 'there's a large parcel here for you. The delivery lady will not hand it over until she can ID you personally. I have had it scanned. Paper only. Shall I send her in.'

'No, I will come over.'

Mrs Wendy Green, took out a photo and glanced at it. She nodded her head, looking at Jonny.

'You need to sign here, please, sir.'

Jonny took the pen and signed his more legible signature. Mrs Green, as promised followed Solomon's instructions to the letter, still clinging to the parcel, checked the photocopy signature that Solomon has somehow obtained and again nodded. She handed over the package and left.

'Never seen that before', Jonny echoed the thoughts of his colleagues.

Jonny took the parcel into his office and closed the door. He examined the outside of the parcel band and extracted the address letter from the parcel's outside pocket.

My dear Jonny Wightman,

Please do not share the contents of his parcel with anyone and make sure you lock it away in your safe. I do not trust anyone but you, Jonny. If anyone else has the combination, please reset it for your eyes only. I want you to read what I have written as soon as you can. Maybe you'll know a lot of what I have written already particularly the historical events so please forgive my reiteration of them. I know you will need some time to check the facts and verify what I have written. I know you are the right man to bring my story to everyone's attention. I will contact you again soon, of course allowing you enough time.

Yours truly, 'Solomon Isaacs'

P.S Remember Private Osborne?

Chapter 9

London

Jonny now couldn't help himself, remembering the papers Mrs Osborne had brought him years ago, and locked the door to his office and ripped open the parcel. There on the table was a full typed manuscript, pages of text, the occasional crossing out and handed written additional notes. Did Solomon want him to ghost the book or write it as a memoire. He began to read what was in essence an autobiography.

**

I have always thought of myself as a victim in many ways. First, a Victim of Birth.

I was born into a Jewish family in Munich Germany after the First World War. My father was one of the lucky ones who had survived the horrors of the trenches with only an infected wound from his own sides barbed wire that he ran into whilst his regiment was in retreat. He had been sent home before the Armistice and took several months to recover from the infected wound. In his absence, my mother had had to help sustain the family tailoring business with my grandfather despite his failing health.

The financial chaos that the Versailles Peace Treaty wrought on Germany soon felt itself in my family. It seemed to us that it was impossible to keep pace with monumental inflation, but we managed to survive and start to prosper again.

Our beloved city of Munich saw the birth of the Nazi Party. To begin with it was just another section of our society that was rebelling against central government but then in 1923, an ex-Corporal from the 1914-18 War tried overthrow the Weimar Republic. His name was Adolf Hitler. History has a funny way of turning bad events into even worse events. That failure crippled the Nazi Party and Hitler was arrested and imprisoned. For us, we hoped that everything would settle to normality. It was a vain hope.

It was there in that prison that he wrote his book Mein Kampf, setting out the world as he perceived it should be.

Soloman Isaacs had been right, Jonny already knew a lot of C20th history and the events that he was writing about, but this was different, it was personal.

I have never read Mein Kampf, only extracts trying to understand later what really happened to Germany. It describes the process by which Hitler became anti-semitic and outlines his political ideology and future plans for Germany. What I never knew until I came to England was that the book was edited by Hitler's deputy, Rudolf Hess, who was far better educated than the Corporal. from Austria.

My family heaved a sigh of relief when the Nazi's suffered the 1923 humiliating defeat. My father had succeeded my grandfather when he died in the 1919 the worldwide influenza pandemic. The family tailoring business continued to prosper as a very successful, respected and profitable enterprise. My mother was allowed to return to teaching general science at the local secondary school. We lived well but were always aware that full emancipation for Jews that had begun before 1914 would remain a contentious issue. There were some days when I heard my parents discussing one Jewish family or another who had sold their business and fled Germany for America or elsewhere, and wondered whether we were going to do that one day, but we remained despite the changing in the political landscape.

The profitability of Isaacs Tailoring allowed me to receive the best education available in Munich. I soon began to take an avid interest in science and in particular that branch that was in its infancy, genetics. Soon, I was spending much of my time, when I wasn't helping my father cutting cloth and running errands around Munich's more affluent neighbourhoods, making notes with my head buried in the science section of the central library. What I began to realise is that I, Solomon Isaacs, had a remarkable gift. I didn't need pen and paper, I could photograph the pages in my head and reference them for later use. This was one gift that I was never going to share, but just hone it more and more, pushing each day the boundaries of my capability. Other kids thought I was an oddball. I took no interested in kicking a ball around in the park or chasing after girls.

One day, I told my mother that I was going to become a research scientist and asked her if she could introduce me to someone in the hospital laboratory where I could work in my spare time. My next vacation job was not helping in the business, but dressed in a white laboratory coat. I was sixteen years old. I was introduced to my first real microscope far more powerful that my previous Christmas present from Mum and Dad. I could see cells reproduce themselves. I could see them being manipulated artificially.

I had never had any interest in girls, but to my amazement I kept thinking about the sparkling brown eyes of the older girl who introduced me to the wonderful world under the microscope. Some days during those weeks we would talk together but that would be all. I was a Jew and she was not. I would think of Fraulein Roberta Bron and her long brown hair and beautiful eyes, when I was not buried in some experimental medical book.

It was a forgone conclusion that I would enter university a good year before my contemporaries. In 1933 I celebrated my seventeenth birthday. That year was etched on my mind for two reasons, firstly, I gained my University place and secondly, it was the year that the Nazi Party took power in Germany and again Munich became the Hauptsadt der Bewegung (the Capital of the Movement). Within that first year of power, during at what was later called the Night of the Long Knives, Hitler started to eliminate some of his most powerful rivals, consolidating his supreme power.

More significantly, the first concentration camp was opened just outside Munich at Dachau. Whilst I went about my studies, our family discussions at the supper table were about our future and whether it was still safe to remain in Germany. It was now obvious to all Jews and to us that the political tide had changed dramatically and that we were gradually becoming a sub-class within German society. For the moment, my parents decided to sit it out and wait and see.

The government, or rather, the Nazi party, controlled everything: the news media, police, the armed forces, the judiciary system, communications, travel, all levels of education from kindergarten to universities, all cultural and religious institutions. Political indoctrination started at a very early age and continued by means of the Hitler Youth with the ultimate goal of complete mind control. Children were exhorted in school to denounce even their own parents for derogatory remarks about Hitler or Nazi ideology. My mother was very afraid by now, seeing what was happening to her children at school.

It was behind this façade that I hid myself and worked as hard as I could whilst I could. My general degree in medical science was achieved with the highest marks ever seen at the university. On graduation day, my parents sat in the auditorium near the front and heard the Head of the Medical School say that in all his experience he had never come across a student with such dedication and sharpness of intellect. He went on to say that the Board of Governors of the School had offered me a four-year research grant and he was pleased so say that I had accepted the offer and that my mentor in his first year would be Doctor Josef Mengele, himself a post graduate researcher. He was unable to say what the research would involve but assured his audience that the benefits to the German people could be immense. For once, in this fleeting moment my Jewish birth seemed to be forgotten.

I remember the clapping and cheering echoing throughout the auditorium as I, very self-consciously, walked forward head bowed to accept the university's top achievement award for 1935. I glanced around and saw Roberta Bron standing clapping unreservedly but well hidden in the mass of adoration surrounding my achievement.

In those first few months I felt no fear within the walls of the University, but in the streets of Munich, it was very different. I was secure behind closed doors, but I couldn't ever forget who I was. It was with this feeling that unless I did something, body and soul, I would have failed my mother and father. I suppose that is why the urge to rebel quietly and unnoticed took hold of me in my spare time.

I couldn't just watch the ranks of marching youth with banners waving, eyes fixed straight ahead, keeping time to drumbeat and song. It was an overpowering sense of helplessness.

A group was formed that was motivated by ethical and moral considerations and came from various religious backgrounds. I knew I couldn't wield a gun or make a bomb, but I could write and analyse the situation. Despite my parents' reluctance to support me, in my walk-in cupboard hideaway at home, constructed behind the wardrobe, I planned the content of leaflets for two of my University contemporaries, Hans and Sophie Scholl. From these small beginnings arose White Rose movement that would spark an underground resistance against the Nazi regime that slowly spread throughout Germany. I would later learn that Hans and

Sophie were executed by the regime. I was proud to have known them.

As Hitler's grip on power got stronger and stronger, I soon became aware that my own life's dream was about to end and with it my tenure of research at University. Adolf Hitler was going to see to that, albeit not directly.

Life for me and my family was now changing rapidly. Fear had spread throughout Munich. Hitler's deputy in Munich, Rohm and his army of loyal and sadistic brown shirts controlled the streets. My family and I were forced to acknowledge that we were Jews by having the Star of David visible on our clothes if we ventured outside. Kristallnacht (the Night of Broken Glass) had sent shivers through every Jewish family as synagogues were torched, books burnt and shops looted.

I remember that night. It started like any other night. My mother had lighted the fire and we sat around watching the flames rise up the chimney, flickering golden shadows around the front room. My father stood to draw the curtains when he heard shouting outside in the street. We all crept over, not daring to be seen through the windows. Opposite, our friend, Walter Sliemann braced across the door of his shop, was arguing with one of brown shirts. Two other brown shirts arrived and with their rifle butts clubbed him to the ground. They continued to kick him then one of them raised his gun and shot the defenceless body of Walter Sliemann deliberately aiming at the Jewish Star of David sewn to his waistcoat. The bullet ripped through his body. The shop window was smashed, and they looted the contents. They walked on down the street laughing shouting *"Don't buy from Jews"*. It was the 9 November 1938, decision time for us all. Reports the next day filtering through the Jewish community suggested as many as several hundred were killed trying to protect their businesses and more than 300,000 men were arrested and sent to concentration camps.

Was still possible to obtain emigration permits? Mum and Dad knew the right people, but had we hoped too much and left it too late to escape. I pleaded with Dad to use his influence to get us out of here before it was too late. The next day, Dad went alone to see if Rudolph and Constance Konig could help us.

Jonny bundled up the manuscript to take home later. He felt it was probably safer in his apartment and in any event, he'd have peace and quiet to work out how he was going to deal with Dr Solomon Isaacs. In the meantime, there was this month's edition of the Journal to finalise in the boardroom.

Chapter 10

Munich 1942

Swaddled in woollen blankets and placed in a carefully constructed cot within a large leather suitcase tucked under the bench seat in carriage number three, seat nineteen, Avyar Heidmann remained silent as he slept to the rhythm of the train wheels as they clanked their way over the tracks towards Switzerland. The timetable told Olga Smit that the Swiss border was three hours away. The baby would sleep at least four hours if not more, the doctor promised so long as you give him this liquid with his bottle at the very last minute before travel. She clutched tightly her own travel papers.

The many weeks of waiting for her visa were over and relief was nearly upon her as she gazed at the passing countryside, mesmerized by the simple beauty of the Bavarian mountains as the tracks followed the river through the valleys towards another world that she hoped would be free from chaos. All she'd known recently was fear that someone somewhere in Munich would destroy her life. She had no reason to think this, but nevertheless worse things had happened in her neighbourhood. She was living next door to a Jewish family and helped with babysitting as both parents' work shifts coincided. This could have been regarded by the authorities as being anti-German. She had done everything she could to look after her neighbour's child, little Avyar, but was this act of compassion a risk too far?

Elsie and Gurt Heidmann had lived next door for two years. Elsie had worked at the Bürgerbräukeller which was renamed in 1939, the Löwenbräu. She was a very popular waitress and that had made her feel safe as did the fact that she's worked there since she left school, but suspicion as to her Jewish background was never far from her mind.

It was not so with Gurt as he had lost his job at the Paulaner Brauhaus in Kapuzinerplatz as a foreman and now with his Star of David sewn to the sleeve of his coat, he was demoted to the lowest job available, loading barrels onto wagons for distribution, despite the manager's protestations and reluctant acceptance of orders from the local Nazi office. Under Gurt's placid acceptance of his fate, lay a fierce temper that had got the better of him two days before his and Elsie's arrest.

He had finished a long shift and was walking home along the marshalling yards. This was Liam, a rundown, neglected, shabby, tough, uncompromising, working-class neighbourhood, but he was used to it. The sound of locomotives echoed through the rundown buildings that lined the track. The autumn chill of the wind ruffled his hair, he pulled his scarf higher over his collar as he left the railway shortcut and continued down the road.

A group of youths started chanting racial abuse behind his back as they passed by. He had got used to this, but tonight for some unknown inner reason, he turned and asked them to repeat what they'd said. As cowards do, they ran off as he cursed the whole world for his plight. Gurt knew at that moment when his temper subsided that he made a terrible mistake. He began to relax as the cracked pavements, litter swirling in rotating gusts and dirt slowly gave way to the pristine boulevard where he lived but knew deep down that those kids would seek to teach him a lesson, one that they hoped he would not forget. Moments later he heard the rubber of tyres squealing as the black Mercedes rounded the corner. He tried to outrun the car but it was in vain, two thugs in long leather coats grabbed him and they wrestled him to the ground and hit him with rubber truncheons, out of the corner of his eye he saw the youths watching and smiling.

'Next time, it won't be pleasant, Jew.'

That night at home, Gurt told Elsie what had happened as they sat opposite each other at the kitchen table. She'd washed his face and bandaged his hand.

'The sheer pain of the first rubber truncheon was something like…,' he hesitated trying to find the words that would really describe the feeling, 'like the dentist's drill when it strikes a nerve, but then the pain spread over my entire body.'

Elsie looked at him. She moved her hands across the table and covered his. Elsie had worked the afternoon shift at the Lowenbrau and put little Avyar to bed in his cot. As she said "goodnight" she looked into his little eyes and saw how remarkably similar they were in colour and shape as Gurt's. "You'll be just like your Dad when you grow up my little one", by which time he was asleep. She stared into space knowing that Gurt had crossed the boundary they'd been so careful to avoid. They knew that formal retribution was not now far away, for both of them. Within minutes they were knocking furiously on Olga Smit's door.

'Olga,' they pleaded. 'Please take Avyar and keep him safe,' as they bundled the little baby into her arms.

Next day before dawn they were gone. She was never to see them again and neither was their son.

Elsie and Gurt Heidmann were arrested to be resettled in the East along with thousands of other Jews rounded up as part of forced labour programme. They had already heard the rumours that had circulated before their arrest about the real purpose of the programme. There and then they pledged to each other that come what may, they would both do what it takes to survive the hell that was to befall them for their only child, Avyar.

Both were young, fit and healthy. On the platform in the freezing night air amongst the downtrodden mass of humanity that had emerged from the wagons after their journey East to Auschwitz, they survived the segregation process. The one day at a time silent look passed between them as they were separated and marched into different barrack huts.

**

Olga Smit remembered very little of the journey to Zurich. She was too frightened and stared aimlessly out of the carriage window trying not to think about little Avyar. She took in the occasional station sign, Furstenfeldbruch then Memmingen as the train headed south. Whatever was she to do. She loved the little fellow and longed to hold him tightly to her chest and

47

rock him gently in her arms. It had been sad to leave her home in Munich but there really was no option. Her husband to be, Marian had died in 1938, killed by a runaway car that didn't stop. The driver was never found. Since then she'd remained in their flat. Yes, she'd been comfortably off. His pension and the lump sum she'd received from his estate, his savings and life insurance.

The war had changed everything for her. All she wanted was to run to safety, but she hadn't anticipated doing so with a baby, a Jewish child, not that his faith mattered to Olga. He was a little human being completely unaware of the trauma and torture that was Germany. Her first step was the Austro-German border near the town of Sankt Gallen in Switzerland.

Her mind slipped back to her formative years when she studied textiles at the Institute near Marienplatz station where she'd boarded this train. It seemed like a lifetime ago. She'd never visited Sankt Gallen, but had been wowed by the quality and ingenuity of the embroidery she seen and touched during Herr Fienfeld's college lecture. She'd written her first essay for her diploma on this little town. She'd been amazed at the machines that are now so common had, at the beginning of the 19th century, been developed here in St Gallen. Her mind raced to the little case under her feet, she had her first purchase of an embroidered Sanktt Gallen ballet dancer tucked safely over little Avyar, along with several others but most of her collection from the St Gallen heydays of the early 1900s were still wrapped in brown papers where she'd had to leave them in the apartment as little Avyar took up the space now. A smile crossed her face as she wondered if he was still comfortable.

The First World War, the Great Depression and now this war had led to the town's steady decline. She looked sadly at the landscape of ruined buildings and disused sheds. One day it would rise again maybe, but only within Parisian haute-couture designers' landscape, she mused sadly. The train slowed as it neared the station. It had followed the river Steinach for miles as it snaked its way towards Switzerland and safety. Her heart beat loudly under woollen coat as the fear of discovery loomed over her, she could hear the carriage doors slide back and forth as the border police checked each passenger. She rearranged her long skirt and coat for the fourth time ensuring that it was only her large suitcase that was visible overhead. The door slid open. There were four others in her carriage compartment. The orders were barked.

'Papiere.' He clicked his heels. She waited, soon it would be her turn.

'Frau.' She stood and reached across. He studied the photograph and looked at her twice. The wait was interminable. She looked at him and then cast her eyes to the floor.

'Koffer.' She reached across as he watched. The man opposite stood and helped to take down the suitcase from the overhead shelf and place it on the floor.

'Offnen,' he barked again. She fumbled for the keys and opened the case. He took a step closer and leaned into the case. His hands searching. She was left with a jumble of her neatly packed worldly possessions spread

49

across the floor. She bent to repack them. Foolishly leaving little Avyar's case exposed.

'Frau Präsidentin, könnte Ihnen gehören. Es Jetzt öffnen. Olga spoke in English. 'Yes, it's mine,' her voice wavering almost inaudible.

A shot rang out further down the carriage. The man looked at her for a moment and rushed out of the compartment, shouting.

'Das ist alles.'

She slumped back into her seat. The rest of the passengers were staring out of the window. A young man ran past dodging left and right. Further shots rang out.

'Anhalten.'

The young man turned to face his pursuers. He raised his hands in capitulation. Those at the window turned away as a volley of bullets ripped into him. His bloodied body fell in slow motion onto the platform as the soldiers gathered around. Moments later the train started to move slowly at first, then quickened its pace and Olga and Avyar left Germany for the last time.

Chapter 11

Zurich Switzerland 1942

Olga gathered her belongings and walked the few steps to the toilet situate at the end of the carriage. She struggled to enter into the tight space and closed the door. The train had slowed to a halt as she took her first look at Avyar in hours. She felt his heartbeat that gently pulsed under her finger. He was warm and still under the influence of the sedatives.

Thankfully, the trains from major cities arrived on the ground level of the station. No stairs or lifts to negotiate. At the gate leading from the International arrivals, there was a cursory glance at her paperwork as she made her way through the throng of people that made Zürich Hauptbahnhof one of the busiest and the largest railway stations in Europe. After the relative silence of the train carriage, the noise of steam gushing from the locomotives, the clamour of echoing announcements and the shouts of commuters, momentarily swallowed her attention. She'd planned this moment in her mind for weeks, but now she hesitated.

Would her presence at the British Embassy be totally compromised when she revealed the existence of little Avyar with no papers. They'd hardly send him back to Germany to certain death, after all she had the letters from her brother in London. She had a home waiting and people to look after her. She also had a great deal of undisclosed diamonds that she's purchased gradually over the year and months leading to this day. No, she'd register at the hotel and then go straight to the Consulate. Her large case was safely stored in left luggage which she'd retrieve later.

Carrying little Avyar, she turned left out of the station on Bahnhofplatz across the river Limmat and right down Zahringerstrasse. Habit had left her with the constant need to look over her shoulder, hesitate at corners, skip across roads and avoid open spaces without people. That was the life she'd left behind but she'd still be careful, she told herself.

The unprepossessing lobby of the Rutli Hotel was manned by a young woman soberly dressed in white shirt and grey skirt. She smiled sweetly at Olga and immediately came around the desk to look at Avyar who was still with his eyes closed. She stoked his little hand that had emerged from his shawl during the walk. Olga had a pleasurable smile on her face as she told the girl he now thirteen months old. However, Olga was aware that time was passing and she needed to be at the Consulate long before it closed at 4 pm. She paid for three nights in advance and asked for a taxi as she was getting late for a meeting. One telephone call from behind the desk and within minutes she was sitting holding Avyar in the rear of the taxi.

She was grateful that here they spoke German. She'd struggle with French or Italian. She was also glad to sit quietly in the taxi rehearsing her plea to the British officials, as the car left the northern end of the Altstadt, or old town, in central Zürich, and made its way along the edge Lake Zürich. She looked out admiring the

Alpine scenery in distance, the winter snow blanketing the higher slopes. It seemed that the city nestled between the wooded hills on the west and east side. The taxi followed the curve of the lake to the west and then over the Schanzengraben canal bridge into the heart of the new town. It stopped outside an austere grey stone building slightly set back from the pavement outside. She looked at her watch, she had two hours to plead her case.

After half an hour of form filling, she was exhausted. Little Avyar was now awake and demanding a feed. She opened the case she'd brought knowing that at some stage he needed a change and food. The receptionist was very obliging and pointed to the first floor where she would be able to attend to his needs. She was descending the staircase with a calm Avyar clinging to her coat lapels when a deep voice announced her name. She turned. In front of her stood a tall straight man in a dark blue suit. His hair brushed back and shining in the lights from the chandeliers.

'Anthony Bancroft. You must be Mrs Olga Smit,' he announced holding out his hand.

She followed him into his office and sat down.

He held the forms in front of him.

'I see you want to join relations in London.'

She nodded.

'Your paperwork seems to be in order, but what about your son. You have said nothing, and I have no birth certificate or other emigration papers.'

'Excuse me,' said Olga standing up and placing the case on his desk. Anthony Bancroft stared as she opened took the keys and slid back the locks removing the bag and bottle that she'd just used. He stood and peered into it.

'This is how I smuggled him away from Munich and certain death.'

He looked horrified at the little bed and then at Avyar. Olga then told him about life in Nazi Germany. The persecution of her neighbours, the daily violence and the disappearance of thousands to Dachau just outside Munich to the north of the city.

'You've heard the rumours of death camps, have you, Mr Bancroft? Well, they are true.' He looked at her. There was silence between them.

'Yes, I've heard the same thing from others fleeing Germany.'

What could the Allies do? They were trying to survive themselves. London had been the target of blitz bombing which had killed hundreds of innocent civilians, but the tide was turning too slowly.

Anthony Bancroft looked at the scrap of paper nestling in the case. He read it aloud. *We, Gurt and Elsie Heidmann give you our son Avyar to take care of him until we can meet up again.'* It was signed and dated.

Anthony Bancroft stroked his brow in thought, fingering the paper and looking at the case. At last, he spoke looking directly at Olga.

'This is a most irregular situation, Mrs Smit. Our main Embassy is in Berne. I alone cannot authorize anything other than your onward journey, not the little boy's.' He witnessed the distress in Olga's eyes as she started to cry.

'What am I to do, Mr Bancroft?' she pleaded. 'I am staying in an hotel. I have no friends here. I don't know

54

the city. I cannot leave him alone again. You can see that, can't you?'

Bancroft sighed. He knew he'd have to do something. Political refugee, persecution, fear. He'd never had a situation quite like this and the thought of letting a defenceless little boy suffer more had made his mind up. He left the room and returned holding a small camera. He faced Avyar who took notice of the funny black object in front of him and stared at it long enough for Bancroft to secure an acceptable image that was in focus. The click and flash soon resulted in the silence being broken by a loudest wail Bancroft had ever heard, as Avyar was reduced to tears rubbing his little eyes.

'These were desperate times that need desperate measures. I'm sorry about that, Mrs Smit.'

His mind was racing back to the case he'd uncovered of forgery of British transit papers six months ago, of the stolen Consulate papers and the men and women who sold entry into the Britain at a price most people couldn't afford.

He stood up.

'Mrs Smit, leave this problem with me and I will see what I can do the help. Come back in two days and make sure you bring your boy with you.'

Whether or not Olga felt any better, she did not know. She felt she could trust Mr Bancroft to do his best, but would that be good enough. He seemed less of a stickler for the rules than she'd been used to. He could have just said 'No', but he didn't. That night in her room at the Rutli, with Avyar asleep in the cot that the hotel had provided, she thought of London, being safe with her family, but then Mr Bancroft had mentioned the devastation caused by the German bombing. After all this, would they still be alive, it was an awful realization that her life would be yet again lost in this dreadful war. The next morning, she was woken by Avyar's cries from the cot. She picked him up and ran the hot water. 'It won't be a moment little one,' she murmured into his ear, smelling the characteristic sweetness of his unblemished skin. With the warm bottle, she sat on the bed as he supped his way through the contents. 'What a little fatty you're going to become.' Avyar smiled at her and she melted again.

To make good use of the next two days, she and Avyar, now ensconced in a second-hand pram she'd bought from a bric-a-brac shop, walked the streets of Zurich. Olga needed money and armed with two stones from her diamond collection, searched the marketplace, making discreet enquiries as she went. She wanted a fair price, that was all. Wartime had boosted the diamond market, but without any paperwork, she knew the price would be discounted. She needed cash now. She'd have to trust her instincts. Each diamond she had was labelled with the number of carats. At least she could rely on that and the prices quoted in the Zurich daily newspaper's business section. The Swiss had a reputation to uphold and when she recounted, for the second time, the bundle of Franc notes back in the hotel, she had been pleasantly surprised how easy it was and how confidential the whole transaction had been. All she had to do was sign a receipt for the money and noted the carats sold. She now hoped she had enough to last until she set foot of British soil.

**

56

Anthony Bancroft left his office at the Consulate early and walked down the street to the corner and hailed a taxi. The rundown neighbourhood, he entered, was safe enough, but not somewhere he wanted to linger long. He hoped that the little man he met before still lived here. He descended the stone steps to the basement apartment holding onto the cold metal handrail. He been here before and had slipped down the last two steps and into the front door banging his head and cutting his brow. Not this time he said to himself. He knocked loudly. The door opened a fraction. Bancroft recognised the face immediately and pushed the door preventing it from being slammed into his face.

'Not here on official business,' he heard himself say not quite knowing how to approach this situation.

'Better come in.'

Bancroft was shown into a small but comfortable front room. Without lights it was hard to see anything until Herr Leeter turned on the corner lamp and sat down. Bancroft followed his queue and sat opposite, unbuttoning his coat and retrieving the envelope from his inside pocket. He handed it the Herr Leeter.

'What do you want of me, Mr Bancroft?' said Herr Leeter rather too formally.

'A little favour, for old time's sake. You owe me one, remember.'

Herr Leeter looked at him and nodded. Bancroft need not have left his name out of the enquiry which resulted in the criminal prosecution of the man who set up the forgery business and preyed on those who feared for their future, mainly wealthy immigrants from

Germany and Austria desperately trying to evade the clutches of the Nazi's even though Switzerland was a neutral bystander to this war. Herr Leeter was down at the end of the criminal chain, but his evidence had helped to successfully prosecute the main men. They never knew who fingered them.

Bancroft explained the situation. He wanted to help but couldn't do what was necessary if he wanted to remain in the Diplomatic Service. Herr Leeter looked at him and Bancroft could see a sadness pass over his face. There was silence between them. Herr Leeter looked at the papers again.

'I've never spoken of this before. Mr Bancroft. I've kept it hidden inside me for years now but seeing that little face. What is his name?'

'From now on it is going to be Avyar Smit.'

'Avyar Smit,' he repeated. 'Not his real name then? Leeter is not mine either. My real name is Leismann. I came here to Switzerland in 1935 during the early Nazi purges of the Jews. Once I had been a graphic artist with a publishing company but that all stopped when it was targeted for anti-Germanic publications and raised to the ground. I worked on the third floor and someone threw a petrol bomb into the ground floor one evening when I was working late. I escaped from the burning building and stood watching from the street, then I realized that my little brother wasn't by my side. I'd pushed him ahead of me but in the confusion of flames and smoke, I had lost him somewhere on the ground floor. He'd only come to walk home with me. He was still in his school uniform. I rushed back into be burning building shouting his name. He'd been trapped

58

under the fallen ceiling near the exit. I tried to pull him to safety. I wasn't strong enough. I will never forget that pain in his face as it melted to blackness.' Herr Leeter put his hands to his head, images of that night swirling helplessly through his mind. He wept for the first time in years. 'Once he'd gone, I knew I couldn't stay any longer, Mr Bancroft,' he muttered through his handkerchief that soaked up the falling tears. 'That is why I will repay your debt.'

Two days later, an unopened package lay on Anthony Bancroft's desk. Mrs Smit and Avyar sat opposite him. He picked up the letter opener and sliced through the envelope and pulled out the papers. He pushed them across the desk to Mrs Smit.

Chapter 12

London 1942

Olga Smit looked at the address. The number 23 bus had set her down two blocks away. There were rows of burnt yellow London brick houses on either side with small front gardens, some well-kept and others suffering from terminal decline. She seen the chaotic effect of the blitz bombing of London, whole streets left in ruins, beautiful Georgian terraces wounded with piles of rubble stacked up in the front gardens, their elegance scorched by indiscriminate incendiary bombs. She pushed Avyar slowly towards the corner shop. She needed to ask directions to Lansdown Road. They eyed her suspiciously when she spoke. Her foreign accent pervaded each word. Anthony Bancroft had suggested that her true background was something she should hide for the moment and that Switzerland was the obvious choice as she could talk about it from first-hand experience and anyway that was the story her papers told.

'You won't find anything there. Gone, they all have, at least those who survived.'

Around the corner she looked at the road. It was a short street lined with scorched and blackened trees, but most of the houses on the right-hand side in the middle of the terrace were in ruins. The remainder suffered collateral damage when the stray bomb landed several months ago. She stood outside the charred remains of Number 14. If her brother and sister-in-law and their two children were inside when it happened, they could not have survived. She returned to shop, head in hands.

'What happened to my brother and his family in Number 14?'

'Your brother?' She looked at the other local customers momentarily. 'Look sit down here. I've just made tea. I'll get you a cup. Not many come in at this time.'

No-one was prepared to talk about what happen in Lansdown Road. It just didn't seem the right time to say anything as they just glanced at each other, not one person volunteered to speak but then the silence was broken.

'Look, I am not sure how to tell you but the sooner, the better. Your brother and his wife and family were in the house when the bomb hit the street, the whole place shook. I am so sorry, but they didn't survive the blast because it was a direct hit. No warning. I think it was a stray. Well, actually, it was two stray bombs. They didn't stand a chance.'

Olga looked straight ahead, no tears, as she held the bottle for Avyar who was sucking away greedily.

'When did it happen?' she finally said.

'A week ago. War is so unkind. One day you here, the next, well.'

She told them her story. Travelling from Switzerland by plane to Portugal then boat to Liverpool. Nothing like that ever happened to anyone round here. They all nodded as other customers came in to listen.

61

'Darling,' said the large rotund lady dressed in flowery pinafore, her hair tied up in a bun, 'you got anywhere to stay?'

Olga shook her head, holding Avyar close to her for comfort.

'Look, my Stan won't mind. He's away somewhere down south, training some raw ones. You know, new soldiers. You stay with me and we'll sort you out. What you need right now is a good rest, you look deadbeat. Oh, by the way Olga, they called me Florrie, short for Florence.'

With relief and a little trepidation, Olga agreed to this act of kindness from a complete stranger.

'Thank you, Florrie.'

'Here, take this.' She handed Olga a small bottle of milk and some biscuits for later.

At breakfast the next morning, Olga walked into the kitchen holding Avyar.

'Sit down, here's some tea and bread. No butter anymore but I've put a little beef fat on it to make it a bit tastier. Florrie sat down opposite her.

'Florrie, what am I to do now?'

Chapter 13

Solomon Isaacs family Munich 1942

Jonny stroked his brow, he'd been reading for many hours, but couldn't stop himself from continuing.

The permits were never granted for me or my parents. My tenure at the University had been withdrawn by the authorities without explanation, another Victim, this time of Nazism. We all knew it was because I was a Jew. Life for us became confused and erratic. We had no income from work as the tailoring business had been confiscated and was now being run by Aryans. Our only source of money was selling our assets one by one until now in mid 1942 there was very little left.

More and more of our German Jewish friends were suddenly disappearing, rumours started to spreading that they were being resettled in the East where work was available for them to help in the war effort. It was true that the industrial giant I G Farben had built a new factory in a place called Auschwitz and needed a workforce. Both my mother and father were fit and both had skills of their own that they could offer until this madness was over.

We decided, before we were ordered out of our apartment and it was allocated to an Aryan family, just maybe we could keep one step ahead of the regime's inexorable Jewish purge. Over the next few days, we gathered our belonging and the few valuables we had left. Most of our furniture had already been sold. My father told us that the Konig family, who had properties in Freimann and Milberts-Hofen districts, far enough outside the central area to be safe for the time being, had arranged to hide us. I will always remember Herr Konig and his wife, Constance. They had been faithful customers of our tailoring business and used to give me little treats when I delivered finished garments to their house. She was a very kind homely person who hated what was happening to her beloved city, but outwardly did and said all the right things to keep her family safe.

Our new home was on the top floor of a small dilapidated house where the ground floor shop windows had been boarded up. From the stone flagged entrance hall, there was a flaking grey painted door with water stains where the last rains had flowed in through the blocked drainage outside. Inside the walls crumbled under my touch as perished plaster exposed the bricks underneath. At least the top floor was dry said my father.

I remember the knock we all had to learn, "tap,taptaptap,taptap,tap". Mannfred, their son, crept up the stone stairs. *"Any other sequence and you need to be out of the window and across the roof."* He told us first day we met at the apartment. There were no other occupants so we were able to sneak out through the rear entrance onto a narrow lane that seemed to be a repository for mattresses, broken chairs and general garbage. No-one would look twice for a Jewish family just off Knorrstrasse so long as we kept quiet and out of site until our papers came though. Dad was still living in hope. Mannfred looked after our needs by bringing enough food and money for us to survive. He told me he'd come by tram always aware that the eyes and ears of the secret police, the Gestapo, were everywhere. He'd have to watch all those getting on or off the tram as it made its way down Furstenreider Strasse. He would get off at different stops and walk different routes each time he came to see that we were all right. I asked Mannfred, several weeks after that first night he'd brought us here, why his family was taking such a risk in hiding us.

'Has your father never told you?'

'Told me what?'

'I'll come in a few days and then we'll go out, just you and me. We'll be safe. I need to show you something.'

Mannfred kept his promise and we both left the building and dodged out of the rear lane into the street. It was very dark. The moon had waned and left the night sky navy blue almost black. I followed like an obedient dog a few paces behind Mannfred and boarded a tram. It took us to Ludwigstrasse. Looking around, he beckoned me to get off the tram. He kept asking me to keep by his side so as not to arouse suspicion as we made our way through the shadows to Odeonsplatz and stopped outside Feldherrnhalle. He pointed to the plaque on the east side of the building and simultaneously we both raised their outstretched right arm in salute for the benefit of the two SS guards on duty that night. This site had become sacred as each year Hitler had decreed that the old soldiers should pay homage to the sixteen Nazis who died at the hands of the Munich police when they stopped the Feldherrnhalle March on 9 November 1923

'What about it? I've seen it many times but frankly I tried to avoid the salute by using the Viscardigasse shortcut over there when I was still allowed to go to University. No point in making that ridiculous salute if you don't have to.'

'Sush, keep your voice down. Underneath you may have read the names of the four policemen also shot that night by the Nazis.'

'Yes and....?'

'There was a fifth policeman shot that day. My mother's brother, Otto. Your father saved his life. He realised what was happening and in the chaos of running Nazi supporters, dragged Otto off the street into alley and stopped the haemorrhaging from a gunshot wound in his chest, with his scarf and waited for more police to arrive and take him to hospital. Now you know why my parents are returning the favour and helping you."

Soon after that night, Herr Konig came to see us.

'I'm sorry, but it is impossible to get you out safely. From what I can gather everyone assumes that you have already been arrested and deported to the East. It is chaotic at the moment. Your only chance to survive for now is to stay here. We'll do what we can but there are eyes everywhere.'

'Herr Konig, thank you for what you have done so far but staying here will bring danger to you and your family,' said my father.

'Look, the ownership of this house is well hidden and Otto is still influential in the local police force. He'll keep me informed. No-one will look for Jews here. Most of the Jewish tenants are being relocated to two new camps, the Jewish Housing Estate not far from here in Knorrstrasse and in the Abbey in Berg am Laim. I've heard from my contact in Widenmayerstrasse at the Office of Aryanisation that only a few Jews remain at large in the city. They've all but given up on pursuing anyone else. We may be lucky as long as we are very careful.'

All I remember now is the fearful monotony of existence. It was relieved by books we'd brought with us but even these I had memorised from cover to cover reciting them over and over again as I tried to sleep at night. The regular visits by Mannfred lightened the atmosphere amongst us each time he came, but the news, he brought, was all very depressing for us and the light left at the end of the tunnel of hope began to fade little by little as thoughts of giving ourselves up by walking into the Housing Estate began to seem a better option.

I don't know what happened, but I can only guess that somehow Mannfred was being watched by the Gestapo and eventually followed. We were awoken by hammering on the door and shouting on the landing two days after his last visit and before we could escape through the window onto the roof, the door burst open and shots were fired into the ceiling. We cowered in our beds.

'Drehen Sie um die Arme über dem Kopf gegen die Wand,' came to order.

We all obeyed, turned away and stood. My legs were kicked apart as I faced the wall. Our rooms were searched as we waited. I am not sure whether I was shivering because of the cold or fear. Minutes later, dressed in our shabby day clothes and coats and carrying a suitcase each, we were bundled out of the building into the cold night air. The noise of the arrests had summoned the curiosity of others who peeked through darkened windows or stood in doorways, amongst those I noticed Mannfred shaking his head in sorrow. We joined a queue of about one hundred others already outside the Jewish Housing Estate and were marched to a side street where three covered lorries stood idling, the engine fumes lingering in the air.

'Schnell an Bord,' shouted the SS officer as he dug his pistol into the back of an old man's neck.

The rear board was slammed into place and the tarpaulin dropped flapping over the rear. In the interior darkness, no-one uttered a word as the lorries lurched and bounced their way out of Munich until the sun rose to our left and the outskirts of Munich disappeared. It was as if we all knew nothing was left for us. Frightened souls clung to the little children and cuddled them into silence. Escape wasn't an option. After an hour or so, we stopped at a railway junction.

We were ordered out of the lorry and lined up alongside hundreds of other Jews clinging helplessly to their cases. Alongside one of the platforms stood a long train of cattle wagons, doors open. Already those at the front were being herded on board, others stumbling and crawling over the uneven gravel beside the rails tried to cling to each other for comfort, mothers holding their little one's hands. Once or twice the crack of a pistol rang through the early morning air followed by the wailing of despair of those closest to the body. Someone else had dared to question an SS officer. As I neared the penultimate truck, I looked along the adjacent railway line at the several bodies that lay motionless with red pooling around them.

No-one dared to look at the faces of the soldiers for fear of a rifle butt in the head, so we pushed each other along until we were all crowded into cattle wagons without food or water. In each wagon at least a hundred of us stood each clinging to what remained of our worldly goods in suitcases and some with blankets tied with string. The books I had tried to smuggle with me were taken and destroyed by gunfire sending the fragments of paper fluttering into the air then taken on the wind into space. I had nothing save the clothes I was wearing. My parents had packed a few personal momentos, but these were to be confiscated within minutes of our arrival. The doors were dragged across the opening and the metal bars were secured with a deafening bang. Some found themselves wedged against the wooden sides where their clothes had been caught in the runners of the door. It was impossible to move and those who tried to clear a space for themselves were quickly set upon by others. It became a savage place to be as human dignity began to dissipate.

The journey East was to take two days, the smell of human waste made me wretch as I watched my fellow countrymen and women reduced to tears. As the hours ticked by, any fight left in them had drained way as if water down a plughole. I watched as the life of two young babies was ebbing away, hour by hour they became weaker. Their mothers had nothing for them. I was helpless to intervene to save them. Eventually the first morning saw them blue faced as they became the first victims of the crush. There was no comfort offered just the pained expression of grief of those around them. I tried to blot out my feelings and taught by mind to become blank, thinking of windowless white walls with no way in or out. It worked for a while but every now and then the rolling and clanking of the wagons disturbed my mind and brought me back to reality.

Chapter 14

The train finally came to a halt, as the wagon doors were unbolted and drawn open, those nearest fell onto the crisp white snow on the platform. Stinking, cold and hungry, they could hardly raise themselves as the snowflakes fluttered through the still air. In front of us stood a line of soldiers, guns across their chests, vicious dogs strained on their leeches as the order for the rest of us to get out echoed down the platform. Searchlights from the high observation towers cast shadows of the hundreds of frightened Jews who stood on the virgin white snow-covered platform. Orders were barked and as one we all trudged along the platform. I immediately recognised one man inspecting the rag bag of human misery as it made its way down the platform filtering bodies to the left and to the right, the cold penetrative eyes of my former University mentor, Dr Josef Mengele, now resplendent in his long well-tailored leather coat with SS insignia on the generous lapels.

I put his arms around my parents and hugged them before we were wrenched apart with a rifle butt. My father and I were separated immediately from the women. I remembered the final touch of my mother's fingers as the women were lead away to a line of long barrack huts.

The air hung heavy with the smell of cooking meat. It was only later that I realised that the aroma was always present in Auschwitz. It was burning human flesh.

'There's only one way to survive here and that is make yourself useful and keep your head down. Eye contact could get you a beating,' whispered one old man, 'particularly by Kapo Gurt Heidmann, the bastard who's in charge of our hut.'

A large man who I had seen the previous night standing behind the German soldiers on the platform, Kapo Heidmann was dressed like us in his striped uniform, stood outside the hut waiting for us to emerge. It was still dark as we lined up to receive our first taste of Auschwitz food. I needn't tell you how awful it was, but you'll eat anything when hunger invades your body as it had ours. Within minutes the meagre ration had gone. Kapo Heidmann looked down on me, he demanded to know what I had done before. I insisted I had medical training and asked to join the hospital squad. He laughed in my face and spat on the ground. He grabbed my arm and lifted me up. I fell as he let go and the first blow hit me on the side of face quickly followed with several kicks to the body. I crawled away trying to escape but he followed. Two soldiers ran past grabbing his arm and insisted he follow them. That saved me from further blows. After he had gone, taking a risk for my own life, I stood for seemed like hours outside the hospital block that morning in the cold, shivering. Kapo Heidmann returned and saw me standing by the entrance and hit me several times with the truncheon he appeared to wield menancingly in circles as part of his job. I refused to move, standing my ground announcing that I and the Doctor knew each other from University. I goaded him by saying that it may be a big mistake and dangerous to ill treat me anymore.

Surprisingly, Mengele recognised me despite the recent bruising to my face, my shabby clothes and frail body gaunt with hunger and still dirty from the cattle wagon journey. As we walked off together into the hospital block, Mengele with his arm on my shoulder, I could not resist a side glance at Kapo Heidmann. It was a gesture that neither I nor Heidmann would ever forget. The same side but rival enemies. I would be taking a great deal of notice in the activities of Kapo Heidmann from now on.

Over the next hour, Mengele showed me the data from his anthropological studies. It struck me that rather than start with a blank canvas, Mengele had started from the false premise that the Ayrian race had the genetic superiority and he was going to statistically prove it. Maybe, I suspected, he had been instructed by his boss, Reichsfuhrer Heinrich Himmler, to find ways to prove the theory, I had no intention of disillusioning Mengele, I had to remind myself that I was there to survive.

That night in the quiet of my hut, I leaned over the edge of the upper bunk and talked to my father who had been shipped out of the camp to work in the factory. He had seen my mother who had been allocated a role in administration, whilst Dad was sorting and labelling the manufactured goods for shipment back to Germany. Both had, like I, been given extra food over and above the meagre rations given to the very young, the old and infirm who were not long for this life.

The days passed into months, I witnessed the use of human guinea pigs for sometimes ill-thought out and what seemed to me as purely sadistic experiments that were carried out by Mengele and his assistant doctors. I was revolted by some, but I could only intervene when I thought my idea may produce a better result. It usually only involved palliative care during procedures.

Chapter 15

It was getting late as the shadows of the building opposite started to cross his apartment window. Jonny Wightman looked at the remaining chocolate bar. He ripped it open and took a large bit.

This section Solomon had headed 'Victim of Knowledge'.

I had the perfect opportunity whilst working in Auschwitz with Dr Mengele to use real human tissue and embryos. I was, of course, a Jewish prisoner to be exterminated in the fullness of time, but whilst I had this scientific opportunity, how could I deny myself?

I will tell you now that I did not and never would be directly or indirectly involved in the invasion of a healthy human being. My persecutors later on would never believe me but, Jonny Wightman, I am asking you to believe me.

Let me begin with what my studies at Munch University had taught me so far. Dr Mengele and I were interested in very different things. He, as I have already said, wanted to prove some races came from a sub-human anthropological base. I discussed this with him on many occasions but never contradicted him directly. Whenever I disagreed with him, it was more of a question that I wanted him to elaborate on, to tell me what he had discarded and why. He would never understand. His ego was high and his patronage came from Himmler himself. I could never believe that he would have overlooked the fact that I was a Jew, but most of the time, he did. We were just two scientists, albeit just for some moments.

When we lived in Munich, well before I went to University, I was aware that nature has been cloning organism for millions of years. Let me give you a simple example, when a plant sends out a runner which is a modified form of a stem, a new plant grows where the runner takes root, a clone. People have been cloning plants in one way or another for thousands of years. Taking a leaf from one plant and growing it into a new plant. It has the same genetic makeup and is another example of a clone. This is where I began to think radically. Could I clone myself? When you are way ahead of the existing field of thought, as a scientist, there are sometimes no natural or legal barriers in place. It takes time to decide what is morally or ethically acceptable and what is not. If it hadn't been for our persecution by the Nazi's, my work would have been advancing rapidly in Munich's academic environment. It might even be said that they missed their chance to start a super Aryan race.

So, one day I asked Mengele, when I thought I had gained enough of his respect, if I could run some experiments alongside his, to my surprise, he agreed. Our equipment was as good as I would have had in Munich. The invention of the electron microscope by Max Knoll and Ernst Ruska at the Berlin Technische Hochschule in 1931 had finally overcome the barrier to higher resolution that had been imposed by the limitations of visible light. Dr Mengele had requisitioned one very early on and had it shipped here from the University only after they received a more advanced version.

One day, he came to me and said that a young 'healthy' woman had been brought into the hospital soon after she had arrived from being rounded up by the SS but had died unexpectedly. He wanted me to carry out a post- mortem to establish the cause of death. It was, of course, very urgent. He didn't want some contagious disease sweeping through his part of the camp, out of control. If anyone was going to die finding out the cause, it was me not him. I had some experience of post-mortem procedures as an undergraduate at the medical school, but it wasn't ever going to be my subject.

I hesitated before being ordered to do so because the autopsy room was adjacent to a labyrinth of gas chambers. Earlier, I had been witness to the horrifying spectacle of the way that my countrymen were being exterminated. A new intake of Jews had just arrived by train and were being herded into the changing rooms as I arrived. They'd been told to remove their clothing and hang it all on pegs. All the while they were being told that new clothes will be provided and hot tea would be served once they'd showered and were clean. Towels were piled on tables to elaborate the lies. A few kapos were needed to encourage each and everyone one of them, old men, young girls, mothers, fathers and babies in arms into the 'showers'.

I was at the autopsy table starting to unravel the reason for this young girl's death for Mengele when I heard the wailing and banging. It lasted about ten minutes until silence came. Then came motor noise of the extractor fans as they vented the toxic, Zyklon B gas into the air outside. Finally, I heard the bars securing the doors being dragged back and the doors were opening. Even having witnessed this before, I still wretched again at the smell of death, urine and faeces hung in the air as the Kapos with rags over their noses pulled and tugged at the dead bodies loading them onto shoots that took them to the crematoria. I stood and retreated into a space I had set aside in my head for such occasions, sitting with my head bowed, so ashamed at my own inadequacy.

The autopsy door opened, and I stood as a young boy about ten or twelve was carried in. He had survived amongst all the dead around him. I laid him out on the table to bring him back to life and started automatically to pump his chest forcing air into him. As I did so Kapo Heidmann pushed me aside and listen to the laboured breathing. There in front of me he placed his hand across the boy's mouth and pinched his nose. His young chest heaved at first then gave way to silence. I stood transfixed at what had happened. There was no way I would again witness such callousness in what was my domain. He was aware as I stared at him that I had revenge in my eyes, but he could do nothing about it.

I turned away as they removed the young boy and walked over to the gurney and I pulled back the sheet and looked at the young woman peaceful in death out of this hell. I discovered that she has died of a twisted gut and that her complaints of stomachache and cramp were ignored as being dietary. I reported to matter to Dr Mengele. He nodded. During the course of that procedure, without him knowing, I removed her ovaries and put them in frozen storage. Strangely, as I did so, I recall whispering to her dead body asking if it was all right. Did she mind?

'At this point, Jonny Wightman, I know you will think that I stepped over the ethical boundary but remember this was a death camp and in the middle of a world war. Ethical boundaries are sometimes blurred at the best of times but these times, here in Auschwitz, were extraordinary.

'I now had the first part of the 'Germ Line'. For your information that is the egg and sperm that combine to make the embryo. I had previously experimented with a technique in Munich to extract the nucleus from a cell and create an enucleated egg. Mengele was happy for me to use the electron microscope when he asked me to set up cultures of various matter so that he could make notes on his own absurd theories. I thought that it should be possible to fuse this egg with another cell using a small electric current. This technique had never been used before and it wasn't to become widely known until the 1960s. I brought that innovation to England in 1946.

Jonny Wightman was now becoming aware that this man had remarkable intelligence, memory, speed of thought and reasoning and the ability to use it. Everyone in Solomon's academic world up to 1942 had thought so. But for his accident of birth, this man would have been known around the world by now. Jonny couldn't really believe what was to come next.

Chapter 16

Stalingrad Russia 1942

Ahead was the industrial city skyline of Stalingrad that stretched either side of the Volga river for 30 miles, it was a scene of mass of destruction, remnants of concrete jutting aimlessly into the sky supported by misformed legions of broken steel and crumbling cement, a chaos of twisted skeletons, that followed days of bombardment by German Stuka dive bombers and barrage after barrage of shellfire. It was 12 September 1942. Klaus Neidman and Captain Johann Bron watched as the oil storage tanks spew flames high into the night sky. The silence that followed the bombardment was punctured by the advance whistle, the company scrambled over the waste land in front. Line after line of German infantrymen from General Friedrich Paulus VIII Corps. The snow was not due until later, but it was beginning to feel cold at night. As they advanced into the streets, it was incomprehensible how anyone could continue in this hell. They were dead. Not a single green leaf survived, everything had perished in the flames. The horror encountered did not stop for days. It seemed like every visible movement was punished by death. Klaus and Johann did not know that this was the beginning of the end of their war. The fight for street after street became house after house. It seemed that any progress was measured in corpses.

The month of September slipped into October and then into November. It was soon clear that General Zhukov's order from the Kremlin to his Red Army 'Not a step back, the only extenuating circumstance is death', had its stoical effect on morale as more and more troops came from the East to replace those who had fallen.

Each apartment block, each warehouse or factory had been converted into a series of well-defended strongpoints. Each manned by a dozen or so man units. Bitter fighting raged in each street. Johann and Klaus cleared bombed out buildings room by room, sometimes having to fire through holes in the floor above them to secure another stronghold. It became clear that they were never going to survive unless they started to think for themselves. The first priority after hours of exhaustion was to find a safe place to rest. They were now alone. They feared their fellow soldiers had not survived this assault. They went into a yard adjoining the building that had just been secured. In the porch lay the skeleton of a horse. It had been stripped of all but a few scraps hanging from its ribcage. Both of them leaped onto the carcass robbing it of the last vestiges cold raw red meat.

Klaus was the first to move slowly away from the courtyard stepping carefully round the immense cesspool of human waste that had nowhere to go, stuck waiting for someone to clear up. There ahead of them, he caught the sight of a human figure crouched over relieving himself. At the sight of Klaus, his wretched face, confused and suffering, disappeared into the darkness. To his right, piled high, he recognised the uniforms of his fellow soldiers. Inside them were the skeletal yellow wax like faces of men who had fallen weeks before in the first wave of fighting. There hadn't been time for burial and there was no time for sentiment. Johann stared into their lifeless eyes. He shook his head and started pulling away at the corpses, searching their pockets. Between them Johann and Klaus stuffed scarves, socks, linings for their boots and a compass and several ID tags. As night fell, the two of them began the slow retreat away from the splintered ruins, monstrous monoliths of concrete bared to the sky, away from the incendiary bombardment that would light to sky and cremate those that had fallen that day.

The advance towards Stalingrad was beginning to falter. Throughout the summer the German army had advanced hundreds of miles towards the city. Killing and burning everything in their path. News of the ruthlessness of the officers and their total disregard for humanity spread amongst the Russian troops and peasants in the countryside.

The morning bombardment from the Russians on two fronts, like a pincer, started before dawn. The frozen wasteland between the two sides now looked like the pictures of the western front in 1915. Craters now we're filled with frozen water hiding the dead men of both sides below in their cryonic state. The night's wind had caused thick drifts to pile against the sides of the craters. Shivering in their sodden uniforms, their feet leadened with snow, clutching feebly the heavy bolt action rifles, the two men waited for the order to advance. This time what lay ahead of them away from the ruins were the waters of the Volga. The natural barrier that had halted advance after advance over the last few months.

Supply lines were stretched too far and too long. Equipment was being lost and Blitzkrieg policy was now beginning to hamper any chance of survival.

A barrage of machine gun and cannon fire erupted in front of them. Men fell either side howling as life was taken from them. Shaking with fear the two men ran onwards leaving their fate in the hands of others. After a while, running and dodging unseen missiles of shrapnel, ice and frozen earth, they found themselves alone and lost again, submerged in the icy waters of the Volga, which flowed unceasingly southwards taking them with it.

Their instinct to survive generated a surge of adrenaline. Thrashing one arm in front of another they were both carried downstream. Clutching at anything floating before them they became prisoners of the flowing waters. As they both fell in and out of consciousness, their plight seemed hopeless until the river started to quicken as it flowed around a large outcrop of rock as it had done for hundreds of years. The effect was to eventually slow the current as the valley opened up again. Both men became aware at the same time that here was their chance to climb ashore. They slipped and struggled to gain a foothold in the shingled mud covered by the shallows on the left bank. They hauled themselves out of the water. Looking around they found themselves surrounded by a covering of low bushes and trees. The earth was cold and the air freezing. Dragging their bodies away from the Volga and further into the tree cover they heard the sound of the banging of an ill-fitting shutter in the wind somewhere in the distance. They moved slowly towards the sound. In a small clearing stood an earth covered dwelling. They had seen many on their way here and had been ordered to destroy the hovels and kill the occupants. It had been a sickening experience. Now they were on their own they would act differently. It appeared to be unoccupied. Nothing moved as they entered into the cold room. Something had burned in the open hearth recently, but the ashes were now damp from the few flakes of snow that wandered down the chimney. It seemed that most of the furniture had previously been burned for warmth. There was virtually none left. Dirty plates with the last meal frozen to the surface were stacked in the sink.

They pulled the meagre blankets over their bodies and lay down on the trodden earth floor. Sleep was not easy, but eventually their eyes could remain open no longer as they drifted off. Only one of them awoke to experience the next day. Hypothermia had claimed the life of Klaus Neidman at the age of twenty one.

Johann wiped the tears from his face as covered Klaus' face with a blanket. Out of the corner of his eye he saw a frail movement from above. He turned and saw the face of a teenage girl. He smiled and put down his rifle. He opened his arms, tempting the child forward. She hesitated and spoke in Russian. He nodded and moved to the fireplace and started to place pieces of wood in the form of a triangle ready to bring heat into the room. The girl watched intently. He looked at her asking for a match. She understood and pointed to the little box which was hidden under a rock in the corner.

He struck the match and lit the kindling. Within minutes the room was full of smoke and warmth. He coughed. She laughed. He went outside and soon returned with a kettle full of snow. She was standing by the fire cradling her hands in front absorbing the heat. She was dressed in a sack with waist ties and long torn stockings. On her head was his beret. It was now so dirty and torn that he wasn't sure which army it belonged to. He smiled at her. Memories of his own daughter lingered in his head as he stared at her for a long time. Catching those moments of her growing up at home in Germany. The laughter of long past days, the sun on her hair, reading her those bedtime stories, helping her revise for exams, watching as she became a women and then.

It wasn't long after they'd buried Klaus Neidman in the forest with a sad farewell that they were both working together preparing a meal. She scurrying back and forth with herbs and pieces of vegetable and throwing them into the boiling pot on the fire. He stirring occasionally, dressed in his soiled winter underclothes watching the steam evaporate from his uniform hanging from a ceiling rafter.

It wasn't until evening as the sun disappeared behind the hillside to the west that they introduced themselves, he was Johann Bron and she was Nadine Rekova. On that discovery they shook hands and laughed. That night she retreated to the warmth under the roof where she had hidden earlier. He lay in front of the dying embers of the fire promising to add more fuel throughout the long cold night.

He kept his promise during a fitful sleep. He stirred early and turned to find Nadine had come down from her perch in the roof and had her arms wrapped around his waist. There was an innocent contentment in her smile. He gently brushed her hair from her face and looked closely at her.

'What has happened to this world', he muttered in Russian to himself.

Nadine opened her eyes at the sound of her own language and hugged him closely.

'You kept your promise.' Looking at the hearth.

'Yes,' he nodded. 'Shall we find something to eat?'

Nadine nodded and wrapped herself in a blanket that she had hidden under the old newspapers in the roof.

'Come,' she beckoned and ran to the door.

Johann followed, racing to put his smoke-dried uniform on, tripping over the threshold as he did so and plunging into the overnight snowdrift outside the door. Nadine couldn't help herself as she laughed and jumped in air with joy and complete abandonment. She ran to help him up and brushed the white coating from his hair and face.

'Follow me.'

After the zigzagging path through the trees, they came to an area that had been cultivated in the past. Under the snow and tree branches and broken foliage, lay rows of vegetables, some clearly frozen but still edible. These were her survival rations. On their return journey, Nadine made Johann cover their tracks using brushwood. Just in case.

This is how life was. Gently, Johann coaxed Nadine to tell him her story.

Chapter 17

Stalingrad Russia 1942

'One day, there was a knock on the door. My parents had the door shuttered from the inside. It got louder and I went to hide in the roof. Finally, it splintered and two men came into the room carrying guns and grabbed my parents and marched them out.'

'When was this, how long ago?'

'Not too long, it was last year. The summer was still with us. My parents never came back after that morning. Daddy had always worried that one day that knock would come. He would tell me stories about terror and repression. He hated Josef Stalin and said the man punished anyone who he perceived there may be a threat to him and that his paranoia knows no bounds. They were afraid of the 'knock' that spelt arrest, exile, imprisonment, conscription or execution.

'I was terrified and lived in fear of the day my parents would disappear. I don't know why they took them away. They were simple farmers tending to the land that we owned. Maybe someone said we shouldn't own land and that inheritance was anti-Soviet.

'One thing my mother told me was never to let anyone catch me as I would be put in a Gulag far away in the freezing wastes of Siberia. She frightened me by telling me that I would be living in bare dirty cells in a brutal world mixing with older and more dangerous criminals, demanding and expecting sexual favours and then turning me into prostitution. That's why I live in the roof. She looked at him, despair in her eyes as they travelled over him.

'You need to get rid of that uniform. There will be revenge killings of your soldiers before this war comes to an end.'

Her words surprised him for someone so young.

'Maybe, maybe not.' Johann paused. He'd been wandering when but now he decided this was the right time. He couldn't remain here indefinitely.

'Nadine, are you prepared to give up your motherland forever and come with me. Never to return in all likelihood. You need to think about that very carefully. I know you have managed to survive and you will probably be able to make a life for yourself after this war is over, but.......'

Johann drew her closer as a father would to a daughter.

'I cannot remain here. I am putting you in great danger. We could do this together, escape, I mean.'

Nadine was certain that this life under Stalin was not something she wanted to endure even if it may change one day.

'I want to go with you. Let's try.'

Nadine put her hand in his and looked into his face, his eyes were soft and welcoming. The decision was made.

The Russian winter was long and cold. The nights were miserably cold and seemed never ending. Dawn rose late and evening came too soon. Surviving on Nadine's hidden vegetable plot and the occasional rabbits they trapped in the wilderness, life gave them new hope. Johann drew on his knowledge of Russia and insisted that to survive they must find a way to move south and follow the river Volga and then west away from the Russian forces. To do this Nadine had to learn as much of the German language as she could for later. The long drawn out darkness of the Russian winter provided hours of tuition.

Whilst Nadine was a quick learner, she had difficulty in hiding her accent. Johann knew that to the south of Stalingrad, the German Army was made up of weaker Hungarian and Romanian armies, under the commands of Petre Dumitrescu and Constatinescu. It might just be possible for him to disguise her amongst them if only contact could be made. They decided that to cross the vast Steppe land, it could only be done under cover of darkness. Their breakout would take place in February.

They had no idea what was happening in the battles around Stalingrad. Johann had thought that it was probable that the German forces were in trouble, in which case so was the escape plan. As dusk fell, miles away in a divisional German army headquarters, unknown to Johann and Nadine, 'Operation Lion' had just begun. German soldiers who were trapped by the surrounding Russian troops in their hundreds were to be saved in one last ditch effort. This Operation was to be a helpful diversion, for no-one would be taking much notice of peasants who were no threat to an army pursuing and trying to capture Field Marshall Friedrich Paulus' German 6th Army.

Dressed in Nadine father's clothes, they packed their meagre belongings in two blankets, including

Johann's uniform, hoisted them onto their shoulders using old leather straps to secure them and with a sad backwards glance from Nadine, they set off south. The ground was hard with a light covering of snow. Their footsteps would be covered again by morning as the light breeze caused flurries of snow-flakes danced before them. At the beginning they agreed to speak only Russian between them, two peasants wandering away from hell.

A plane passed overhead, its engine roaring it onwards towards Stalingrad. It was followed by several more. As they disappeared onto the horizon, gunfire erupted from the ground lighting the night sky. A token gesture of defiance. Nadine and Johann plodded on. That night they had to make as much progress south as they could. Soon it was clear that they had put several miles between them and the smouldering city with its stench of death and destruction. They saw houses that were no longer houses, the rags and torn coats of men that lay motionless in wretched foxholes, tangled machine guns torn out of clutching hands that blasted their owners into tiny fragments, their mess tins and helmets scattered like confetti that had seen jollity on their owners faces listening to the music that once formed part of their existence, their fragile life. This was long ago in another world far away. In one such foxhole, Johann and Nadine decided to rest up for the daylight hours. Using the tangled frame of a machine gun, long abandoned as the bullets ran out and all that was left were the empty belts, Johann constructed a small enough space for them to sit and tear the hardened bread into bite size pieces to be washed down with cold tea. The sun rose yellow and crimson through the scarred desolate landscape was they closed their eyes that first day.

One thought pervaded Johann's mind as they awoke the next evening. He needed a weapon for self-protection. Everything around them was rusted, even the watches had stopped for these men. Time was something that didn't matter anymore. It scarcely mattered for Johann and Nadine, their time was measured only by the hours of daylight. Neither knew how long they were going to have to endure the foot chilling steps through the snow. Ahead lay swathes whiteness dulled under the moonless sky. Johann keep checking their direction on his stolen compass, he had no idea the miles that separated the two fighting fronts and when he'd see or hear the terrible barrage of fire that would inevitably mean the deaths of others in this stagnant world. He never mentioned his constant fear to Nadine as she seemed to be able to focus on what was important and be guided by that alone. She had already scavenged extra coats and managed to find boots that fitted with the help of additional socks. The dead would be glad to see them being worn again, she would say as they huddled together day after day each time waiting for night to fall again.

'I've been calculating,' said Johann in German. He insisted that was to be their language of choice the further away from Stalingrad they walked. Nadine was understanding most of his conversation but stumbled over words she'd not heard before.

'Calcul…. What is that?

'Adding things together, mixing numbers to make sense of things.'

'Like what?'

'Well, we have been walking, save for the occasional rest, for four nights at about 3mph for eleven hours. Therefore, I calculate we are one hundred and thirty two miles from where we started.'

'I've never walked so far before, I should be very tired.' She laughed.

'Are you? Very tired?'

'Only when I hear your calcul..., calculation.'

He laughed and gave her a hug.

Far away in the early morning sky, they both heard the approaching drone of a light aircraft getting louder as Johann's curiosity got the better of him and he climbed out of their hiding place in wake of a burnt out Panzer Tiger I. The morning sun was bathing the frozen wasteland all around. Johann recognised the plane and waved his arms painfully above his head. The plane turned and descended for a closer look at this sole man now dressed in Wehrmacht uniform. It swooped overhead again recognising the uniform of the second person. Unknown to Johann and Nadine a report had already been made about another large group of German soldiers some miles to the west near the Don Heights and it now reported the position of these two lone figures.

Chapter 18

Munich Germany 1944

In the distance could be heard the muffled sounds of bombs exploding. Somewhere fifty of so miles away people were dying in flames and dust as the rubble of burning buildings toppled into the streets. That night the whole sky to the west was a gigantic sheet of fire. In the following days people was being dug out of the ruins, wedged amongst fallen beams. Some are still alive but unable to move but it was the dead that bore the agonies of their fate.

To the Allies, Munich was not only a German city that housed many high-ranking Nazis, it was a symbol of the Nazi regime. The Allies needed to send a political message. The targeted area were the two airfields but the city surrendered to the massive collateral damage.

On the night of the 24 April 1944, Munich was set alight for the last time. There on this night two hundred and sixty bombers let loose their loads.

The next morning with fires still burning, the stench was unbearable. Everything smelled of smoke. Civilians were being pulled out of shelters and being buried in shallow graves in the gardens of destroyed homes.

Out of one such charred shelter crept a tiny boy. His hair was matted with tar that had dropped from the shelter roof as the buildings above fell upon his refuge. He wore only a filthy soiled pair of flannel bed clothes.

He stumbled into the arms of a white hooded nurse and was immediately wrapped in a blanket.

Chapter 19

Munich Germany 1946

Captain Stuart Campbell stood before the Matron in charge of the orphanage on the outskirts of the ruins of Munich. With him was his wife, Naomi. She had spent the war hidden in the depths of Whitehall as a coordinator of relief amongst the thousands who had lost everything in the Blitz of London. Families were still trying to find what happened to the loved ones as the flames had engulfed street after street and the rebuilding had hardly started, so great was the restoration of order and the removal of broken houses and streets.

Her husband was still trying to find those who were responsible for perpetrating such horrors as he had witnessed travelling through southern Germany and Poland. Confusion and identity changes allowed some to escape. Stuart was meticulous in his efforts, lying awake at nights assimilating the situation. He barely talked about what he'd seen but occasionally Naomi was awoken at night by his restlessness.

That day he had asked her if she could see if there were any ways the Allies could help in minimising the terrible traumas these orphans had suffered at not only the hands of the Nazis but the Allies who had tried to stop the madness.

She wandered through the corridors of this vast building, watching the staff, stepping out of the way of children running and doing what children do best, being energetic and enthusiastic despite their circumstances.

Naomi rounded on corner, sitting on the stone balcony plinth overlooking the vast play area was a young boy, no older than six or seven years old. He was lost in his own world repeating words to himself. She stopped and observed him closely. He had dark hair, very thin and, even for one so young, an intense bearing. He looked up and saw her looking at him. He curled into a defensive ball and stopped muttering. Naomi walked slowly over to him. She held her arms slightly forward in an open welcoming gesture. He didn't move. A good sign she thought to herself. She stopped in front of him gently lowering her head to his level.

No words passed between them. She saw his body relax slightly but his eyes were fixed on the carved stone he was sitting on. Nothing that was obvious to a casual observer but she knew.

In her halting German she asked his name.

'They call me, Karl', he said quietly.

'Hello Karl. My name is Naomi. How are you doing?'

'My real name is not Karl. Schatzi, that's what my mamma called me and my other mamma.'

'Good to meet you, Schatzi.' Naomi held out her hand. Tentatively, he reached out and touched her fleetingly. He then sat on his hands protecting them from further intimate intrusion.

'Are you not interested in playing with the other boys or girls?'

Schatzi shrugged his shoulders.

'You speak very good English. Did you learn it in school?'

'No. I listen to the ladies dressed in the white uniforms with red crosses. They speak in English.'

'How long have you been here?'

Momentarily, he was silent.

'Two hundred and sixty one days, eight hours and....'

Schatzi looked at her wristwatch upside down.

'...Ten minutes and thirty one seconds.'

Naomi considered his response and all she could say was.

'Wow!'

'What does 'wow' mean?' he asked innocently.

'It means 'that is amazing', it is an expression of surprise.'

'Wow.' He repeated and laughed loudly.

'Schatzi, when I saw you earlier, you were talking to yourself. What about?'

'I was thinking about Charles Darwin and his philosophy on the origin of species. My father had a copy in German and I read it many times. I can recite many pages from the book. I used to go and sit for long times in the shelter we built in the garden. That was where I was when the bombs fell. Shall I tell you?'

Naomi nodded.

Schatzi then started speaking very quickly in German. Naomi couldn't understand much of what passed his lips but enough to realise what he had said was true. He stopped and looked down at his lap as if transferred into another zone forbidden for others to enter.

He then started to speak in Russian reciting pages of Darwin's work.

'My daddy taught me Russian. I think that is why he was sent to the war in the East.'

She remained silent.

'Wow, wow, wow,' he shouted and burst out laughing again.

'Wow,' repeated Naomi.

Full of confidence, Schatzi asked Naomi if she had read Karl Marx, John Stuart Mill, Alfred Krieger, then Adolf Hitler's philosophy about the Aryan superiority.

Naomi was shocked by the last sentence.

'Do you believe he was right?' she asked as if talking to an adult with years of experience to make some kind of value judgement.

'No. No. No. That's because he was prejudiced by being poor here in Munich and being told by his Jewish art teacher that he had no talent and all around him he saw Jews in businesses making money. He sent my Daddy to fight in Russia. I never saw him again. That isn't fair.'

Schatzi looked at Naomi for the first time although he didn't appear to be looking into her eyes but beyond in the distance.

After a moment, Naomi said.

'Do you want to come with me to see the playroom?'

He again shrugged and nodded his head dismissively.

'How about you show me around your home?'

Schatzi shuffled his legs to reach the ground and stood up. He wandered down the corridor. Naomi following. Occasionally he'd look back to make sure she was still there. They reached the entrance to the garden. The smell of newly mown grass hung heavy in the summer air. Slowly he walked to a bench overlooking the ornately manicured garden of this former manor house.

He sat down awkwardly again sitting on his hands. She followed his lead, it was not very comfortable but she persisted.

'Would you like one of these?' as she opened her hand and offered him a boiled sweet.

He took one and popped it into his mouth. He sucked it thoughtfully.

'My mammas and daddy died in the war. Oh, I already told you. Sorry. I am an orphan.' He suddenly said.

'I know. How do you feel?'

'Sad. I liked them very much.'

Sometimes he talked as if an adult, then at others as the child he was Naomi considered his response.

'What do you like doing the most?'

'I like thinking the most'

'What do you like thinking about?'

'Us.'

'What is 'us'?'

'You are silly. 'Us' is us. You, me, them, people, everyone.'

Naomi was not so astonished, this time, but to hear a ten-year boy utter those words was quite remarkable.

'Schatzi, would you like to meet my husband, Stuart? We could take you on a little outing if you like.'

'No!' He shouted and started shaking uncontrollably.

Naomi put out her hand and took his gently in hers. 'It's all right. I understand.'

She withdrew her hand when he had calmed down. She then felt his little fingers stroking the back of her hand. The sensation was something she had never experienced before. It generated an intense feeling of protection for this little boy whom she didn't know at all but felt belonged to her and her alone.

Chapter 20

Munich Germany 1945

Captain Stuart Campbell listened to his wife's description of her encounter with Schatzi.

'I want you to find out as much as you can about this little boy Stuart, you won't believe the... I don't know how to describe the feeling, darling. It was out of this world. I know that seems totally irrational but that was it.' She relaxed back into the chair and folded one arm behind her head and looked into space.

Stuart leaned forward and took her hand in his.

'Darling. This is not easy. I'm dealing with criminals not lost children, but I will ask one of my staff to interview the Matron of the orphanage and see where we go. O.K?'

'Thank you.'

Sleep did not come easy to Naomi that night. She could not get Schatzi's face out of her mind, however hard she tried. Morning eventually came as a great relief. She had agreed to meet one of Stuart's army colleague's wife for a day trip into the countryside. She couldn't wait for it to be over. However, what she hadn't anticipated was that her companion was a child psychologist who had spent her career in Great Ormond Street Children's Hospital in London before the outbreak of war.

Naomi and Ruth spent the whole day talking. Naomi explained to a complete stranger that she and

Stuart had been unable to have kids and Ruth had confided that she and her husband had agreed that even if they could they would be reluctant to bring a child into this world because both her and her husband had come from violent and disruptive backgrounds and couldn't take any more. They loved their work and so it was.

Naomi described the experience of yesterday, in detail. Ruth listened over a long lunch at the Metropolitan cafe overlooking the ornate garden of what could have been Eden if not for the pinnacles of half destroyed buildings surrounding the square.

'Naomi, this little boy shows the classic signs of autism.'

'Autism, what on earth is that?' said Naomi in confusion.

'I attended a lecture at the beginning of 1944. I think it was March. It is a new understanding of the lack of social motivation and social intelligence. Your Schatzi sounds like a classic apparently. He didn't like being held or touched. They remain insensitive to social cues.'

'Well that is not quite how I saw him. He seemed self-possessed and was articulate.'

'Yes, what I did learn was that there were very many variants. Sometimes their IQs were low and yet savants, as the professor called them, had amazing talents. Some can specify the day of the week on which any date in history fell, others although unable to read music, can play on the piano, any composition after just one hearing. There is something about them that illustrates an important fact about the structure of the mind.'

'So, are you telling me that my Schatzi may have genius genetics?' Naomi laughed.

'Maybe.'

'Tell me more' insisted Naomi as she sipped yet another cup of coffee, thinking where do these Americans manage, in all this chaos, to supply coffee, chocolate biscuits and other luxuries that she had been deprived of for so many years.

'Well, there was Blind Tom, a slave child born in 1850. He could sit at the piano and his little fingers used to take possession of the keys. Tested by musicologists, he could replay compositions of twenty pages having heard the piece just once, faultlessly. Like Mozart, he could perform on the piano with his back to the keyboard.

'Another example he gave us was a girl called, Nadia. She started drawing at the age of three. She had a sense of space, an ability to depict appearances and shadow and perspective. Most children even if they can draw cannot perform these details until they are at least three times that age. Then there was Stephen who was plucked from the London school for the developmentally disabled. He could master line and perspective at the age of seven. He could copy the masters but not just faithfully but using his vivid memory he could improvise a Matisse, a Van Gogh.'

Ruth continued to give examples she had heard about. Naomi was intrigued. She couldn't wait for Stuart to return so that she could see Schatzi again and see if he had a talent she could nurture.

It was late in the afternoon that Naomi and Ruth bade each other, goodbye. Vowing to meet again soon.

Naomi was waiting in the foyer of the hotel when Stuart walked in briskly with his usual air of confidence. She called out shyly. He turned and strode towards her and embracing and kissing the top of her head. He pulled away.

'Before I forget, one of my lads did some digging. You know how fanatical the Nazis are at keeping records. Well, your little Schatzi, was born in unusual circumstances. It seems the family covered up that the child was their daughter's. It would have brought shame on a party member and rising Wehrmacht Captain. He was introduced as the parents' son. Eventually, someone found out and like a good Nazi reported them. Father was sent to the Russian front to face certain death and mother and daughter were disowned by the party and thrown out of their seconded house and left to fend for themselves.'

'Oh, how awful for Schatzi. Poor fellow. Not a great start.'

Stuart took his wife's arm and lead her to the terrace.

'You met Ruth today?'

'Oh, Ruth was great company. Thank you.'

'What was so great?'

'Well, did you know she is a psychologist?'

'No. I knew she worked at Great Ormond Street and recently prepared a paper on some aspect of child behaviour.'

'Oh well she didn't mention that, but it explains a lot. She seemed to know a lot about syndromes called

Autism and Asperger. I found it fascinating. That's why we had a great day.

'I would like to visit the orphanage again, Stuart. Soon. I want to spend time with Schatzi. Can you arrange it, for tomorrow?'

'Just go there, they are just happy to have others around. I shall go there in the morning, if that's all right with your schedule?

'I have a meeting with my team at nine. Apparently, they have taken more suspected Nazis into custody awaiting interrogation. I will probably be late.

Chapter 21

Auschwitz Poland 1944

Now I had to find a surrogate mother who could be confined for 9 months in Auschwitz. `Impossible', I hear you say, and I agree but for an unusual event that occurred a year before our liberation.

On the 3 March 1944, some ten months before the Soviet army entered Auschwitz and liberated the our family together with more than seven thousand remaining prisoners who were mostly ill and dying, I found a young woman clinging almost unseen to the underside of the steps leading to the first floor of the hospital. It wasn't unusual for the doors to be unlocked and unmanned these days. Things were changing slowly, imperceptibly to most, but I could see and feel a change of atmosphere. It was not an unusual morning for me when I came to start my 5am shift. I was always looking over my shoulder. It was part of being a German Jew and as usual I did so that morning. Out of the corner of my eye I saw the outline of a body. I looked around to make sure no-one else had noticed it. The moon hovered above the lifeless trees surrounding hospital block and the stairs and hallway glowed white. It was very cold and she was shivering despite the German trench coat pulled tightly around her, her hair and face were matted with dirt. Her brown eyes wide with fear. I bent down, the young woman shrank back afraid of my touch.

'It's all right, you're safe with me, I am a prisoner too,' I said holding out my hand. I crouched there for some minutes trying to make her feel safe. Eventually, I put my arms under her shoulders and with what little strength I had left was able to pull her upright and guide her upstairs into safety.

Her story was remarkable.

Her name is Nadine Rekova, and with a German officer, Johann Bron, they were making their way from Stalingrad to find the retreating German army. Their journey had taken them past the Red Army encampments near the Donskaia-Tsaritsa river. Their campfires had help them find their way towards Kamyshevka where they were able to find food and shelter in abandoned ruins of a small village that had been occupied by the German 317st Infantry Division a few days before. It was unsafe for them to remain, but for a few precious hours of sleep before continuing into no-man's land again continuing westwards. They struggled along night after night, freezing weather chilling them to the bone. Johann was now suffering from frostbite and a bout of dysentery which slowed them further. Nadine did her best to encourage him to keep going, but the day before she reached the German lines, he refused to move.

He had lost hope and curled up in a disused tin shed and closed his eyes. Nadine was grief stricken when he insisted that she continue alone. She left him with the remaining scraps of food and her best thick woollen blanket, hoping he would survive and they'd meet again but not really believing it. Without Johann to help when she reached a German outpost, she was taken into custody as a prisoner. It was unusual that a single woman survived, particularly as she was Russian but her story of helping one just one German soldier and her vehement hatred of the Russian regime, lead her from one interrogation to another with more senior officers each time. I think her knowledge of the Russian army advance westwards may have spared her. Eventually, she was sent with hundreds of others of all colours and creeds to us in Auschwitz. She did her best to disguise her Russian roots on the journey through Eastern Poland. Times were beginning to become chaotic, even in this camp. Records that were normally immaculate began to breakdown as the gassing of prisoners was given the top priority.

I asked her what she thought had happened to Johann. She shrugged her shoulders and tears fell through the mask of distress. She hoped he'd been found alive, but didn't really expect it.

In the hospital, there was little hope for any of us. I hid her in one of the old disused laboratories that was cluttered with obsolete equipment no-one had thought of getting rid of and told her to stay put. I tried to explain to her that she had no hope of living more than a few hours if she was discovered.

She survived the night and I had come up with a plan to try to save her from the gas chamber.

My next waking hours bothered me greatly. I had an opportunity to make history. Here in this horrible place called a hospital where science held the glove of the devil each day. Was I going to join the band of his followers? I wrestled with my conscience, tossing and turning throughout the night about what was the right thing to do. Save her by imposing on her my relentless quest for scientific progress or try my best to protect her which would possibly mean a few weeks of life and then the certainty of the gas chamber. Could I persuade her to undergo an operation? I had lain awake trying to think of the best way to explain to her how I intended to try to keep her alive and fit. I wandered across the frozen earth towards the hospital the next morning, I had decided what to do, but only if I had her consent. I would explain the procedures, but I would not tell her the whole truth.

I had been horrified by the passing of the **Law for the Prevention of Genetically Defective Progeny** on 14 July 1933, which legalized the involuntary sterilization of persons with diseases claimed to be hereditary, weak-mindedness, schizophrenia, alcohol abuse, insanity, blindness, deafness, and physical deformities. The law was used to encourage growth of the Aryan race through the sterilization of persons who fell into the quota of being genetically defective. One percentage of young people between the age of 17 to 24 had been sterilized within 2 years of the law passing. All these statistics had been carefully documented and I came across them when I entered University. Remember genetics was to be my chosen area of research before my family lost their status in Munich and came to end our days here.

Early on in Block 10, as this part of the hospital was referred to, I discovered that from March 1941, sterilization experiments were conducted here by **Dr Carl Clauberg**. I soon found out that the purpose of these experiments was to develop a method of

110

sterilization which would be suitable for mass use on millions of people with a minimum of time and effort. These experiments were conducted by means of X-ray, surgery and various drugs. Thousands of victims were sterilized. Aside from its experimentation, the Nazi government sterilized around 400,000 of its own people as part of its compulsory sterilization programme.

Mengele was not involved in these experiments. It was Clauberg's field and he was reporting directly to Berlin and Reichfuhrer Himmler concerning the success of one of these methods, intravenous injections of solutions containing iodine and silver nitrate. I saw the bodies of these human volunteers with some horrendous side effects lying hidden stacked behind the hospital buildings waiting their turn in the gas chambers. In the end, radiation treatment became the favoured choice of sterilization. Specific amounts of exposure to radiation destroyed a person's ability to produce ova or sperm. Many suffered severe radiation burns during these experiments, so extensive as to cause a lingering painful death.

I had to paint a bleak picture, after all Nadine Rekova was a Russian and would undoubtedly be used in due course. I left out some of the most brutal pictures that still remain in my mind today, as I explained all this to her. She shivered at the thought of being a human guinea pig but agreed to my plan. Maybe I overemphasised the alternatives. I don't know but to me there was no other way to save her.

My plan was to ask Clauberg if I could carry out an artificial insemination using a surrogate mother. I couldn't approach him personally, so I pleaded with

Mengele to put forward my case. I told him, I thought it would be extraordinary to have this information, particularly for those Nazi's who wanted children but were unable to. This was their way to help to perpetuate the super Aryan race.

My argument was that it would be a much more acceptable than the Lebensborn or Fount of Life initiated by the SS in 1935 with the goal of raising the birth rate of Ayran children of persons classified as racially pure and healthy. The regime encouraged anonymous births by unmarried women at their maternity homes and facilitated adoption of these children by SS members and their families. They could rightly say that the children were theirs. Clauberg's answer came back as an enthusiastic 'yes'.

You may ask how Nadine remained hidden until the experiment. Well, we Jews have been hiding from the regime in a lot of cases right in front of their noses, dangerous but true. The first day, I put her in a nurse's uniform that had become available. The previous owner of it befell what would undoubtedly become Nadine's fate one day if I didn't intervene. They were all 'volunteers' from the camp so no questions arose as they were potentially living on borrowed time.

Here I must get technical about what I did, Jonny Wightman. I removed three of the eggs I'd taken during the autopsy from the liquid nitrogen storage and placed them under the microscope. I removed the nucleus from all three. I already suspected that genes were known to be the discrete units of heredity. They also generated the enzymes which controlled metabolic functions. I knew there was something else involved

112

that made it all work but what I didn't know then was that DNA was that elusive element.

It was me, Solomon Isaac, who took the massive leap into the dark, born of trust in my theories and the unusual wherewithal to carry them out.

On Clauberg's orders, I had collected semen samples from SS Officers including the camp commandant, Lieutenant Colonel Rudolf Hoss. These were frozen until ready. Clauberg was totally unaware of the true nature of my experiment but as others were involved at his insistence, I had to keep him fully appraised of the artificial insemination progress. Unusually, he had been very cooperative in making sure that Nadine and several other female volunteers, received a good healthy diet prior to the operation, but then, if it worked, he'd be receiving another plaudit from on high for his work.

I had been spending time on other matters for Mengele during this time most of them in the post-mortem chamber looking at grossly contorted faces from the nauseatingly unnecessary and for the recipients excruciatingly painful procedures. I was required to preserve and pack for dispatch to Berlin the organs for further research following the experiments. It was an awful experience and one I will never be able to erase from my mind, only time has blurred some of the images, Jonny Wightman.

I spent as much time as I could with Nadine. I came to cherish those moments. If I were honest, I think I began to fall in love with her. In some ways, she reminded me of Roberta Bron, especially as her eyes began to sparkle as her body started to recover. Nadine was very insecure and had told me what had happened to her parents and that she never wanted to return to Russia. You must remember, Jonny Wightman, that we both realized, from the hushed words of new arrivals that the war was beginning to be lost by Germany, but in the panic that would undoubtedly follow, where would we be?

Chapter 22

By January 1945, it became clear that the Nazi regime was being cleared from eastern Europe and retreating back to Germany. By the 17 January, Mengele and his notes disappeared from Auschwitz. Panic set in and the German SS began a murder spree, shooting the sick, blowing up the crematoria, the bath houses, and as much evidence of the holocaust as they could hide.

An unreal silence descended on Auschwitz. There was no chatter from the birds. They had flown years ago disgusted by the smoke and the smell. Inmates unused to the lack of barked orders, were milling around, heads down lost in their own misery.

As soon as I realised that Nadine myself and our baby were free, we stumbled around, stepping over skeletal bodies where life had once been, through the stench of blue smoke rising lazily from the smouldering ruins of former killing ovens now bent and twisted by the explosions that had taken place over the last few days. We carefully climbed the threshold of several huts and I searched the faces of bewildered men gaunt from hunger and too weak to smile. My father wasn't where he should be. I panicked, pulling up the blankets as I raced along the hut. We'd been through so much, I could believe he hadn't survived. Tears cascaded down my face. At the end of the first tier of bunks in the fourth hut, hidden under a lice-ridden blanket appeared a face, my father. I lowered my head and slowly lifted him, with the shallow embrace, his face lit up.

'Solomon, my son.' He was so very weak, I thought the sight of me would kill him. I nodded and held him a little tighter, taking the bottle of water and sugar from my pocket and held it to his lips. Most of the liquid dribbled over his stubbled chin but he revived a little and his shrunken eyes looked at Nadine and her blanket swaddling the little baby. A puzzled look crossed his face as Nadine showed him the baby's face for the first time. He looked into the eyes of the child. It took him back to the first day he picked me up in the hospital in Munich.

'Sorry, Dad, what did you say?'

His father mumbled again, 'He looks like you, many years ago.'

'Dad. He's your grandson. This is his mother, my wife to be, Nadine.'

My father straightened up as if his heart had started to beat properly for the first time in years. More sugared water passed his lips, as he held the bottle in his withered hands. His strength appeared to return. He held up his hands to Nadine's face and stroked it gently and said very quietly, 'Thank you, my dear.'

Over the next few hours, we all searched for my mother. We came across a group of women wandering around, and in their midst, I saw her. A sign of recognition passed over her eyes and she stumbled forward from within the group and we all collapsed on the frozen ground that had witnessed so many deaths. There was no strength left to shed tears.

On the 27 January, into the compound rolled several Russian tanks and a convoy of trucks, what confronted them were seven thousand starving skeletons, dead bodies strewn for all to see and hundreds of thousands of women's dresses, men's suit and shoes of all sizes from little infants to grown men. Even I had never seen this side of the camp.

As I looked around me, it was becoming obvious that our ordeal had not ended with the opening of the gates.

**

Jonny put down the manuscript and rubbed his eyes. When was this meeting? He picked up the covering letter. Looked at the date and wondered when Solomon would contact him again. He had no idea where he was staying. I like the guy wherever he is, he thought to himself.

He retrieved the next page and started to read.

The phone rang. Jonny Wightman put down the papers under the footwell of his desk. He'd come back to them later....

Chapter 23

Jonny poured himself another coffee and picked up more pages of `Stealing the Staircase to Heaven' manuscript. Solomon was right when he said it needed Jonny's writing skills as the writing moved from first to third person, every so often. Perhaps, Solomon moved from one to the other when things changed in his mind from being very personal to more about others. It didn't matter at this point.

**

Just before the Russians liberated the camp, the Nazis rounded up as many of the fittest inmates as they could to take back to Germany to work, but with a camp this large and in such chaos it was easy for some to hide. The Isaacs had managed to evade the route march out of the camp towards Germany and watched helplessly as tens of thousands under SS guard disappeared through the gates. Once it was clear that there were no more SS soldiers around, he attended to the sick and infirm who remained within the barbed wire compounds. Some food, medicines and dressings remained and were made use of by tending those who clearly had a good chance of survival. They were all gathered together in one block and received extra food. They were suffering in the main from starvation, sickness, loss of body fat and severe weight loss.

This field hospital was within days supplemented by the Polish Red Cross and many doctors and nurses from nearby Krakow. Solomon Isaacs continued to work helping the children whilst his parents became hospital volunteers, delivering water, washing patients, preparing meals and cleaned the rooms

On the cold grey morning of the 30 January when through the open gates of Auschwitz, shuffled the Isaacs family and Nadine Rekova carrying a grey blanket swaddling the baby. All were clutching blankets tightly around their skeletal frames. The wind from the East had died a little as they walked away from hell towards main highway out passed the piles of the frozen bodies of those who hadn't survived.

The Isaacs had been checked by the Russian NKVD, as the KGB were formerly known, then given certificates of their captivity in the camp allowing them to travel. They also received papers from the local Polish administration. They had eaten well that morning as they headed west. They did not realise that, as the war was still ongoing in the central region, their next home was going to be a transit camp in Katowice.

It was on the third day that two soldiers came looking for Solomon Isaacs. They found him sitting by a table scribbling furiously with a pencil, notes of his experiences of the past three years.

'What is your name?' barked one of the soldiers.

The sight of the British Army uniforms surprised but heartened Solomon. He stood up and bowed his head and told them.

'Come with us and bring those notes.'

Solomon stumbled into line followed by the second soldier. He was led into a small drab room. Seated at the desk in front of him was an officer inspecting various photographs. Solomon was ordered to sit and hand over the papers. The officer, who had introduced himself as Captain Campbell, started to inspect them carefully. He obviously spoke and read German fluently. He looked up and his blue eyes pierced the air between them. Campbell scanned the scribbled notes again and instantly knew the man in front of him was `intelligence gold dust'.

'So, you are Solomon Isaacs. You worked at Auschwitz for two and a half years in the medical centre and hospital.'

It was not a question but was said with some menace that Solomon could not understand.

'Who are these men?'

Three photographs were being swivelled around so Solomon could see them, instantaneously Solomon recognised the camp Commandant, Rudolf Hoss, Dr Carl Clauberg and Medical Superintendent, Josef Mengele and told the Captain.

The interview continued for several hours. Solomon answered all the questions with rapid details that Captain Campbell found both astounding and disturbing.

'I want you to go away and write everything you can remember with descriptions, times, dates. Anything,' ordered the Captain.

'Am I a prisoner again, Captain?'

'Certainly not, you are helping the Allies and this British officer to bring these criminals to justice.'

120

'May I make a request so that I can help without the worry of my family?'

The Captain was unused to being looked at so passionately. He nodded.

'I would like better resting conditions for my family with better food if I am of help to you capture these criminals.' He hesitated then continued and 'I would like someone to listen to me and take notes more quickly than I can write. This may save you a great deal of time.'

Again, the Captain nodded. In the meantime, he would rearrange life for the Isaacs family that day. He would also order his counterpart in intelligence gathering in Munich to uncover as much information about Herr Isaacs and his family and particularly the son, Solomon.

Chapter 24

Solomon Isaacs stood in front of the stenographer, his shoulders back and started to pace the room.

'Ready?'

The stenographer nodded her head.

'Mengele was fascinated with twins. His face came alive and the death mask gave way to a more animated expression. One day, he beckoned me over as he knew me from Munich University and that I was fascinated with genetics. We became for a fleeting moment two doctors with a scientific goal. There was a tender touch to his hands that I had not seen before.

'He became fanatical when he drew blood from both pairs. He told me he had found 14 pairs of Gypsy twins. In fact, they had been rounded up by the SS guards from all sections of the Auschwitz complex.

'One morning when I returned from my barrack, I was intrigued to see that he had placed two of the identical twins on his polished marble table and had put them to sleep. There was a smell of chloroform in the air. They lay there, peaceful in their ignorance, these gentle beings who had not even lived more than a few years and had trusted the gentle touch of Mengele and the luxury of a handful of sweets.

'As he injected a large dose of chloroform into the hearts of each of them in turn, I stood rigid. I was too shocked to utter any cry of pain as he began dissecting and meticulously noting each and every piece of the twins' bodies.

The stenographer looked up at Solomon, horror in her eyes. He waited before describing experiments to change eye colour, artificially conjoining bodies to create Siamese twins. Almost all of the experiments ended with the disposal of the little corpses in the crematorium.

'There was such a veil of secrecy that Mengele was able to carry out these crimes unchecked over the time I was in the camp.'

Solomon Isaacs held his hands to his head as he described some experiments he witnessed and gave detailed accounts to the stenographer. Tears streaming down her face. Graphic details of injection of lethal germs, sex change operations, incestuous impregnations, removal of limbs and organs, every experiment was logged over the next few days.

There was one subject and series of experiments that Solomon kept strictly to himself, hidden deep in the memory of himself and Nadine.

After the third day of dictation, Solomon was asked to attend a meeting of several officers from the armies of Britain, America, Soviet Union and Poland. His evidence had been distributed amongst the Intelligence corps of each army. An alert for the apprehension of Dr Josef Mengele was sent to all.

Solomon had seen Mengele leave Auschwitz disguised as a regular German infantrymen. He told them that rumours had spread that he was travelling to the Gross-Rosen work camp. This was early February 1945. Unknown to those in Katowice, Mengele had been captured as a POW and held in Munich. He was then released by the Allies as they had no idea that he was in their midst.

Solomon Isaacs remarkable ability to recall events and faces, led eventually to the capture and execution of ten members of the extermination camps at Auchzwich-Birkenau. Two of those identified by Solomon Isaacs were fellow Jews, Gurt and Elsie Heidmann, who were eventually detained by the British.

In return for his cooperation, Solomon, Nadine, their baby and the Isaacs seniors were granted travelling visas to England. Solomon was to report in due course once Captain Campbell had finished his intelligence work in Europe to him at the University of London, Kings College, where Campbell had been a research doctor before he was seconded into military intelligence in 1939. In the meantime, they'd be looked after by the British Army refugee office.

Chapter 25

Olga stood by the window looking out at the green pastures beyond the small garden of her cottage lost in what might have been, had her brother survived the blitz. Avyar was now just thirteen years old and about to sit his common entrance exams for senior school. His adaptation to life in England had been easy, especially here away from the destruction in London and the massive clear up operation, he knew nothing else but for Olga it was one of hurdle after hurdle as she struggled to deal life in England alone, save for him.

It had started when she realised that no-one had done anything to search 14 Lansdown Road and bury her brother and family. It's a matter for the Council, Florrie had told her. You better go and talk to them.

With Florrie by her side as moral support and as translator if things got too technical, they sat in front of Mr Greenhurst. He explained that the Council staff were overworked and short on the ground and often relied on help for local residents and the Home Guard. He'd see what he could do. He also showed them both what Prime Minister Winston Churchill had said last year to the newspapers.

Florrie read the editorial headline out loud to Olga. *'On the way back in my train I dictated a letter to the Chancellor of the Exchequer, Kingsly Wood, laying down the principle that all damage from the fire of the enemy must be a charge upon the state and compensation be paid in full and at once. Thus, the burden would not fall alone on those whose homes or business premises were hit but would be borne evenly on the shoulders of the nation. Those so affected should make their claim to the Exchequer.'*

'Well that's a start, eh, Olga.'

'Any idea what the payment is Mr Greenhurst 'cos this lady has nought?'

'Not really, we haven't had much call in these parts. My boss said he thought it was somewhere around a hundred pounds.'

Two days later, Florrie and Olga stood in the road as an old flatbed lorry and four men assembled with two Home Guard volunteers in front of the ruins of number 14.

'Better not stay here, luv. Maybe things you'd better not to see, when we start to look underneath this lot.'

It had started as a cloudy dull morning, but as the lorry filled with debris, the sun came out as they looked on.

'Florrie, you get back to the shop. I'll be all right here. Can you thank Mrs Ogsby for looking after Avyar and tell her I'll be back as soon as I can.'

An ambulance arrived just after lunch. Two men dressed in white overalls walked towards towards Olga.

'Sorry, luv but they've found four bodies in there,' said one of the men. 'Seems they were together in the back kitchen when it happened. Wouldn't have known a thing about it by all accounts.'

Olga put her hand to her mouth as they carried the first body to the ambulance. It was one of the children she presumed as the ambulance man seemed to be able to carry the cotton shroud with ease. Tears streamed down her face as the final body was carefully placed in the back of the ambulance. She felt an arm around her shoulders as Florrie returned with a mug of hot tea.

'Come on let's go home, shall we.'

'No, I want to see all of it, their home, their clothes, the childrens' toys, feel their presence. I need to touch their life, otherwise they'll be no closure for me.'

They both sat on the pavement and looked on as the second lorry of debris left to be joined by another. As dusk was approaching, the site of Number 14 Lansdown Road was level. Personal items broken, dirty and scorched had been piled in the back garden at Olga's request. She walked towards them.

Olga blinked out of her reverie as there was a knock on the cottage door. She walked through the sitting room and opened it.

'Hope I'm not intruding, Olga,' said Rees, the landlord of the only pub for miles. Amroth's New Inn was the focal point of the little village and Rees was not only the pub's owner but also Olga's landlord. He was the one who'd taken her and Avyar into the community and given her a reason to live. Whilst there was nothing outwardly amorous in their relationship, they both needed each other's company. She had no-one save Avyar and he'd been left with two young children when his wife had died several years ago. Being a tight knit Welsh community, it wouldn't sit well if they were seen together too often and too quickly. They often joked it would take ten years for the locals to accept that they could spend time alone with each other. They had their own chaperons, the whole village of Amroth. They often laughed at the absurdity of it all.

'No, not really. I was looking over the green fields, thinking about my first days in London. It makes me so sad, occasionally.' She rested her head on his chest and he put his arms around her shoulders.

'I know he said. You'll never forget and you shouldn't. That's what life is about. I find myself, at the most odd moments, thinking of Rita until the girls tell me not to look so sad.'

Olga pulled back and wiped a tear. Rees was tall, well built with a dark complexion. Olga always jibbed him about his complete lack of dress sense. He seemed to be colour blind, but gradually she'd taken over dealing with his wardrobe and sometimes now he looked almost elegant but not quite yet.

'Look. Milly's said she can't come in tonight. Can you fill in?'

Olga nodded. They both knew that for tonight at least they could enjoy each other's company after closing. Early on, he'd asked her to work at the pub whilst Avyar was a weekly boarder at a little preparatory school down the road in Begelly. The three children played together whenever they could at weekends and in the holidays and Olga did the babysitting for Rees' girls. None of the villagers would see anything wrong with that.

One weekend, Avyar stood in the kitchen uneasily moving on the balls of his feet uncertain what to say. He blurted out unexpectedly.

'We were learning about the war, Mum, at school on Friday.'

'What part, darling?'

'Some nasty things that happened in Germany. My friend, Andrew said he was a Jew and two other kids said they were. Am I a Jew, aren't I, Mum?'

Olga knew the day would arrive soon and here it was. She and Rees had debated this very moment in private. Olga had never had the courage to say anything save that she had escape Nazi Germany to save him and that one day he'd be reunited with his real Mum and Dad. Her enquiries after the war as to their whereabouts had always stopped at a dead end of silence.

'Come and sit down, here next to me on the sofa.' She took his hand and clasped her other hand over his.

'Yes, Avyar. You are Jewish.' She told him that his real mother and father had given him into her care as they knew she was able to get out of Germany and that they were about to be arrested by the Gestapo and transported to the East. She had tried to find out what had happened to them, but nobody knew. She told him how she had smuggled him out in a suitcase.

'That is amazing. I was quiet for so long.' He laughed at the thought.

'When we arrived in London, our whole world was turned upside down again. I'd lost my brother and his family, a home in London. I decided that with V1 and V2 rockets still falling, we'd be better off here away from it all.'

'Tell me about my other mum. What is she like?'

'I used to babysit you whilst they were working. They'd bring you into my apartment before going to work. I loved holding you, feeding you, cuddling you.

Your mother was tall with blond hair and deep blue eyes. She was always smiling and laughing.' Olga didn't mention the tensions that all Jewish families felt during those months. Rumours of transportation spread, no-one was safe. Avyar needed to hang onto good memories at this age.

'What about Dad?'

'Your father worked at the Lowenbrau factory as a manager. He was dark with short cut hair. Strongly built, towered over me like a giant. I used sometimes to think I must be a dwarf,' Olga quipped. No mention that he lost every vestige of self-respect when another non-Jew, who was ill-equipped for his job, took over and he was reduced to working with is hands and his strength, that would be for another time.

Avyar listened intently as Olga related stories about life in Munich leading up to their escape. Olga kept tightly hold of his hand, looking into his young eyes, wondering what impressions were forming behind them in his mind.

There was a knock on the door and in strode Catherine and Ruth, Rees' daughters.

'Come on, Avy, you're late. You haven't even got your coat on. Sorry, Mrs Smit we are meant to be in Saundersfoot. Going to the fayre.'

After they'd left, she hurried to the New Inn fastening her coat as she ran along the road, tears were beginning stream down her face. Rees was holding forth behind the bar as to why England had managed to beat Wales at the Arms Park in Cardiff. She heard him blaming the referee.

'Stupid idiot didn't see that forward pass.'

'Olga. You look awful. What's the matter?' Olga burst into uncontrollable sobbing.

'Sorry lads. Give me a minute.' They disappeared into the back room behind the bar.

'Oh, Rees. I've just had *THAT* conversation with Avyar. I feel such a fraud. I didn't tell him everything. I am ashamed at my own weakness.'

Rees took her into his arms and stoked her hair.

'Olga, you have done your best for Avyar. You have asked the right people. The Foreign Office letter says what we all now know, behind the Iron Curtain there are no official figures for survivors and the Nazi roll call of inmates was not wholly accurate in the last years as the killings reached their peak.'

Olga looked into his eyes.

'You think they escaped and ended up being deported to the Soviet Union or did they end up in the gas chambers like the other millions.' She pulled away from Rees.

'All I'm saying is you cannot do anymore. If you want my opinion. I think they are dead. Wait until Avyar raises the subject again.'

'What and tell him another story?'

'No. Look, darling.' He took her hands again. 'Tell him about your enquiries. Show him the letters. He'll understand.' Rees pulled her to him.

In August 1959, Avyar Smit entered senior school. Olga held back her tears as she waved goodbye at the railway station in Carmarthen.

'He'll be back soon. Half term is only a few weeks away,' comforted Rees.

'I know but the house will seem so quiet without him even though he seems to be out most of the time. I blame your girls.' Olga smiled at Rees took his hand and walked away from the station.

Before Avyar left, he'd said, 'Mum why don't you and Rees get married? I like him a lot. He'd look after you now I'm going to be away for the next few years and you need a man about the house. Catherine and Ruth would love it too. Well?'

'You three have been plotting, have you?'

'No, but you have to admit it's a good idea.'

Rees wasn't the sort of man to raise the subject. He thought too much about what Olga had suffered and what effect it would have on his girls. It just didn't seem right to ask. He wanted to but....

Chapter 26

Solomon Isaacs knocked on the door.

'Come.'

A huge smile crossed Captain Campbell's face.

'Captain.' Solomon proffered is hand.

'No longer, Captain. Just plain old Mister, now'

'How are you, Solomon?'

'I'm really very good, thank you.'

'And Nadine and the baby? Bring any pictures?'

'Nadine and Stewart are both great,' said Solomon handing over the latest photograph.

'He's the splitting image of you, Solomon. It's unreal. Same bone structure, underneath the puppy fat. Same eyes, hair colour. An exact copy.'

Solomon laughed. 'Everyone we meet says the same thing.'

Solomon explained how he had settled into life in London. His mother was a supply teacher in Wandsworth and his father was busy making suites for a tailor in Savil Row.

'Tell me about you research? It's ok, I am cleared to the highest level, so anything we discuss stays in this room.'

Solomon began.

'So, let me tell you what I have been researching into as part of my Doctorate. There is a great deal of research using animals, so the technology does exist to remove cells and look into their constituent parts. My theory is that if you take a donor egg and remove the nucleus, then with another whole nucleus you can fuse the two using electric pulses. Once this is complete you need to implant the fused cell into a donor female and then allow the natural gestation period to take place.'

'That's the theory, all I have to do is develop the hardware and the technique. There are some immense possibilities. Solving infertility, producing animals that give us more food and less fat, engineering crops that are immune to diseases and so on.'

Solomon stopped abruptly and looked at Campbell whose smiling face took him by surprise.

'Well, I hear your command of English is now impeccable, so the time has come for you to put your research here in London and your life's ambition to the test.'

Campbell knew already much about Solomon's work but just listened intently to what he described and when he'd finished.

'I have secured a special clearance for you to work in a top-secret research programme in the beautiful Wiltshire countryside at a government scientific establishment, Porton Down.' He passed across the table a document for Solomon to sign. Official Secrets Act stuff. You'd better read it. Once in, you are never out.'

Solomon scanned the pages and then signed.

Campbell then went on to describe some of the work about chemical weapons and research to eradicate some world health diseases being carried out at Porton.

'However, Solomon, the government want us to take the lead in cloning technology. They have given you a team of specialists. I will introduce them to you when we meet here next week. Would Wednesday suit? Say eleven in the morning?'

Solomon nodded, surprised by the turn of events.

'But what about my lab, notes, instruments .....'

Campbell stopped him with a raised hand.

'All seen to. No need to worry. They will be waiting for you at Portion. You will have a brand new facility that was finished last week. Final security checks are being carried out as we speak.'

Chapter 27

Doctor Solomon Isaacs knocked on Campbell's door at precisely eleven.

'Come in. Ah, Solomon, meet your 'family' as I like to call them.'

The four others were all standing.

'This is Dr Raymond Philp. Raymond's special talent was born out of his research as a microbiologist. Last year at Cambridge, he has recently been able to create an enucleated egg. The one you were talking about last week a cell without a nucleus.' Solomon shook hands and Philp sat down

Campbell then introduced Solomon to Jeff Andrews. A very tall lanky man.

'Jeff will be your engineering genius. You tell him what you need that hasn't been invented and he will invent it. Quite brilliant. You know the new handheld calculation devises. Jeff invented some of the 'bits in the middle'. Sorry, Jeff, bit crude to say the least.'

Jeff smiled and leaned forward to take Solomon's hand.

Turning to the small balding man, Campbell introduced him as Alfred Maidstone.

'Alfred is here to see that once you have secured a technical problem breakthrough, the necessary protection from worldwide patents is undertaken. He is a genius at technical drawings and description. He will

136

assist Jeff if anything is to be developed for your use inside the facility. That needs to be added.'

'Finally, may I introduce Simon Gray. He spends his days bent over his microscope searching for each individual's built in programming cells. I think that sums it up, Simon?. He has just completed his PhD at Cambridge under the tutelage of Raymond. Something to do with profiling that I am told will replace fingerprinting in due course. Isn't that so Simon?'

'There we have it, your team. They know all about you too!'

Solomon took a position in front of them as coffee was served.

'Well, Stuart told me last week that my English had improved. I hope that it will be good enough so that we don't ever misunderstand each other. My dad, who is a wonderful tailor, said to me once, and it has always kept me in good stead, 'measure twice, cut once'. That is my scientific yardstick, metaphorically speaking, and I am sure it is and will be yours. So, let our quest begin.'

Chapter 28

Jonny started to read the recollections of Solomon based on the papers he'd managed to obtain from his defence lawyer, Sir Julian Greenage, at the time.

R v Solomon Isaacs

Sir Ronald Buller had not long been appointed Attorney General for England & Wales. He was educated at Eton College and Oxford University. Now, over-weight and aging gracefully under his wig, his hair was thinning and turning white. He stood slightly stooped but with an overpowering demeanour that came from his aristocratic background. He toned this down by black rimmed glasses that he kept taking off and putting on for effect.

'If it pleases your Honour, I represent the Crown and the Defendant, Solomon Isaacs, represented by my learned friend, Sir Julian Greenage. The Defendant is charged with offences under the Official Secrets Act 1911. It will be revealed that he did deliberately and with considerable forethought stole confidential papers and give them to a member of the public.'

He turned to the jury and walked over to them, pondering purposefully allowing his slightly podgy hands to pull at the outer lapels of his gown.

'Each of you have probably read or heard about the allegations made by Mr Wightman in his newspaper about the untimely death of Private Osborne and the

138

claims made against Officers of the Armed Forces and the Ministry of Defence, but I ask you to put this behind you and concentrate solely on what you hear in this courtroom.' he continued.

'In England and Wales jury trials are used for criminal cases. Here we are dealing with a very serious criminal case. The twelve of you are here to uphold the right of the accused to a fair trial. The right to a jury trial that has been enshrined in English law since Magna Carta in 1215. I tell you this because this court would normally be a sea of many faces, but as you can see there are not many of us here and the court recorder will hand the transcript of these proceedings to the Ministry of Defence for safekeeping afterwards. You will also have been asked to sign an acknowledgement that you are bound by the Official Secrets Act. You will hear over the next few days, details of work that is carried out by our scientists for the security of this nation in these troubled times. You are not here to judge the right or wrong of these matters. You are here to decide whether and only whether the Defendant is guilty as charged. My learned friend will no doubt seek to persuade you that there are other more important issues at stake, but let me assure you the law is very clear and the Defendant broke that law.'

The slight bespectacled figure of Sir Julian Greenage stood. He was many years Buller's junior, but not all of it showed hidden under the weight of his wig which he straightened. His hands splayed firmly on the desk in front of him. He looked towards the jury. His voice for a slight man carried effortlessly across the courtroom towards them.

'I am here today to tell you that there is a defence in English law which I will call necessity of circumstances and coupled with that whether disclosure was necessary in the public interest so as to avert damage to life or limb. I will go further in this case and suggest on the evidence you will hear that my client was exposing serious and pervasive illegality amongst some of his colleagues and members of the armed forces.'

If Buller had taken exception to slights being made to his country's integrity, he didn't show it as he stood to call his first witness. It was obvious that Greenage knew him of old. It was interesting watching him trying to provoke the old man. Sometimes Buller was downright rude. Greenage left him to shout and bluster. The jury looked sometimes intimidated by Buller, yet his disagreeableness appeared to strike a cord with them. They were trying a case of what he referred to as 'heresy' and he represented the Crown.

'Commander Yardley, you've told the jury what to your knowledge happened in this case and you referred to the documents that they now in front of them, but can you answer me this. If you had been the Defendant what would you have done?'

'That is very simple, Sir, my understanding is that the Official Secrets Act does not allow for any public interest defence. Mr Isaac should have reported it me or my superiors.'

'Thank you, Commander. Please wait there, Sir Julian may have some questions.'

'Indeed, I have. Commander, may I remind you that my client was very unhappy about the disregarding of levels of Sarin used in the experiments and you have been a little vague over the question of dosage. I have in my hand a memorandum about limiting dosages to be used in Sarin experiments. The jury may have already read about your refusal to take any notice but I would....'

'Your Honour, this is completely unacceptable, I have already asked, and you concurred, that the jury put past matters out of their mind.' By the time Buller had finished his sentence his face was already showing the signs of bluster.

'Let me ask you another question. If Mr Isaacs had reported his major concerns to you, what would you have done?'

'I would have reported the matter higher up the chain of responsibility.'

'Would you have told them of breaches of the Nuremberg Code. You were in charge, weren't you, Commander? Or did you let the scientists 'just get on with it' on their own. Make their own rules. It was your job to ensure compliance, isn't that what civilised nations do?'

Buller interrupted again raising his voice gradually into a crescendo.

'That, your Honour, is slur on the Commander's position. I demand an apology.'

Ignoring Prosecuting Counsel, who was still standing ominously behind his table, the Judge told Commander Yardley to answer the question.

'I had received a request from my superiors to ensure that we used the lower range dosage. So far as I know this was adhered to.'

'My client says that the dosages were reduced, as you say, but to only 200 from 300 milligrams. Were you not told that the dosage should be ten times lower than that?'

Commander Yardley hesitated.

'Tell the jury what levels were to be used, Commander.'

'10-15 milligrams were suggested.' Yardley lowered his head.

'Thank you.' Sir Julian turned to Buller and nodded and then asked the Commander.

'You are also accused by my client of not observing the Rules of Informed Consent. What do you say to that accusation?'

Yardley set out the Nuremberg Code principles emphasising that his scientists had done all they could to explain the risks and answer any concerns of the volunteers.

'At what point did you turn a blind eye to changes in the way these Informed Consents were obtained?'

Buller was on his feet again.

'Your Honour, he pleaded, Sir Julian is now blatantly suggesting that the Commander took no notice of his superiors in the Ministry of Defence and Nuremberg Code. This is nonsense and is not acceptable, I want it removed from the record.'

'Sir Ronald, it may not be very palatable to hear that those at Porton Down may be a law unto themselves, but we are here because it is alleged those ignorances caused the death of a young national serviceman. You may carry on, Sir Julian.'

Sir Julian cross examination of Commander Yardley eventually extracted all the worries that had prompted Solomon Isaac to breach the Official Secrets Act.

Sir Julian decided that his client would not give evidence. It was patently obvious that Buller would unnerve him in cross examination and undermine Sir Julian's belief that what had been done by his client was not only justified, but because of the breaches of Codes within Porton Down, was in the public's interest to be published. He hoped it would also ensure that tighter controls on human experimentation were introduced.

In his summing up, the Judge instructed the jury as to the law as it applied to Solomon Isaacs' actions. The jury must then apply the facts as given to the law and reach a decision on that basis. The emphasis was clearly that Solomon Isaacs was guilty as charged.

As the jury retired, Sir Julian went over to Solomon as he stood in the dock.

'Let me tell you. They are under no obligation to and should under no circumstances obey the judge's obvious biased directive to convict you, Solomon. They should listen to the judge's opinion, but should be guided by their conscience, personal convictions and above all salient facts of a case that you and I put to them. Have faith. I'll see you later.'

Two hours later, the Court reconvened. The Usher took the verdict slip from the jury foreman and passed it to the Judge.

'Please stand, Mr Isaacs. The jury have found you guilty of the three offences under the Official Secrets Act 1911 that you were charged with. You have, by your actions, jeopardised the national security of your adopted nation. I hereby sentence you to Life Imprisonment with a minimum of 35 years. Take him down.'

Jonny started to read the supplementary notes that had been added.

Chapter 29

Jonny had now completed much of his further research and investigation into Solomon's story and was now ready to talk to him about the 'Stealing the Staircase'. He rose early. Today he was dressed more soberly than usual. Blue tie, white shirt and grey suit. Unlike Solomon Isaacs, Jonny Wightman needed his recording machine, he couldn't rely on his memory.

When he arrived at the Carlton Hotel, his watch told him he was twenty minutes early. Time for coffee and a little relaxation. He sat away from the entrance and surveyed the atrium flooding sunlight onto the sweeping mahogany and stainless steel staircase and luxurious plain blue carpet that swept upwards to the first floor landing balustraded in both directions to the various luxury suites on the first floor.

Jonny sipped his coffee taking in, as only a journalist can, the comings and goings of staff and customers alike. Each time his mind wondered to the last words of Solomon's letter arranging this meeting 'Jonny Wightman, you have read my story. It was I who gave Mrs Osborne those papers in 1953. That is why I chose you to give my life's work to'.

At noon precisely, a figure appeared hovering over Jonny's table. His bald head and grey hair and stooped demeanour belied the picture Jonny Wightman had in his mind. Solomon Isaacs smiled down from above. Jonny rose to greet him taking his hand.

'We meet at last.' These were the only words Jonny could think of.

'Yes, indeed, we do.'

A pot of coffee and biscuits were delivered to the table.

'Do you mind,' said Jonny producing a small discreet recording machine. 'I won't remember the details, but I suppose you'll recall every word.' Solomon nodded as a smiling Jonny pushed the record button.

'First of all, you promised you'd tell me "why me".'

'I did, didn't I. Of course you remember You remember Mrs Osborne and those papers I smuggled to her years ago.'

'I had seen so much horror with Mengele and his colleagues' experiments that I couldn't let it happen anymore. I wasn't part of that team of scientists, but I heard things I didn't like and made it my business to find out more. That interference ruined my future and my family's, but I don't regret it one bit. Your assessment of deemed consent, breach of the Nuremburg Convention and the use of young innocent conscripts was so well researched, I knew I could trust you implicitly.'

'Thank you, Solomon, but I must tell you that whilst I have been able to check very much the whole of your manuscript, there are still some loose ends that I cannot verify.

'I expected that. Such as, exactly?' quizzed Solomon, knowing the answer. Jonny opened his brief case and took out his notebook.

'First, what happened to Captain Bron. Did he die in Russia? Second, what happened to Roberta, his daughter? And now thirdly, who was responsible for you being uncovered as the whistle blower at Porton Down?'

'Jonny, these maybe loose ends but don't you see, I want to know as well. My book may provoke answers for us. What are we to do next? Put my book out there. Let everyone read it.'

'You want me to ghost it for you?'

'Yes, I do, if you are willing.'

Solomon explained that he had turned *Stealing the Staircase to Heaven* into a work of code and been allowed to keep the book as his reminder of the years he'd spent in Belmarsh. Jonny's mouth hung open thinking of the huge mind in front of him as he recalled the thousands of words that had been decoded and typed into the manuscript over the few months since Solomon's release. He now knew that the contents were accurately recalled by Solomon and would stand the test of the legal team that would undoubtedly be employed to advise the eventual publishers on, amongst other matters, the intricacies of defamation.

Solomon leaned across the table and paused the recorder, he then continued.

'Since the day I walked out of Belmarsh, someone has had me tailed, hence the use of Mrs Green as my delivery lady,' said Solomon. 'I am used to looking over my shoulder, as you may have gathered so it wasn't hard to spot the team at work.'

Solomon told Jonny about sending the Scotland Yard his typed copy of the original book taken from Belmarsh as a surprise.

Jonny burst out laughing thinking about the faces at Scotland Yard. Solomon smiled momentarily then became serious again.

'There may be some things in the book that someone somewhere high up is very interested in. I really don't know.'

'Solomon, I understand your worry, but isn't it just possible, probable, that Category A prisoners after their release, are monitored for a while. You were in breach of the Official Secrets Act, after all?'

'I suppose you may be right, but this feels like something more sinister to me,' said Solomon reluctantly guiding his paranoia to the back of his mind but still not convinced.

Chapter 30

Sitting around the oval highly polished table sat five men and one woman. In front of each stacked high were four hundred and twenty one sheets of "Stealing the Staircase". Pictures of former senior partners of the firm, some in suits, others in court regalia, hung on the wall, looking austerely down on the gathered few.

Solomon sat next to Jonny Wightman, now dressed as he was for their first meeting in a dark suit, blue tie and crisp white shirt. They'd met earlier across the street over coffee so that Jonny could explain the basis of the meeting. He'd also said it was an unusual request in his mind. That of meeting with lawyers was what the publisher did behind closed doors. Later, they had been joined by Rufus Alroyd, the head of what, euphemistically, he called the *trouble section.*

'You're going to be cross examined by some of the top lawyers in the field about certain aspects of your book. Remain calm and just answer the questions, full stop, nothing more. I'm not at all concerned but we, as publishers, need their OK.' Solomon looked at Rufus.

'I understand. You're pumping thousands into this publication and its promotion. You also want me to be able to stand the pressure outside in the real world. Isn't that part of today's exercise?'

Rufus smiled. Solomon had hit the nail on its head.

149

'My name is Hazel Plowright, Head of our Defamation Department, we have read your very incisive and remarkable story. Defamation, calumny, vilification, or traducement, whatever you want to call it, is the communication of a false statement that harms the reputation of an individual person, business, product, group, government, religion, or nation. In this case, you have covered quite a lot of ground and the devil lurks in the detail as you all know too well. She let the words hover over the table.

For the next three hours, Solomon was subjected to vigorous cross examination by Hazel Plowright, in particular, and the other two lawyers. They'd obviously divided the book into sections with Hazel taking the largest chunk. Every potential false statement was closely scrutinised and not once did Solomon hesitate or change what had been written. The pages were turned, the margins ticked against each cross-examined section until finally silence came. Hazel Plowright looked at her two male colleagues and turned to Rufus Alroyd.

'You have our blessing, Rufus.' She then turned to face Solomon again.

'Dr Isaacs, if I may say so and even if this sounds condescending which it is not meant too, I would love you to join our team here as a Consultant whenever you wish and good luck to you.' She passed her card across the table. Solomon, who was quite exhausted, managed a smile and bowed his head.

'One more thing before we wrap up this meeting, I have to say that casting my objective mind aside, I am truly sorry for what happened all those years ago, Dr

Isaacs, but I have to warn you that the journey you are about to take will undoubtedly need all your strength and may reveal more ugly truths but I'm sure you realise that. This manuscript will be a "bombshell" to some of those you've loved. I can see some problems ahead, Dr Isaacs.'

Chapter 31

'So, the manuscript stands,' said Rufus as he settled into his chair and loosened his tie. A week had gone by since the meeting with the lawyers. 'Now the marketing strategy.'

'Rufus, forgive me but was all this prepared weeks ago, you don't usually act so, how shall I put it, expeditiously.'

'Actually, Jonny, we started on this as soon as we saw the first draft. Solomon was right about the lawyers meeting. We just wanted to get the measure of his strength.' Rufus looked across at Solomon apologetically. He passed across the table to Solomon and Jonny a chronology of dates and proposals for gaining maximum coverage.

'We, at Grange House, can do so much but it can be somewhat ineffective without your involvement, Solomon. On page one, my team have outlined what we think is the best way forward. You are an unknown and this is an autobiography, so in theory did doesn't come high on our sales projections. However, it is an exceptional piece of work so first, we need produce and print ARCs (advance reader copies). They are more expensive to produce than the actual book, but with the promotion to the *good and worthy* of the trade and other hand-picked celebrities that I suggest on page two, I think we'll overcome that problem.'

Solomon and Jonny looked at page two and were astounded at the list of who's who and the venue booked for the occasion, not only was this going to be a UK launch but worldwide.

'You up for a well-rehearsed speech, Solomon?'

The rest of the meeting discussed flap copy, cataloguing, provision of post launch promotions at various high-profile book outlets, advertising and press releases in major newspapers around the world, in-store placement, trade shows, internet promotion.

'We'll provide a team for Facebook, Twitter and blogging for you. You just won't have the time to do this at first but as these platforms develop, a continued presence will be needed.'

As the meeting was drawing to a close, Rufus turned to Jonny. 'We think that once the launch has been completed, the Metropolitan Journal should come into the mix after all your name is credited by Solomon in his *Thanks to* section effusively. Can you write something that you can print and we can syndicate to similar journals around the globe.'

Jonny had already thought of this, hoping he'd be asked, and produced several close typed sheets and passed them to Rufus with a wry smile.

'Always the journalist,' said Rufus putting the papers with his bundle. 'So, 21 October, then.'

Chapter 32

Jonny Wightman did not now know that his life was about to change again dramatically because of Solomon Isaacs but in a completely different way to that which he expected.

Solomon had arranged to see Jonny the next day at noon. Solomon had said it was urgent but didn't want to speak over the phone.

Jonny was early and contented himself with catching up with domestic politics in an interesting article in the New Statesman. Two shots rang out. Jonny jumped to his feet to see Solomon stagger out of the open lift door and crumple to the ground, rolling as he tried to regain his balance.

Jonny ran over to him as everyone else seemed to be running for cover in the panic and confusion that followed. Solomon raised his head, as Jonny shouted for someone to get a doctor. He knelt beside him trying to stem the flow of blood from the hole in his chest.

'Jonny, I recognized the tail....' mumbled Solomon as he gave in to death.

Solomon Isaacs never finished the sentence that he had wanted to tell Jonny Wightman.

'I'll find whoever it was, Solomon. I promise,' murmured Jonny into unhearing ears. He looked around and grabbed one of the spent shell casings, looking towards the entrance as a darkly dressed figure

154

melted into the chaos and disappeared through the revolving door into the street.

Later that day Rufus Alroyd rang Jonny.

'What a tragedy. We are all devastated here. Look, I have spoken to Hazel at the lawyers. I am going to postpone everything, let the dust settle, as they say and see where the police investigation goes.'

'I agree, Rufus. Sensible decision.'

Chapter 33

Russia 1942

Johann Bron was picked up by soldiers of the Red Army twelve hours after he had insisted that Nadine carry on towards the retreating German lines. He now became one of 91,000 German soldiers taken prisoner when the German General von Paulus surrendered. Tired cold and malnourished, he survived only to be forced-marched to a camp in Bektova on the outskirts of Stalingrad. Johann watched as hundreds died on that march before the long train journey east into Siberia where the temperature hovered around 30 degrees below zero at night. Before the journey, the box cars lining the marshalling yards were loaded up. Men were crammed together with barely enough room to breathe. There were no windows, nowhere to sit, no food or water. Those who survived had endured the torture for five days. When the box car next to Johann's was opened, no-one appeared. Eighty six men were dead. Those from Johann's box car that had survived were ordered to assemble the dead on the platform. They were piled six foot high. Rigid toppled mannequins frozen in statues of death.

Several months into his captivity, it was so cold that the Russians forced Johann and his contingent of the Germans to build barrack shelters from the frozen dead bodies of other prisoners, solid as rocks with no fear of ever thawing.

Johann's main fear was falling ill. There was within the group a doctor, but he was ill-equipped to administer much medical help as the only supplies were for the guards and camp Commandant alone. Under Stalin's regime to be a Commandant of the POW camp was no honour. Only the cruellest and debased men were chosen. Better to have them in Siberia than near civilisation. Commandant Chukorov was built like a hungry bear. Facial hair masked scars from the fierce life he had lead in Moscow. His eyes were persistently blood shot from the copious bottles of vodka piled high outside his quarters. Johann had kept to himself his command of the Russian language for fear of being used by one side and hated by the other. Better to blend in and keep out of harm's way, if he was to survive.

Chapter 34

Jonny sat back in his office after wandering around London in and out of coffee shops dazed by what had happen to Solomon Isaacs.

Jonny knew now that he was the only one who could provide the ending to Solomon Isaacs' life story. And maybe discover those "loose ends".

He had deliberately made himself scarce after the shooting. He needed time to think. He knew that in the normal situation the Jewish faith teaches that traditionally, burial takes place as soon as possible, within 24 hours. This is not always possible and, given the fact that many modern Jewish families are spread out around the country, it usually becomes necessary to wait a day or two until all of the mourners can arrive. Jewish funerals cannot take place on Shabbath or on most Jewish holidays. He knew that Solomon was essentially, a loner, especially after being in Belmarsh Prison, so that it would be unlikely that the delay would be anything other than Police and Coroner procedures.

To Jonny, Solomon's story now had become even bigger. Over the next two days, newspapers had been covered with ideas as to motive and opportunity. They had little to go on. Jonny read every word written but could find nothing of substance.

Jonny Wightman made his way into Southwark Coroners Court on the mild April sunny day.

In the crowded courtroom, the first witness was the police officer who attended the scene. He described the deceased as lying outside the lift door in the hotel's foyer with a serious chest injury and produced a single shell case in a tagged plastic evidence bag. He told the court he expected that the second shell case had been retrieved before the perpetrator vanished through the chaos and into the street. A local doctor staying to the hotel had already pronounced Solomon Isaacs dead and laid a blanket over the body. Several witnesses, including Jonny Wightman, were then called to described what they thought had happened and finally the autopsy report by Doctor Grimond confirming two bullets entering the chest, one penetrating the heart, the other the right lung, had caused Dr. Isaac's death. He stated that death would have been instantaneous. A jury of five men and five women returned a verdict of murder.

'What'd you know, you're not telling here, Jonny.'

'David, how nice to see you again. How's life at the Standard?'

'Same old stuff. Boss said I had to come to see this one. Been several shootings this year already. Silly sod thought there may be a connection. I'm wasting my time here. The shooter's gun wasn't the same as the others. Modus operandi, you know, same gun makes them important in their world.'

'See you around, Jonny.'

Back in his office, Jonny fingered the spent cartridge case turning it round in his fingers. According to the pathologist's report it was a bullet fired from a Walther P38. Jonny began his research hoping it may take him somewhere. Accepted by the German military in late 1939, Walther began mass production at their plant in Zella-Mehlis mid-1940, using military production identification code '480'. After a few thousand pistols, the production codes were changed from numbers to letters and Walther was given the 'ac' code.

It would be impossible, thought Jonny, even as a very long shot, but if he could have the hammer indentation on the cartridge in his pocket matched with the Walther then he'd have Solomon's killer. Even better if he could somehow get hold of the bullet in police custody, but that was going to be impossible. There were thousands of P38s taken as souvenirs after the war and many kept by Wehrmacht soldiers and those escaping Germany in the immediate aftermath of its defeat. He knew somewhere in Solomon's past he'd find the answer. He returned to the page about the P38. Nothing would point to the killer, but Jonny wanted every detail. Maybe something would find a place.

From an engineering perspective the P38 was a semi-automatic pistol design that introduced technical features that are found in other semi-automatic pistols like the Beretta 92 and its M9 sub-variant adopted by the United States military.

The murderer must have known a lot about the gun to use it so efficiently. Jonny read on. You could chamber a round, use the safety-decocking lever to safely lower the hammer without firing the round, and carry the weapon loaded. This lever can stay down keeping the weapon safely 'ready' with a double-action trigger pull for the first shot. The firing mechanism extracts and ejects the first spent round, cocks the hammer, and chambers a fresh round for single-action operation with each. The killer must have known that an old P38 was dependable, most likely untraceable and was meant to be very significant as the weapon of death in Solomon Isaac's case.

'Here we are again,' thought Jonny, 'back in the 1940s. At least that's what the gun suggested.'

Chapter 35

The Coroner released Solomon's body for burial. Jonny was going to be an interested bystander hidden from view, camera at the ready, no doubt with several policemen scouring the mourner's faces for clues. He visited the Edgwarebury Jewish Cemetery in the London Borough of Barnet, the day before Solomon's ashes were to be interred. He walked around amongst the tombstones, occasionally stopping to read a life now forgotten. Over in the far corner near the outer perimeter, he noticed two workmen digging unmarked patch of ground.

'Warm day,' he commented.

'Aye, always a rush these jobs. The dead can't wait here.'

'Do I know the person for this plot?' asked Jonny.

The taller man took a piece of paper from is pocket. He read 'Some gezzer named 'Solomon Isaacs'.'

Jonny bade them 'fairwell' and searched around for a well secluded vantage point. Just to his right was a rank of five storey Georgian houses, one of which had scaffolding clinging to the front and several men working. Jonny walked over the road.

'This the new flat conversion, I've been told about?'

'Only one round here, mate. Must be the one.'

Jonny smiled at the man.

'Look, I'm in a hurry today. Any chance I could look at the first-floor balcony flat tomorrow?'

'Why not, you won't be the first.'

'Ok see you at 11ish'

As usual, Jonny did his homework. He didn't know much about Jewish custom and tradition, but he was about to find out. Jonny was certain that Solomon's funeral would be graveside only, not as in other cases where they would start at the synagogue and then progess to the cemetery.

As to who would be present, Jonny couldn't wait to see. Could Solomon's murderer be one of the 'officially' designated as mourners: parent, child, spouse, or sibling, but that didn't prevent other from being graveside. Who would be amongst the Nihum Avelim (comforting mourners)? Jonny asked himself. Who would place the earth over the coffin? That would be interesting, thought Jonny. He recalled that Jewish tradition teaches that one of the most important *mitzvot* (commandment) that can be performed is helping loved ones find their final resting place. This is both a symbolic and actual act. Their presence at a funeral would be a powerful act of service and love, 'or something else more sinister', added Jonny. He'd told Rufus and those from Grange House to present his apologies, but he'd be there in spirit.

Perched high in the Georgian building, taking photographs of the internal layout and view from the balcony, Jonny didn't recognise any of those clustered around Solomon Isaac's graveside. His powerful camera clicked away. He moved from room to room to change the angle. Fortunately, it was a cloudless sky and the sun didn't cast too many shadows. He watched the simple bio-degradable casket being lowered into the ground. The simple polished wood with glued corners, no nails whatsoever, slowly, inevitably, disappearing into the darkness. It wouldn't be long for Solomon Isaac's body to filter through the rotting coffin giving the earth its nutrients in a natural fashion.

As the gathered few made their way from the cemetery, Jonny noticed others, not directly at the graveside, slowly drift into the surrounding streets. His camera clicked away, catching their furtive glances. One, he thought he recognized, from somewhere but where?

Chapter 36

Solomon Isaac's had given Jonny his whole story. It wasn't meant to end with him being gunned down in a London hotel. Within all those pages he'd learned about what Solomon did and what he'd achieved, but he never expected to have to find out who killed him and why.

Jonny sat back in his study at home. He had installed a large white lecture board on one wall. At the top was a photograph of Solomon staring at him. Beside the main photograph were others that Solomon had included in the manuscript.

'Come on, Solomon, speak to me,' said Jonny out loud as he fingered the other photographs in his right hand.

He took a black pen and scribbled a list of important names from the 'Stealing the Staircase' manuscript down the right-hand side that he knew had entered and passed through Solomon's life, however briefly. He put them in the best chronological order that he could, putting dates from first to last mention.

He went over to his copier and placed each of the other photographs on the platen and enlarged each. He then pinned each one against the name on the right had side. Several names had no matching photographs. He then printed out all the worthwhile photographs taken at the funeral. On his desk he tried to match them with

165

the ones that Solomon and given him. It was an impossible task.

Tomorrow he'd ask, Rod Taskny, to photo-enhance each and then add life's natural aging process to each of those photos of Solomon's by the appropriate time span. He looked at the dates on the board and noted the approximate age they would be now.

As his head whirred, Jonny fell in and out a sleep. Tired and unrested, at 5 am he could not stay in bed any longer. He showered, dressed and cantered down the stairs into the street, holding his portfolio bag of photographs above his head to avoid colliding into some of the other early risers as he crashed through the front door and onto the street. As fortune would have it, the first taxi he hailed stopped and he got in.

There was no-one at 'Photo Blending Tech Limited' when Jonny arrived. He knew Rod was usually early but checking his watch realised that he'd have to treat himself to breakfast first. Sitting alone at 6.00 am in the morning in a London café is a little depressing, thought Jonny. Still the double expresso with two white sugars was doing the trick, particularly when sitting beside it was a cinnamon and current bagel piping hot and melting the two servings of butter.

When Jonny saw Rod, he vainly banged on the window to no avail but followed him as he tapped in the lock code and opened the door.

'Mr Wightman, my dear fellow. You're keen, Jonny. Must be important.'

'Thought I'd catch you first thing,' he said as he hauled the portfolio case onto the empty desk and laid out the photographs.

'I need some enhancement first, then I need you to age the faces.'

Rod examined them carefully.

'Actually, Jonny, you caught us at a great time.'

'Really, I always thought you said to me and I quote 'the timings not good, Jonny', he laughed.

'Well, this time it is, here let me show you why.'

Rod walked over to his computer and turned on the screen. A few second later a green page appeared and in the centre were the words 'Synthetic Face Ageing' staring at him.

'It's the latest technology in age progressions. We been playing around with it over the last few weeks and it works. Look.' Rod produced the picture a teenage girl.

'This was taken over thirty years ago and this one is what the computer produced thirty years later. Now look at this one.'

There in front of Jonny were two almost identical pictures of the teenager thirty years later, an original of now and the enhanced one.

'That's unbelievable.'

'Yes, it a pretty powerful piece of kit. It is the hand that guides the computer programme that counts. We must be able to produce corrections or alterations with flawless detail in order to create an accurate age progression picture. The most accurate renditions use the anatomical knowledge of child growth development; and some medical knowledge of what to expect due to diseases, alcohol and drug abuse, or other serious illnesses. I know that will be impossible in most of your cases, but it does need a great deal of background lifestyle, likely socio-economic details etcetera to get that close. We knew a lot about that teenage girl.'

'You want me to research each of the backgrounds of those in these early pictures?'

'As best you can. It really will help to get an accurate age enhancement. Sorry, Jonny but over to you. What I will do in the meantime is get some clarity into these early photos before we attempt to use them. See you in a few days, eh?'

'I'll send you an email, all the background information I can on each person.'

As soon as Jonny got home, he rang his senior researcher, Rachel.

'Sorry, Rachel, been tied down on another matter. Will be out for a while. In the meantime, I need you to get as much information on the people in the photographs I'm sending round by courier as you can. I've named each one, but I need to know, lifestyle, schooling, routines, fitness, friends, the lot. As usual it's urgent.'

'What are you up to. Trying to find a murderer, Jonny Wightman?' Rachel always used his full name when she knew there was something important being researched by her boss. She'd worked with him for years and understood at this stage not to ask too much, but she knew what he was doing.

A week later, Jonny knocked on Rod Taskny's door at Photo Blending Tech Limited.

'Here's the background info you wanted on each of the old photos. Best we can do, Rod.'

'Thanks, Jonny. Anders here is the guy we use on this bit of kit. Anders used to be part of the old artists system.'

'Which is the best, Anders?' asked Jonny.

'Personally, Mr Wightman, as an artist I could produce an image for the public to view and compare with a person already seen. It leaves a bit to the imagination to record and retain a similarity. But, a computerized image, based upon a photograph and limited by the software used to create it, is viewed as an exact image, leaving no room for the mind to readjust that retained image. In other words, the age progression made by an artist allows the viewer to imagine who it could be, while a computer-generated age progression image leaves little room for those similarities which may evoke recognition in someone's mind.'

'Yea, I see that, but you didn't answer my question.'

'Well, with this new software, I can do both. It asks a lot of questions as Rod had said, hence this bundle you've just given me about each person. You will be amazed with the results, said Anders holding up the package.

'I'll leave it to you and look forward to being amazed.'

Back in his study at home, Jonny tried to add significance to each name, but he couldn't be certain he was being objective enough. Solomon had tried to be objective, but sometimes Jonny had his doubts. After all, it was Solomon's story and some things may not manifestly what they seem to be. He'd learned that from the many stories he'd covered over the years.

Grey is a very difficult colour to be precise about. How good was Solomon with the colour grey?

Chapter 37

Jonny remembered that part of the manuscript about Solomon's wife, Nadine, and her escape from Russia with Captain Johann Bron. They had both assumed that he'd died in the battlefields of western Russia in 1942 and so had Jonny. Could he still be alive somehow?

No stone unturned, Jonny started to do his research. He'd used his contacts in the police force to trace the old man to Munich. Would this trip help him? He hoped it would.

Jonny took the morning Lufthansa flight to Munich and landed at noon. He walked through airport control and bought tickets for the S-Bahn at Munich Airport Centre. Much more convenient than taking a taxi and suffering the inevitable traffic delays as the trains ran all day every ten minutes. Forty minutes later he arrived at the Hauptbahnhof. Rachel had booked him into the Hilton Centre located above the Rosenheimer Platz S-Bahn line from the airport. Jonny didn't leave the station but took the elevator directly from the station into the hotel. As usual the front desk staff were friendly and helpful. Jonny had been here before on an abortive first effort to locate Johann Bron, but now he had an address of a care home some hour's drive outside the city.

The next morning, Jonny, found the hire car in the basement carpark and headed to northwest out of the inner city passed the Nymphenberg Palace veering north towards the Olympic park and arriving at a gated two storey 1970s building more in the form of a school house dormitory than a Care Home. He waited patiently in reception and was shown into a large bedroom with the wall littered with photographs, pencil sketches and paintings. In the corner was a large bookcase with what appeared to be a collection of the world's literature in several languages.

'Captain Bron will not be long. It's his day for physiotherapy and we are running a bit late.'

'It's not a problem. He seems to be well read,' said Jonny pointing to the bookcase.

'Oh yes. The Captain also speaks several languages fluently. You find him a fascinating man, Mr Wightman.'

With that the matron left Jonny alone. He started to study the pencil sketches that were clustered together all dated between 1945 and 1952. They'd been folded and rolled many times until finally they'd been allowed to see the light of day permanently.

Captain Johann Bron threw out his hand as he walked purposefully into his room. Jonny shook it generously. Bron stood proud and tall for a man of his age, his head slightly stooped. He had deep blue eyes and a kindly face masked behind years in a Soviet camp, thought Jonny.

Please call me, Johann, and I will assume, Jonny, will do for you.'

'I see you've been examining my drawings?' said Johann standing beside him, in English with the barest hint of a German accent.

'You drew them!' said Jonny surprised.

'After my capture, I was taken to one of the camps near the coal mines in the Siberian town of Vorkuta. It was there that I started drawing, as a record of that terrible time. It gave me hope and a little peace, as when I was sketching my mind was totally focused forgetting all other thoughts.'

As they moved from one drawing to another, Johann added some description.

'That's the latrine. It was a long deep pit with a log across it. For fun the Russian guards would wait until it was loaded with prisoners, then they would roll the log causing them to fall into the cesspit where we were supposed to drown in their own shit. Some of us survived as you can see,' he said smiling.

'That's barbaric.'

'I know, but they were paying us back in some small way for the German Army's treatment of them and their citizens as we butchered and killed our way across their land towards Stalingrad in 1942 and 1943. It was their revenge. Look at this one,' said Johann pointing to two sketches side by side.

'We were starved most of the time. One of ours found a way of supplementing our diet. The cattle corn we were occasionally fed would not digest so at night they would sneak to the cesspit and strain that ocean of shit for the undigested corn kernels to grind, washing them as best we could, mixing with sawdust and make cornbread.'

173

'A picture of revulsion,' said Jonny looking at Johann Bron. 'What's this one?'

'Even worse, Jonny. I didn't witness this personally but drew the story. A soldier described to me one night how he was forced to work burying the dead from a Russian field hospital just before we were shipped East. He heard one of the sick saying that he must have his leg amputated but asked to keep the leg because it still has some fat on it for stew.'

'My God, sorry, but did he get...... get his leg back?'

'The leg disappeared and later someone brings him a cup of stew.' Johann drew back from the wall and sat down.

'Jonny, back then no one saw this as an irrational statement. Life was hell, he knew he eating his own flesh in that stew. He never asked. You must remember that the men who surrendered at Stalingrad were already in very poor shape. There had been no consistent food for weeks. Cannibalism was a common occurrence. I don't know if he ever survived the war. Most prisoners didn't, despite the Russian statistics that you and I have read.'

There was a pause as Johann ran his fingers through his hair and then placed them in his lap as if remembering some other awful detail and finally lifted his eyes and looked at Jonny.

'This broken army, my broken army in threadbare rags for uniforms, with no supplies, was forced to march in temperatures approaching -50F at night for miles, without food. So, by the time the Russians got us to the holding camp, hundreds had fallen or had been shot for not marching. Our main fear was getting sick. Getting sick was an automatic death sentence.'

'Johann, you survived.'

'Yes, I did indeed.'

He smiled, remembering with fondness the moments with Nadine before the night he told her to save herself.

'You were one of the last to be released.'

'Yes, I still don't know why, many others had gone home by 1950. I think it was the political hostilities between East and West Germany that made things worse. It was Chancellor Konrad Adenauer who succeeded in concluding negotiations for our release. By the end of 1955, I was one of the last prisoners of war to come home.'

'What did you come home to?' asked Jonny, knowing it was a chilling experience for Johann, but he wanted to see if this man held other secrets in his heart. Jonny hadn't told him anything other than he was researching pre and post WWII experiences.

Johann looked at Jonny. His face became contorted, the smile had got lost in the agony of realisation that he came home to nothing and was lost in a world that had changed. He'd been a prisoner of the time he'd spent in the Army, then a prisoner in a gulag and then in 1955 he had been a prisoner in his own freedom. Not knowing what to do, where to go and who to see.

'Nothing that was familiar to me,' said Johann sadly. 'I was an only child, I found out that my mother and father had died when their house had been bombed and obliterated following blanket incendiary firestorm that enveloped everything in this beautiful city. My wife and family had been condemned to live like refugees after the Nazi's stripped us of everything and sent me to the Eastern Front. The house they were living in suffered the same fate. Everything had gone.'

Jonny nodded. There had been no mention Nadine in the story so far. Was Johann going to say anything?

'Sorry, Johann, can we go back to your capture by the Russian Red Army. You must have been one of the lucky ones to have survived alone in no-man's land between two opposing armies. How did that happen?' pressed Jonny.

'I was lucky, yes. I haven't ever spoken of this before, Jonny. What kept me going was hope. After running away from the Russian counter assault at Stalingrad, I stumbled across an old farmhouse.'

Jonny listened to the story that came from Solomon Isaacs' manuscript. Although some of the details sometimes varied, Johann told Jonny about Nadine. He noticed a sadness in Johann's eyes as the remembered Nadine Rekova. Jonny had already decided not to mention what Solomon had said or what he'd learnt about Nadine. He didn't want to muddle Captain Bron's thoughts at this stage. The right time would come.

'War puts some interesting people together just by chance and circumstance.'

'It does, when you least expect it. I believe those months living off her hidden vegetable garden, gave us both the physical strength to endure what was ahead of us.'

'Johann, you mentioned something that intrigues me, some moments ago when you were talking about

176

the Nazi's. You said, 'they stripped us of everything'. What did you mean?'

Johann got up slowly, his knees creaking as he rose, and walked to the desk. He rolled back the top and took a key from his pocket and unlocked a drawer and pulled it towards him. He turned and in his hand, he held some medals, a commission certificate into the German Army with a Swastika emblem at the top and handed them to Jonny.

'That's who I was before….Rising star of the Wehrmacht. Look at the date. A Captain at 23 years old.'

'Before?'

Jonny noticed hidden in the same drawer what looked like a Walther P38.

'Before. Yes, before some Nazi reported us for a son being born out of wedlock by my daughter, Roberta. We tried to bring him up as our own, but someone found out and told the authorities.'

'Who was the father?'

'Roberta would never tell us, but she loved little Schatzi. It means 'treasure', I think, in English. He was a little treasure. So bright, always asking me things. He had his head in a book most days as soon as he could read. I used to tell him words in Russian, he'd soak them up like a sponge. I used to tell my wife he was a genius. He was the son my wife and I never had between us, but I thank my Roberta for giving him to us for those few years. But they're all gone now. Just me left.'

'Have to go too often these days. Old age can be a bugger, Jonny. Excuse me, I'll be back.' Bron disappeared to the bathroom.

Jonny took the opportunity to inspect the Walther. Good working order, he thought to himself. They talked more about the war and his survival for another hour, then Jonny switched off the recorder.

'Thank you for your time, Captain, it's been a pleasure to talk to you. Take care of yourself.'

'You too, Jonny.'

Just as he was through the door, Jonny, turned.

'Do you get away from here at all, Johann?'

'No. Not much. The odd pre-arranged trip, it's not a prison here, you know but it's not easy for me these days.'

Jonny walked through reception towards his hire car and on the spur of the moment walked to the front desk.

'Excuse me. Just been seeing Captain Bron. He a remarkable fellow. So much history, I couldn't get a word in edgeways. He must be sad sometimes not be able to see the outside world, a man like him.'

'Oh, he gets out, not very often but when he wants to. Just back from a week away, actually, we do have records just to keep an eye on some of them. They're sometimes very forgetful but not Captain Bron. Here let me see. It was some time ago. Don't know the exact dates. It's a bit vague, somewhere in France, by the look of things. An address in Caen, sounds like a hotel or bed and breakfast, Port de Plaisance.'

'Yes, that's what he said,' lied Jonny. 'I'm glad he gets out. Thanks.'

Chapter 38

Jonny thought long and hard about Nadine and Johann Bron on the flight back to Heathrow Airport in London. He knew that both would want to be re-united. A lot of water had passed under the bridge, still, maybe it was a good thing he hadn't told Captain Johann Bron just yet. Solomon wouldn't have wanted it, he told himself.

Jonny wondered what Johann Bron had done in his time away from the Care Home. Had he been to England what did he do and who did he see? Why didn't he tell Jonny?

Later that day at the board in his flat, Jonny added the photograph of Captain Johann Bron for the first time and then stared at the other names. The one thing he had to keep reminding himself was that whatever was in 'Stealing the Staircase' was almost certainly accurate and came from a man who had a remarkable memory for details and dates.

'So, where next, Mr Wightman?' Jonny said to his empty office at home. If evidence pointed to Johann Bron, the Walther P38 would be available for forensic examination later.

There was the sound of the intercom.

'Parcel for your Mr Wightman. It needs to be signed for.'

'I'll be down,' said Jonny already halfway out of the flat, keys jangling in his hand.

He carried the parcel to his desk, ripped it open and stared at the first photograph, with his heart beating fast laid out the rest covering the whole surface. He couldn't help ringing Rod immediately.

'They're amazing, Rod. I'll call in one of these days so you can see the difference, if any, between fact and fiction, your fiction.'

Slowly and methodically, he fixed them onto the board next to the names from Solomon's treatise. 'It was almost always someone you know', he said over and over again staring at the new images.

'One step at a time,' Jonny recited to himself. He tentatively pinned a photograph of Captain Johann Bron on the suspects' side. He had a gun, not necessarily, the gun, but Jonny was almost certain he'd been in England at the time of the shooting but did the image of the murderer fit the old man. Jonny's recollection of the dark figure gave him nothing but for now the all-important motive was missing.

'Rachel. Hi, all OK? Could check passenger list and entry and exit records for a Captain Johann Bron coming from Caen, address in Munich. Ship, I would think but if that doesn't bring up anything, nearest airports in the area.'

'When?'

'Last three weeks.'

'Thanks.'

Jonny opened the page he'd marked 'Nadine's story'. His rough notes were in the new folder. He added Rachel's lifestyle resume and the new photograph

181

of her which tallied almost exactly with Rod's version of ageing. The woman at the graveside was Nadine. He rifled through the rest of the file then remembered he'd put her latest known address and telephone number on the board. 'Amazing what information you can get on people these days. Nobody's privacy is sacred these days'

'My name is Jonny Wightman.'

'I know who you are, Mr Wightman. The question is 'what do you want with me?' Her tone was harsh yet not dismissive.

Jonny was not surprised by her tone realising that she would blame him for the revelations that put Solomon into prison. It must have been shocking for her, but Solomon did save her life in Auschwitz.

'I'd like to meet, please. At your convenience.'

'For what purpose, may I ask again?' This time her slight Russian accent came to the fore as she raised her voice authoritatively.

'According to interviews I have had with the police, they seem to me to be making very little progress in finding your husband's killer. I want to know more. You know who I am and why I am interested. Please can we meet.'

There was a long pause and Jonny held his breath.

'OK, Mr Wightman, Mona Lisa Café, 417 Kings Road, Chelsea. Shall we say lunch on Thursday 12.30, suit you?'

'I'll be there. Thank you. Mrs Solomon, I will be sure to book a table away from flapping ears. Unless I am mistaken, I do believe there's an overflow room upstairs.'

Clutching a photograph of Nadine, and the one enhanced by Rod, Jonny recognised her sitting in the corner. He handed her a blurred, black and white photograph of her with Solomon taken in 1945. Then Rod's update, followed by his taken at the funeral in full colour. She stared at them as he laid them on the table, moving the cutlery and plates to one side.

'Would you like a drink?'

Two dry white wines arrived with the glasses frosting at the edges.

'Cheers.' Nadine clinked her glass in recognition of Jonny's chivalry.

'Where did you get this one?' said Nadine holding up the small 1945 photograph.

'My office obtained it from immigration records. We have a lot of contacts and information passes both ways,' lied Jonny.

'Nadine, tell me about Solomon. Things that are personal that I cannot read about in the public domain.'

'Mr Wightman, surprisingly, there are many things I still do not know myself. We both had to sign the Official Secrets Act as soon as he finished his doctorate at University here and from then on, we never discussed his work.'

'But he did come home each night after work.'

'Not always, as he's told you, he was stationed in Wiltshire. I saw him each weekend. I never wanted to move to Wiltshire. He understood that and I honestly don't think he wanted us there. It was hard at first, but I got used to it. I think our son, Stewart, suffered more. He used to rely on his dad answering all his questions. I wasn't as good, they were always about scientific things.

I must have spent a fortune on books over those years. I'd get Stewart to write down the questions and wait for Solomon to telephone.

'You know he saved my life.'

'I escaped from Russia with the help of a German soldier, Johann Bron. I never heard from him again. I left him in a snow-covered field. He'd run out of hope of ever making it home to Germany. After that, I ended up in German camps and finally in Auschwitz.'

'Forgive me,' said Jonny glancing at her left arm. 'No number?'

'Surprising really, but it was 1944 and things were beginning to fall apart. After he had put me in a nurse's uniform in the hospital, Solomon came up with an idea that would give me the possibility of survival. I had to do the right thing for the Nazis.'

Her face coloured and she looked away from Jonny, embarrassed at the memory.

'Sorry, I know this is bringing back painful memories. Please stop if you want to.'

'No, it's all right.' She continued, 'The right thing was to become pregnant with an Aryan child with a proper bloodline. Solomon assured me that he'd be the father and would marry me if we all survived and that they'd never know. Stewart was born just before our freedom came. The chaotic last few days when the Germans realised they could not defend their actions in Auschwitz and fled, leaving Solomon and I and Stewart hiding in the hospital block.

'A British officer, Captain Campbell, helped us resettle in England because Solomon had helped identify a number of war criminals. Solomon then went to work for him after his doctorate.'

'Stealing the Staircase' had told Jonny how his son, Stewart had been conceived.

'Forgive me for prying, Nadine, but you and Solomon never had any other children.'

'We tried but there was something wrong inside me. I never found out what. I don't think they knew exactly. Solomon kept the Reports. I read them but they were too technical. Anyway, I had Stewart and he was a handful, but I was grateful for him.' She smiled.

'You said on the telephone that you knew who I was. How did you know me?'

'I read your piece on Mrs Osborne's son back in the 1950s, the one who died during the Porton experiments. It caused waves throughout the Ministry. They closed down various experiments immediately. Everyone was under suspicion for breaching the Official Secrets Act. The interrogations that followed were very upsetting for me and Stewart despite the fact that we knew nothing.

Solomon was hauled into interview after interview. It lasted for months. Some nights he'd be allowed home, under house arrest, looking worse than the day we were freed from Auschwitz, dark rings under his eyes from sleep deprivation. I'd wake up at night listening to his whimpering, rolled into a feotus ball next to me. He was inconsolable most of the time. Just sitting in the lounge staring into space.'

'Was he the only one under suspicion?'

'I don't think so. He mentioned seeing some of his colleagues, coming and going. They were kept apart from each other, I think. He never talked about it. One day, I came home and he was sitting in the bath, fully clothed, no water, flicking the safety switch on a gun he'd rescued from the camp, a reminder of dark times. I asked him what he was doing. He looked at me and said, 'I was wondering how many of us this thing had killed'. We had no bullets for it, so I wasn't afraid, just sad.'

'Can I see the gun?'

'I don't carry it with me, you know,' quipped Nadine, the taking another sip of wine.

'Yes, of course.'

They arranged to meet again, next week.

Nadine's flat in Pimlico was on the top floor with no lift, 43 in heavy brass stood glistening as the automatic hall light reflected off its surface. Jonny caught his breath before pressing the bell.

'You must be fit,' were his first words of greeting.

Nadine was dressed in a grey trouser suit with white blouse emphasizing her full figure. This time she had let her grey hair fall loose around her face. The smell of roasted coffee beans hung in the air as Jonny surveyed the room.

'How do you like your coffee? No let me guess. Black, one sugar,' Nadine called from the kitchen.

'Perfect. Where did you get these pictures? They must be quite valuable.'

'Maybe,' said Nadine handing Jonny the mug of coffee. 'They are mostly signed prints but artist's editions or else edition artiste. I like the two early Dali's, particularly the Don Quixote. The swirls of the pen are so free.' She stood gazing at the picture.

'I'm a more traditionalist,' said Jonny moving towards the water colour of the sun setting over St Mark's Square in Venice. It was numbered and signed with 'A E' in one corner.

'The most beautiful city in the world.' Solomon took Stewart and I there just before the trouble at Porton. Her face now became sad and the lines around her eyes became exaggerated. She collected herself and opened a cupboard in the bedroom and returned with a box. Inside covered with a white duster was a Walther P38. She handed the box to Jonny. He took the gun out of the box in its plastic wrapping.

'That's funny, it looks better now than when Stewart last played with it. He loved running around shooting imaginary enemies. Solomon always told me to keep it wrapped that's probably why. More coffee?' she took Jonny's mug.

'Interesting piece.'

'Yes, I'd never be part with it whilst….. Solomon wouldn't like me to let it go. He always said that it was for Stewart when he went, so now it's his bit of personal history.'

'Where is Stewart these days?'

'Still working. I don't think he'll ever retire. Some hush-hush work on genetics in Cambridge. Just like his father. Have you ever met him?'

'No. I assume that's a picture of him over there on the mantelpiece. If it wasn't for the hair colour, I'd think it was Solomon.'

'Oh, his hair is now the same colour as Solomon's. Your right, I can't see anything of me in him.'

'When did you last see Solomon, Nadine?'

187

'On the day they released him from prison. I waited at the end of the street. I wanted to see him again just once. He had cut himself off from the world after Porton. Didn't want me and Stewart to suffer the ignominy of having to visit him for years. Stewart was only nine at the time. At first, I was angry. He had no right to cut us off.'

'Why do you think he wanted to remain, how shall I put it?'

'Hidden?'

'Yes, cut off from you, Stewart and his previous life. You must have been very upset with him.'

'At first when he refused to see us or talk to us. Thirty five years is a very long time to be apart, I'm sure he made up his mind as soon as he was sentenced that his life was over. I know he felt betrayed after all he'd done to invoke justice into a cruel world.'

'You must have angry with me, too,' said Jonny.

'I was. If you hadn't published. If Mrs Osborne hadn't come to your office. If Solomon hadn't had a conscience. If someone at Porton hadn't fingered him. "Ifs", they swirl around your head and grind you down like an unyielding foe. You have to live with them but also look at the good that happened afterwards. I don't know but I have to content myself, as you do, I assume, that other sons like Mrs Osborne's, are still alive.'

'Yes. I really did not have any choice. Solomon did what he thought was right.'

'I know he did but…..' Nadine looked around at her existence. What might have been, as her gaze settled on the waters of the lagoon in Venice, bathed in the orange glow of the brush strokes of the setting sun.

'Nadine, would you have any objection to me setting up a meeting with Stewart?'

'No, of course not. I had to explain to Stewart. Bit at a time as he grew older, the tragedies that had befallen us throughout our lives and then why his father was in prison. There was nothing that I hid from him.'

Chapter 39

Jonny turned to the board on the wall. Nadine Isaacs' name was added to the possible suspects. Motive was possible. Opportunity and weapon were also ticked for the moment.

Jonny parked his black convertible in the Addenbrooke Hospital carpark and unfurled the soft top and secured the roof. He loved this little car in London, but long journeys could be uncomfortable for his long legs. He walked towards the large information board and surveyed the buildings looking Treatment Centre on LV 6.

At the Department of Medical Genetics' reception desk, Jonny asked for Professor Stewart Isaacs.

As soon as Professor Isaacs appeared out of the lift and walked towards reception, Jonny thought he was about to meet the man behind 'Stealing the Staircase'. Every little thing about Stewart, face, build, his gait, his demeanour, everything was Solomon, his father. It was unnerving and amazing.

'I am sorry to trouble you in such trying circumstances, Professor.'

'It's all right. The past few weeks have been very difficult but none more so than things that happened long ago. Anyway, my mother has told me a lot about you, Mr Wightman,' said Professor Isaac as he took Jonny's hand.

190

'Jonny, please. May I call you Stewart?'

'Of course, everyone does. Professor is so lofty, I think. Come, I've put everything on hold for an hour or so. You have my undivided attention.'

Jonny was shown into a study lined with expensively bound books, a fine mahogany desk with red leather inlays behind which Stewart took his seat.

'Fascinating subject, genetics. Not that I know much about it. What exactly do you do, Stewart?' confessed Jonny trying to get a nagging thought out of his mind about something Solomon had written which worried him, one of those loose ends.

'Me, these days co-ordinate the young ones. We adopt a broad approach to 'Medical Genetics' here. Taking what my father and others after him started. He had a vision and I have a vision, a different vision. Mine is applying genetics to diagnostic and therapeutic approaches to disease. The ongoing research here addresses a broad range of monogenic and multifactorial genetic disorders. Many research programmes and clinical activities are run jointly with other departments at Addenbrooke's and elsewhere. We used to share the Department of Pathology here, but I fought to separate it and so the University of Cambridge Department of Medical Genetics was established here a few years ago. We have close interactions between the Department and members of the NHS East Anglian Medical Genetics Service including NHS consultants and the Directors of the NHS Molecular and Cytogenetics Laboratories. Medically qualified members of the Department also have clinical duties in the NHS Clinical Genetics

Department. Sorry, too much information, anyway, there you have it, Jonny. It's big and very important.'

'Certainly is, and therefore I must thank you for your time.'

'Mother said that you were trying to enlighten the police as to the person who killed my father.'

'No, not enlighten them, at least not at this time. As I told your mother, the police appear to have very little to go on and, further, they are unaware of my interest at the moment. Of course, once I have anything to say to them, I will do so but until then, everything stays with me.'

'My mother told me years ago when I was growing up that there had been a newspaper report that exposed unethical Porton Down experiments and that your work was based on a leak, shall we say. Yes, the least said about that the better. It has caused a lot of heartache for my mother. She was very angry, and I think still is.'

Jonny searched the Professor's eyes for any indication of deceit in the statement. He wasn't sure as the Professor turned away from his glance.

'Yes, that was my work. As a young reporter in a minor provincial newspaper that day is etched in my memory. I can tell you that I had no idea who leaked those papers at the time and I wouldn't know for a very long time afterwards. Actually, after your father was released from Belmarsh, he came to me with his life story which admitted it was he who delivered those papers to Mrs Osborne. Your mother told me a little of what happened to your father afterwards, but it was and still is, totally shrouded in the Official Secrets files at the

Ministry of Defence. Everything was done behind officially closed doors in 'camera'. I was..........'

'Let me stop you there, Jonny. I used to lay awake at night after my father did not return to live with us. I couldn't understand why he'd abandon me. Left my mother and me to fend for ourselves. Oh yes, we were provided for by some Ministry pension scheme. As I grew used to it, my mother told me more and more. When I heard about your report, you were on my 'hit' list for elimination in my child's eye, of course,' he said smiling.

'I understand, Stewart. You have to realise that Mrs Osborne had no idea who had delivered the information, all we knew is that her son had died in....'

'Yes, I know. I know you had no choice, I just wish I hadn't lost my father.'

Stewart walked over to a locked cabinet and punched in the code. The spring-loaded door swung open. He retrieved a large yellow folder brimming with papers.

'Brought those from home this morning. Never showed them to anyone, not even mother. It would have upset her too much. You will be the first. Don't start reading it here, it will take too long to assimilate, take them with you, I don't need them now my father's dead.'

Jonny took the folder and started to open it.

'No, leave that for later.'

Stewart gave Jonny a rough resume.

'I am sure you'll have some queries for me once you read the details.'

'Stewart, before I go can I ask you another question?'

'Of course.'

'Were you aware that your mother kept a gun from the war?'

There was a hesitation before he answered.

'Yes. A Walther P38, if I remember. Haven't seen it for a while. Used to run around with it, playing cowboys.'

'Yes, that's what your mother said. Remarkable condition for such an old piece. Anyway, thanks for being so forthright in such circumstances, Stewart. It was a pleasure to meet you.'

They shook hands outside the lift as the doors opened and Jonny squeezed in amongst others dressed in white coats. On the ground floor, he walked to the reception desk with the new file safely tucked into his briefcase.

'There was a conference in London last week. Something about 'advances in hereditary disease prevention'. I thought I recognised Professor Isaac there, at my hotel?' Jonny asked the receptionist as he was leaving the building.

'Yes, Professor Isaac was one of the main speakers. It wouldn't have been at the hotel, he always stays with his mother.

Did Stewart lie about not seeing the gun since childhood? Maybe he hadn't seen it for years and yet he had a mind and recall, many of us would be grateful for half its capacity. Jonny shifted another name and photograph into the suspects' column as soon as he arrived home. Solomon's book had certainly made

Stewart angry for himself and his mother, was that motive enough? At the moment it was. He put a tick in that column. Maybe the file from Professor Isaacs would help.

The yellow file contained undisclosed details of the court case against Solomon Isaacs. There must have been someone in the courtroom taking illegal shorthand notes for this amount of detail. Who had arranged this unauthorised intrusion into a court case held in camera? Someone who wasn't happy with the proceedings or the outcome?

Chapter 40

He looked at the board again, inadvertently pushing the photograph of Captain Campbell up and down until it fell to the floor. He picked it up and took a closer look.

'What have you got to say, were you in court. You were his "mentor"?'

Jonny placed the three photographs on the table, one of the frail old man being helped along the path at the cemetery and placed it next to Rod's aged enhanced up-date. Definitely the same man. What was he doing at the funeral? Yes, they knew each other years ago in Germany and then back in the UK when he gave Solomon the opening for research at Porton. Had they kept in touch despite the Court case, despite the obvious disapproval of his colleagues? Was it Campbell who compiled the court case notes and why?

Jonny had read the file Stewart had given him several times. Solomon's manuscript revealed that during WWII, when he met Campbell, it was as a result of his employment in the Intelligence Corp in Germany and Poland.

By reputation and having to deal with them, Jonny knew that British Intelligence is the oldest, most experienced organization of its kind in the world, the unseen hand that has influenced world events. Despite losing an Empire, the British retained much of intelligence infrastructure that then existed and given that benefit to NATO and Europe. It was this need to protect the Nation that at some point had become too powerful within its own walls and at its core was the 1911 Official Secrets Act.

It's all right to punch above your weight, admired and trusted by the CIA and feared by the Russians but to keep a cloak, with the help of the various Ministries of Whitehall, that protects the identities of the shadowy figures in and around the Porton Down establishment, Jonny thought it all went too far in the case of Solomon Isaacs.

Inevitably, Campbell would have involved in the evidence collecting against Solomon, but Jonny was concerned that Campbell may also have been caught up in the witch hunt that followed by the suits from MI6.

Campbell was an old man now living under the same roof as his adopted son, Schatzi. Jonny opened the file of names and addresses that Rachel had put together. He leafed through it and found Stuart and Schatzi Campbell's address, 'The Barn Ropers Lane Middlehurst Kent'.

Jonny typed it into his computer. Multimap located the property and gave him directions. 'Shall I telephone first or just think of an excuse once I'm there?' mused Jonny. No, Campbell, wouldn't appreciate a surprise at his age. Jonny picked up the telephone. After five rings it was answered.

'Campbell residence, how can I help?' said the female voice at the other end.

'My name is Jonny Wightman. I was a friend of Solomon Isaacs and I would like to meet with Mr Campbell Senior as I have some…'

'Wait a minute, I'll see if Mr Campbell is available.' A minute or two passed as Jonny waited.

'Thank you, Annie.' Jonny heard a quivering voice and a door close. Campbell picked up the telephone.

'Yes, Mr Wightman, what can I do for you?'

'I really don't want to talk on the telephone, Mr Campbell and I apologise for disturbing you, but I would like to drive down and talk to you about Solomon Isaacs, if I may. I saw you at his funeral with your son and I am trying to thread some pieces together about his death.'

'Mr Wightman, I've told the police all I know. Nothing more to add.'

'I think you may have more to add. I was his friend and I am trying unravel loose ends. Please spare me some of your time.' Jonny sensed a softening in his voice.

'Oh, yes, very well. Where do you live?'

'Central London.'

'Come for lunch on Thursday. Noon suit? I'll get Annie to cook us something nice.' There was a pause.

'You know I admired Solomon, very much, but he did upset many people, still had an amazing mind yet, he suffered so much and never complained. I blame myself for what he did. I suppose I should have realised certain things about Porton Down, but I suppose that's easy in hindsight. He thought that innocent servicemen shouldn't be put through what he'd seen in Auschwitz,

198

even though those experiments were not carried out in his department at Porton.'

'Me too. I have been learning a lot more about him as the days go by since his untimely death. It's very kind of you to spare me the time. See you at noon on Thursday.'

Clearly, thought Jonny, Campbell wanted to talk to someone. What could he now add?

Chapter 41

Jonny was sitting opposite Stuart Campbell at his dining table. The room as oak panelled and would have been dark save for the sunlight cascading through the leaded windows that graced one end of the room overlooking the lawn with willow trees edging the small stream that seemed formed the southern boundary of the Barn. A former hop storage building that was converted into Stuart Campbell's house many years ago had been recently redecorated and smelled clean apart from the steam rising from the crock that stood in the middle of the table pervading the air with a mouth-watering mixture of lamb and mint.

'As usual, Annie, this looks magnificent,' said Campbell as he served generous portions for both of them. Annie brought around the vegetables, serving Campbell first then Jonny.

She smiled to Campbell

'Where would I be without you, Annie?'

'I must thank you for seeing me and being generous with your time. You suggested we talk as we eat. Did you mean that?'

'Hang on a moment. Let me turn these damn hearing aids up. Ah that's better. Of course, but don't let the food go cold.'

Jonny told Campbell about his research into Solomon's death and Campbell related what Jonny already knew about the interrogations after the war ended in Germany when he was in intelligence and the meeting with Solomon and the subsequent return to Britain, but Jonny wanted to move on to something that had been troubling him since there was so sign of Schatzi Campbell and no mention of him since he arrived for lunch. Hoping not to upset his host and remembering the photograph taken at Solomon's funeral, Jonny plunged in.

'I saw you with a younger man at the funeral, I assume that was your son, Stuart?'

There was a long pause while Campbell keep eating. Finally, his fork hovered over his plate and moved his chair back a little, crossing his legs and lifting his glass of wine to take a large sip.

'Yes, that was Schatzi?'

He told Jonny how they couldn't have children and how his wife, Naomi, had fallen for this orphaned little boy.

'Jonny, there were thousands of children who found themselves abandoned, orphaned or lost in Germany after the war ended. Families had posters put up all over the country. The British Government estimated that there were over 50,000 orphans. We found many just wandering the countryside as we drove around. Some living in trees, boxes, abandoned houses, sheds and anywhere that offered them shelter. It was devastatingly sad. Many, we took to rescue centers.'

'How were you expected to cope?'

'Sadly, it wasn't my job. I personally couldn't do anything. Naomi realised the awful lack of help for these youngsters and did her best to encourage short term fostering from places as far away as the Netherlands and Belgium. It was quite a task. Many wanted to adopt but without papers and searching records, it wasn't possible in case someone returned to claim their child. Many of the records were destroyed in the saturate bombing from our side at the beginning of the end.

'It was difficult enough for me to organise for the Solomon family's paperwork to allow them into Britain. There were still restrictions on Jewish immigration from before the war.'

'Naomi must have taken a chance with Schatzi. Did you adopt?'

'No, we couldn't. We fostered Schatzi to begin with and then adopted him years later when there was no evidence of any family being found alive.'

Jonny savoured the last mouthful of the lamb stew for a moment.

'Did you or your wife know about Schatzi's prodigious mind when you fostered him and brought him to Britain?'

'Yes, in a way. One of my colleague's wife was a psychologist and they talked about him at length before we brought him to England. Then in London we learned more at Great Ormond Street Children's hospital. The first thing to be done was to overcome the long term physical and intellectual effect that this war had on Schatzi. It was severe to say the least. He'd survived the Allied bombing campaign against Munich.

Almost all the schools, hospitals and teachers had disappeared. His body was suffering from malnutrition, although the nuns did their best, supplies were short.'

'How long were you in Germany?'

'Two years on and off. Naomi came home first with the necessary paperwork for the fostering of Schatzi and I stayed on chasing war criminals, with some success thanks to Solomon's amazing ability to remember and recall events and faces, but some did get away in the chaos, I'm sad to say, especially that evil man, Mengele.

'You never talked to him afterwards about the indictments issued for war crimes, I assume.'

'No, I couldn't. Actually, I kept my own diary. I know I shouldn't have but…. Bit of a mess, I fear.'

Stuart Campbell pushed his plate away and walked and picked up a tattered notebook from inside his roll-top bureau.

'You can borrow this. It's not for the public domain, even after all these years. Background, shall we say,' said Campbell as he sat down and handed it to Jonny.

'Thanks, I'll read it later.'

'Stuart, one thing has been puzzling me. Were you required at Solomon's trial. It could have been thought that as you were responsible for him being seconded to Porton Down that you were in some way responsible for what happened. Is that a fair comment?'

'No. I mean, yes. it's a fair comment, but remember, he was vetted by MI6. He wouldn't have got the research job without their say so.'

'What happened after Solomon was convicted, to you, I mean?'

'The University was pressured by MI6. I sure of that, but I was allowed to continue teaching but only academic stuff. Demoted you may say. Eventually, I was pensioned off, bags packed, office cleared. Gone, far too young to retire.' said Campbell. 'Yes, Jonny, I was angry, very angry.'

Nothing in his voice changed but Jonny was sure, whatever Campbell said, he blamed Solomon Isaacs for what happened.

'And how are you coping with Schatzi now?' said Jonny changing the subject.

'Since Naomi died six months ago, he's become, how shall I say, 'lost'. She made him well enough to cope with life and achieve some great work, but I'm afraid to say I'm too frail and too old to guide him at the moment. Annie does her best, but she's not a Naomi. Solomon's funeral was the first time I had succeeded in getting him out of the house since she died.

He stays in his study most of the time now working on some scientific challenge relating to the treatment of Alzheimers using stem cells. He tells me what he's doing and the theory seems as if it should work in practice, so I have told him to get back in touch with the University and ask them to put it to the test. They started testing two months ago. It could be a major breakthrough, if he's right and very often he is.'

'It may not be appropriate, but can I meet him? You said you'd told him I was coming so it wouldn't be so unsettling.'

Ignoring the request, slowly Campbell pushed himself upright grabbing his stick from beside the chair, his knee creaking under years of usage and the weight of his own body.

'Old age is a battlefield, Jonny and one we do not survive,' he said as he straightened and turned and wandered slowly over to a bureau, again took the keys from his pocket and opened the top drawer. He handed a tattered glue notebook to Jonny.

'Naomi's diary. Another part of our story, Jonny. There's not much left for me now so maybe it can be of some help to you in finding the murderer although I'm not sure how.'

Jonny wasn't sure either, maybe the next question would help.

'Stuart, daft question, I suppose,' said Jonny innocently, 'but most war veterans keep souvenirs from their time in the forces. Do you have any?'

'Oh, I kept an old Walther P38, but haven't seen it since we moved here years ago?'

Chapter 42

London

Back in London, Jonny, moved Campbell's photograph on the board. He ticked "motive" and "weapon" from his interview with Stuart Campbell but the man he'd seen disappearing into the street after the shooting was too nimble, or was he? "Motive", Campbell's University position was certainly ruined by Solomon's whistle-blowing and even if he was old he undoubtedly still have connections to the intelligence service. Jonny scratched his brow and sat down, opening Naomi's diary.

Jonny opened the first page. It was headed 'How shall we cope?'

Saw Ruth's boss today, Professor William Caines, Head of the Child Psychology Department. Very polite. She'd told him a lot about Schatzi and how we'd been allowed to foster him. He asked lots of question about Schatzi. I told him everything I could.

Without too much patronising, he told me that Stuart and I are blessed with such a child but there'll be many times that we won't believe him. At seven, he would have preferred to help him earlier but said it's never too late. He told me that lot of his colleagues, in the field, have a great deal to say about Schatzi's condition so I must read as much as I can.

I asked if everyone like Schatzi were the same and needed the same treatment. Each case is different. If in doubt ask me. Regular weekly consultations started. Schatzi was apprehensive at

206

the first two meetings but soon couldn't wait to see Bill, as he called him.

The next page was headed "New beginnings". Jonny was starting to understand how difficult life was becoming for Stuart and Naomi Campbell.

Professor Caines confirmed that Schatzi's condition was incurable and would last his lifetime. I remember the words "He'll never outgrow the problem". We would have to be there for him as long as he trod this earth. I was determined from the day I fell in love with Schatzi in the orphanage convent in Munich, that I would accept and enjoy the quirks that made me laugh out loud on that first day. 'Wow'. I laughed again to myself today remembering that short introduction to my life with my son. It probably won't be the last time this little word lights up a bad day with him.

I cannot compare Schatzi with others, he is too bright, even for Stuart, with all his University degrees, let alone Professor Caines, Bill, to understand. Today, I vowed to myself again that come what may, our child was going to be unconditionally loved and accepted. It's not difficult to remember Professor Caines' words sometimes. They seem to be absorbed word by word for later. Today, he said that there will be times when you feel uncomfortable and intellectually troubled. Always remember, the first time he hesitated then stroked your hand. He needs you, you're his protection, his programme of routine, you organise his life so that when he wants you, he can come. That's his security. He hates disruption, unscheduled changes. I know you have created a safety zone at home. He needs this to feel safe and secure. One step at a time.

Jonny was both troubled and uplifted. He couldn't, in all honesty, imagine that he could find the strength to do what Naomi did for Schatzi.

I've tried to be as consistent as I can, but it troubles me that he may not respond in the same way in new environments as he grows. When we went to Professor Caines' last session, the buses were not running so we had to go by black cab. Schatzi threw a tantrum. He refused to get into the black cab. He's been in cars before, but this was different. People in the street thought I was abusing him in some way as I grappled to force him. Several passers-by stopped to watch, uncertain what was going on. It felt awful. I felt awful. I told the taxi man to leave. Schatzi quietened as I held him tightly, stroking his head. Then he said something that made me take his hands in mine before we walked for a while. I thought I was going to die if I had to get in that black hole, Mummy. In Black Holes, you get sucked in as they implode. Why did God invent them?'

The next page was headed 'His Disability is an Ability? I need to....' Naomi had never finished the heading. Maybe she never knew whether she could accept this truth, if it was one.

He relies on me. We went for a drive. He stared out of the window to the side watching the images fly by merging into each other, mesmerising, his eyes flicking back and forth. It would have made me feel sick, but he seemed to be memorising each individual item as it passed by. Suddenly, he said to me that I was his foundation and what he'd become would be down to mummy. I said to him that we should see how far we could go together. Then came one of those Schatzi moments. When we were driving home, a car overtook us, I said, 'he's got his foot to the floor'. Schatzi started stamping his foot onto the floor, saying, so have I mummy. He didn't stop till we got home.

I must be careful how I speak to him.

Jonny leafed through the pages picking out bits and pieces over the years.

How will I not let him down? I bought him some new science books. Stuart had recommended them. I still marvel at his ability to concentrate to the exclusion of all else for hours on end. He forgets to eat so I have to remind him and bring him to the table. Today, it was a six-hour marathon read of 'Advances in Medical Science'. He is only ten now, I need to remind myself. As we were eating, he said, 'as Dad's not here, Mum, can you tell me if I'm going to live forever, now that they think they have discovered something called the aging gene. What if I was able to manipulate it for you and me to live longer? I told him to talk to Dad as I thought it may be an interesting line of experiment.

I'm feeling sad tonight. Schatzi asked if, when his real mum gave birth to him, he hurt her by being so big. I told him it would have been a very joyful time and any natural pain would have been forgotten immediately as he lay on her body and she cuddled him. He then put out his arms and I cuddled him. He lay his head on my body. I don't know if he was remembering. I think he was because he said that he'd died just then and come back to me.

Mummy, why do I find it difficult to play with other children? Do you? Yes. You're just very sensitive. Do you want me to show you how? He was silent. I must learn how to teach him to play in structured groups to begin with. I'll arrange a birthday party for him.

Today was his birthday. Eight children were invited and all of them came. Schatzi was the centre of attention and loving it, until the music started. I could see he was in difficulty when he put his hands over his head then seconds later as I got to him, he banged both fists against the table in the restaurant. We had to end early.

209

Why did we have to leave my party early? He'd forgotten what had happened. Be positive. You have huge advantages over other children. You can hear, smell, taste and touch much better than me or Dad. That means sometimes, if they all come at once, like at your party, you need to shut them off. That's what you did. It worked.

I am trying to teach him to read social clues from the outside not the inside. There's no magic pill, as Professor Caines told me very early on. He's been a rock and full of good advice. We don't go to see him now that Schatzi is older. One day I'll take him back but not now. I know that I am to Schatzi, that in his own way, his heartbeat and the centre of his universe, as he has become mine, that's why today was a real breakthrough. He'd just finished reading 'Is God real?' and put the book down. 'Mum, you must let me make my own judgements and mistakes'. I don't believe in God anymore; he has made too many faulty judgements.

London University have asked Schatzi and me to an interview. It's got nothing to do with Stuart, in fact, it's not his College. He wanted no input, but he does know details. He's very proud. All he said was that Schatzi was very young to be considered but they really didn't have any choice, his results were prodigiously good. Stuart and I know he's a genius and they are about to find out.

We waited outside the admissions office at Senate House London. I'd bought a suit for Schatzi. He felt uncomfortable but eventually I persuaded him it was the right social thing to do. He could wear his old jeans and scruffy sweatshirt once he had been accepted. Mum you have to be with me to begin with. Of course, I'm your foundation, so you said. You are. He laughed. The preliminary chit chat was unbearable for Schatzi. He fidgeted and moved around in his chair as if plagued by ants. Things changed when he was asked about his aspirations. For the next ten minutes Schatzi was lost in his world. Explaining the theory and detailed experiments he wanted to undertake to establish a myriad of still unknown facts about DNA.

A letter came this morning addressed to Mr S Campbell. On the back was the insignia of The University of London. You open it, mum. It simply said that Professor Hutton would be delighted if Mr S Campbell would join his team and study for his undergraduate degree at the same time as the preparing for his Doctorate in the field of genetics on a subject matter to be agreed after further discussion with his colleagues.

Jonny put down the Naomi's journal. Even he was tempted to say, "wow".

Chapter 43

Hampshire England

Jonny closed the blinds to shut out the gloomy evening sky and poured himself a whiskey. Campbell had possession of a Walther. Jonny hadn't seen it. Where was it now?

Jonny sat down and started to read through Campbell's notebook. Jonny's gut instinct told him there was something here somewhere and Jonny's instincts were usually right. After he read them, he was struck by the sheer numbers of individuals that Solomon had described and their crimes. All those responsible were named. Jonny recognised many of those named from the manuscript, others were unknown to him.

He knew about the two Jewish prisoners who were accused of brutality and murder against their own people in Auschwitz. Gurt and Elsie Heidmann. Strangely, Campbell had made a comment 'Solomon very uptight here'. What did Campbell mean? Campbell would expect another call from him now he'd read the diary. Perhaps this time, he could meet Schatzi.

He'd never been able to meet Doctor Schatzi Campbell. On the spur of the moment, he rang Stuart Campbell to thank him for lunch and to ask him what his notes meant by the use of the words "Solomon very uptight here". Annie answered the telephone.

'Oh, Mr Wightman. It's terrible.'

'What?'

'Schatzi's dead. The police are here and the local doctor. After you left, I went to give him his evening meal and there he was lying on the floor. Mr Campbell is devastated. He just won't say anything coherent, so the doctor's given him a sedative. Shock, you know.'

'I am so sorry. Anything I can do, please ask. Please tell Mr Campbell that I rang to thank him and you for a lovely lunch. I'll call again soon. Goodbye and tell him I'm so very sorry.'

Jonny read all the obituaries of this genius scientist, winner of a Nobel Prize, awarded the OBE by the Queen for services to science. Not one mention appeared as to the reasons for his death 'causes as yet unknown' was mentioned. Jonny would have to read another Coroner's Court decision, unless he died a natural death. Jonny didn't think so.

Schatzi had joined his mum at the end of inky black hole that had drawn her in some months ago. Stuart Campbell had inferred that he had been unable to do much about his son's melancholy over the past few months. Jonny felt a terrible pang of guilt about his intrusion into Campbell's life in his quest to unravel Solomon's murder. So he was surprised to be asked to attend a very private burial in the local churchyard in Middlehurst. Campbell had invited him specifically as he wanted him to stay over at The Barn. Jonny was intrigued by the invitation thinking that they did get on with each other and had Solomon as a point of contact.

Stuart Campbell looked amazingly well despite losing his wife and son in quick succession. Annie guided him to the car and assisted him into the front seat. Jonny was surprised when she took the driver's seat and led the way back to the house.

'Please sit down, Jonny. Scotch?' he handed Jonny a generous glass full and sat back behind his desk.

'Cheers.' Jonny raised his glass. 'To Schatzi's life and what he achieved against all the odds.'

'Thank you, Jonny. I'm sure Naomi's diary gave you an insight into how difficult it was. On a lot of occasions, I was just a bystander, but I'd like to think she knew I was there when things were bad. A lot of couples' marriages don't survive the pressure, you know.'

'I'm sure you did your best to give him as normal a life as could be.'

'I'd like to think so. He hated travel but very occasionally he'd pluck up the courage to come to London to see me, on his own. I'd always meet him at the station although once he arrived early and surprised me in my office, so, yes, he led a normal a life as we could provide. Anyway, I asked you here because there is a gap in the diary that I want to try and fill in for you. It something to do with Solomon but I don't know what exactly. Sometime before Naomi died, she said to me that Schatzi wanted to go back to where he was born.'

'A trip to Munich?'

'Yes, apparently, he had told her he'd like to find the place where they met for the first time but insisted that they go together. He never liked plane travel and would only feel comfortable if she was by his side. Naomi asked what I thought. I said he's free to do what he wants. We cannot stop him. I also said it would be good to have her with him as I thought it would be very traumatic for him. She'd accompanied him abroad before to important conferences and, of course, to Sweden for the Nobel prize presentation. I went with them for that one. I was so proud, I cried for the first time in ages.

'It was several months before Schatzi received a letter from the WASt advising him that he should contact the Administrative Headquarters of the Munich Central Council in Marienplatz. He wrote to them. Yes, they had a Johann Bron in their records as the former resident with his family in Brienner Strasse in 1942. This is what prompted him to go back to Munich,' said Campbell, 'but it was only later that he told us. I think he was trying to be protective of us.'

He gulped a large mouthful of scotch and refilled his own glass. He looked into the amber liquid as he spun the glass in his hand watching it spill around the sides, he sniffed the aroma lifting off the surface. Stuart Campbell took a deep breath and Jonny was sure he could see a tremble in his demeanour before he raised his voice defiantly.

'If Naomi and I could have foreseen the future, that trip would never have taken place, Jonny. Never.'

Chapter 44

'It's OK, Schatzi. Just buckle up and relax. We'll be on the ground again in ninety minutes.'

He sat back and closed his eyes and thought about the past few months. Without confiding with his parents, Schatzi had long had the urge to try to trace exactly what had happened to Captain Johann Bron, his first daddy. He remembered him being sent to the Eastern Front and having to move to a new home in Munich. He had drawn a blank from all his enquiries in England. His adoptive mother, Naomi had told him that before they could adopt him, they had to satisfy the adoption agency that he had no surviving relatives and that Stuart had used all his contacts in the military to try to find out what happened to Johann Bron. All the evidence suggested that he had never survived the long route back to Germany with Nadine. Schatzi accepted this for most of his life but now he had a strange need to seek further.

After trawling through his own adoption file and not learning anything new, he completed an enquiry form and wrote to Deutsche Dienststelle (WASt). He had discovered that it had unique records of the Wehrmacht and received numerous and extensive documents from other military and military-like associations, including the surviving stockpiles of the Waffen-SS and the police associations. At the end of

WW2, it had been under the supervision of the American Military Control Commission and their headquarters were now in Berlin.

Schatzi had high hopes that their 'home-displaced person' section with particular reference to those coming from the East would give him some leads. He'd been told by the WASt that their files contained no information coming from Soviet Russia naming Captain Johann Bron as a fallen soldier.

Settling into their hotel room at the historic Torbrau 4-star hotel in central Munich, Schatzi lowered himself onto the beckoning double bed. The receptionist had told him that Marienplatz Square is just a 5-minute walk away.

'You all right? See you in the Schapeau restaurant for dinner, Schatzi. Is seven OK, darling?'

'Fine. I'll be at the bar after a shut eye. I'll get your usual, Mum?'

Schatzi flicked on the TV, surfing the channels. He settled on a local news channel and closed his eyes. Soon he was sound asleep. He woke with a start as the alarm sounded in his ear and realised, he been asleep for too long. Mum would be waiting at the bar wondering if he was ok. He hated rushing, nevertheless his mother had taught him to take a deep breath, look in the mirror and just get on with it.

'Sorry I'm late. See you ordered Munich's finest. Thanks.'

He took a sip, wiping the foam from his mouth and savoured the rich flavour.

'You know, Mum, it's the law and as a matter of pride that breweries here make their beer with yeast, barley, hops, and water. They don't usually add preservatives.'

Mrs Campbell leaned forward and took her glass from the table, holding the crisp white wine to the light.

'I prefer things a little more subtle, Schatzi. I'd be the size of a side of a house if I drank that beer every day.'

'I know. Not everyone's favourite, this dark Weiss beer,' said Schatzi holding up his tankard, trying read the faded motto printed on the glass. 'It's the brewing of the wheat in such a way as to make it smoky looking rather than pale.'

I was looking up some facts before we came.

'Schatzi, you know I'm not a great lover of beer and its history.'

Naomi knew not to interrupt Schatzi when he was in full swing.

'Sorry, Mum, but there's no city in the world that clings to a beverage the way Munich clings to beer. Münchners, with a little help from their visitors, consume a world's record of the stuff: 280 litres a year, per capita (as opposed to a wimpy 150 litres in other parts of Germany). The rest of Germany say that Bavarians never open their mouths except to pour in more beer! The Münchner response is that settling questions of politics, art, music, commerce, and finance, as well as the affairs of the human heart, requires plenty of beer and lots of good, unfussy food.

'Some of Munich's most notable events have floated on the suds, Mum. In 1923 there was Hitler's Beer Hall Putsch, in 1939 an attempt to assassinate Hitler and, more recently, the Beer Garden Revolution, when the proposed closing of a neighbourhood beer garden at 9:30pm was seen as a threat to the civil liberties and prompted mass rallies by infuriated Münchners.'

'Schatzi, facts and figures, always your strong point but not so with food. Come on what's on the menu tonight?'

'You're going to have to forget your calories and get ready for high cholesterol,' said Schatzi with a broad smile, draining the last suds from the tankard with a noisy breath in.

Naomi studied the menu.

'I see what you mean. Dumplings, potatoes, dozens different types of *Wurst* (sausages), roasted meats flavoured with bacon drippings, breads, and pastries. As you say, not good for my figure, Schatzi.'

'Mum, your figure is great. In Munich, the Munchners have an affair with sausage.'

'Here we go again', thought Naomi, afraid to stop her son from talking, now that he was totally relaxed for the first time since landing. She didn't want to interrupt his enthusiasm.

'It is of ancient lineage, wurst having been a major part of the national diet almost since there were people and livestock in the area. Bavarians tend to view their wurst with some superstition, nostalgically adhering to such adages as 'Never let the sunshine of noon shine on a *Weisswurst*.'

'How do you know all this? You were only little when you left. I don't remember things when I was 6 or 7.'

219

'Ah, Mum, you're not me. It is a childhood association. My favourite is *Bratwurst* which came originally from nearby Nuremberg and is concocted from seasoned and spiced veal, calves' brains, and spleen. You need to eat it with a foaming mug of beer.'

Naomi looked quite ill at the thought of the contents.

'OK, that's enough for me. Let's order?'

Naomi slumped into bed a little overcome after three large glasses of wine and fell into a deep slumber only to be woken by Schatzi at 9 o'clock saying he was going to the Town Hall in Marienplatz, he'd meet her later in her hotel lounge. He's taken on a different persona, she thought to herself, almost unexpectedly she saw her child as just a typical middle-aged man of the world. It was quite disconcerting. All she could say as he left her was, 'Be safe, Schatzi.'

He entered the palatial cavernous entrance hall and sauntered over to the reception desk. In fluent German he asked for the Housing Records Division explaining that he was rehoused during the war and eventually adopted and had lived in the UK since 1946. The receptionist looked at him, he was clearly nervous, hopping gently from one foot to another as he waited for her to locate the correct person in the building.

'What names and address are you looking for and give me any other details?

He started slowly giving her details of streets, neighbours' names, shops, schools, type of buildings colour of the paint work. She started to type in all the details and then stopped, letting him continue, amazed at the details she was listening to. Finally, she said 'and you were six years old!'

'Please take a seat, a colleague will be down in a moment.'

'Danke.'

She watched him as he carefully sat down brushing imaginary dust off the seat. He carried no bags and didn't seem like an activist, but there was something she couldn't put her finger on. Her eyes watched him furtively look around, taking in everything as if he was 'casing the joint'. She dialled security. Explaining that she had her doubts about the man who had just confronted her.

'Wie kann ich dir helfen?'

'No, I don't need any help, I am waiting for someone from Housing. I used to live here as a little boy until the bombs came.'

At that moment a lady dressed in a sharp grey suit interruped them

'Es ist ok, er ist gut.'

She lead him to the marble staircase and they ascended to the first floor. Through the door she walked into a large airey room full of filing cabinets and desks occupied by similarly dressed women with their heads in papers. Schatzi followed through the throng and sat down at the lady's desk.

'Strange request after so long, Dr Campbell. Let me see what we can do to help you. Ah, yes. Here we are. You traced this originally through Berlin?'

Schatzi nodded in agreement.

She turned the screen around so that he could see as the addresses and information flew passed. Schatzi's eyes caught every passing piece of information.

'Stop,' he shouted, pointing. 'Back a bit. There.' He reeled off all the addresses and links and dates. The only information he didn't reveal was 'Johann Bron made the same request in 1956'.

'That is amazing, Mr Campbell.'

He turned to go but before, gave her a very formal double handshake and bow, in thanks.

'I have found the old house we used to live in and the children's home where we met, Mum.' He hopped from one foot to the other trying to control his impatience. 'Can we go now?'

Miles away, Captain Johann Bron received a call from the Gerhardt Steiner, he listened intently particularly at the description and the questions asked and finally sat down, replacing the telephone receiver and disconnecting the call. He was quite shocked and looked very pale when the nurse came to bring his morning coffee.

'Captain Bron, you look unwell. What is the matter, where is the pain?'

'I am quite well, thank you. Just a bit dizzy. Got up too soon, I think,' he lied, thanking her for the coffee. He waited until she had closed the door and picked up his telephone again.

'Sorry about that, Gerhardt, coffee arrived and it was a bit of a shock to say the least. Look, I know it's short notice but could you get to my old home in 72 Brienner Strasse, you know the one just off Königplatz where your Dad and I used to assemble in the early days in the Party's mass rallies.'

'Not the Brown House, then,' laughed Gerhardt Steiner.

'The national headquarters of the Nazi Party. Not on your life, Gerhardt, stay well clear of 45 Brienner Strasse.'

'Johann, what do you want me to do?'

'You're looking for the man you described to me. I am thinking it may be my grandson. He is about the right age and what's remarkable is that photographic memory I remember so well. The offspring of my daughter. The one that got us into trouble, you remember your father telling you?'

'My god, Johann, sorry about the shock. I thought he died, at least that's what we were all told, including you. I only rang you as agreed if anyone should be searching for you.'

'Yes, I know. Look. What I want you to do is follow them, photograph them and let me know where they are staying. Complete dossier. Can you do that for old times' sake, Gerhardt?'

Chapter 45

Munich

Gerhardt Steiner was the son of Johann's friend who helped his family after they were 'excommunicated' by the Nazi's in 1942. Johann had found Gerhardt on his return from Russia in 1953 and was sad to find that his father had been killed in the bombing of Munich in 1944 when his own family went missing. Gerhardt had remained a loyal friend and now nearing retirement from the Munich police force, but would be able to do work like this for Johann without any official involvement.

He arrived in 72 Brienner Strasse and parked on the opposite side of the road to number 72 and a few doors down. A perfect position for observing activity in and around the house. He had only to wait a few moments before a taxi arrived and a middle-aged man and older woman alighted. The taxi waited. Gerhardt turned his camera and started the video feature, pausing occasionally to ensure he had perfect clarity on some stills. The two people climbed the stone steps to the blue painted double doors and pressed the entry phone. Moments later the door opened and a well-dressed lady holding the hand of a young girl opened the door and after a brief conversation allowed them in. Gerhardt waited.

After half an hour or so, the front door opened, and mother and son stood looking from the front step and then descended to the waiting taxi. Gerhardt pulled out behind the taxi followed at a safe distance. This was easy surveillance for an experienced policeman. The taxi moved away from the middleclass housing of Brienner Strasse through Konigsplatz and out into the high-rise post war housing developments that were thrown up after the streets of early 20th century rubble was cleared in the wake of the 1944 bombing. The taxi stopped outside a bleak grey midrise apartment building. Shabby was the best description, Gerhardt could think of.

Schatzi got out of the taxi, leaving Naomi in the back seat and walked to the corner where the access to the rear was reserved for car parking. He disappeared out of view. Gerhardt had no second thoughts and opened the door and followed. He was dressed as if he lived in the area. Old jeans and sweatshirt hidden under a well-worm leather jacket. Hands in pocket he approached the car park. He saw Schatzi crouching in the corner near the rear boundary cutting the car park off from the gardens beyond. He slowly walked over to him. Schatzi was in his own world and did not hear him approach.

Gerhardt noticed he was crying. Unsure what to do, he started the walk silently away and then had second thoughts. Johann wanted proof; this was his chance.

'Sorry. You all right.'

Schatzi was shaking with fear and curled himself into a ball. Gerhardt proffered his hand and Schatzi withdrew further.

'Bad day, eh?' Gerhardt said crouching on his knees and waited for a reply.

Naomi saw Schatzi and ran over putting her arms around him as Gerhardt watched.

'It ok now, Schatzi,' she said tenderly and then looked at Gerhardt.

'He was here in 1944 when the area was bombed. Only one to survive around here,' she offered as an explanation.

Gerhardt wandered slowly back to his car and slumped down behind the wheel, thinking of Johann Bron and wandering how he was going to deal with this. Definitely his grandson, he thought.

Moments later, Naomi, with her arms around Schatzi, emerged from the car park and got in the taxi.

'You still want to go to the old Children's Home?' she said hoping that he'd say 'no'.

Schatzi unfolded himself from her arms and sat upright and nodded 'yes'.

Gerhardt followed the taxi as it made its way in a south westerly direction out into the countryside heading towards Starnberg, according to the main signposts. Gerhardt had to hang back as the road became sparsely populated of vehicles of any kind. After travelling through pine forests that surrounded the metropolitan area, the taxi slowed and took a left turn onto a minor road and headed back towards the city. Finally, it slowed and passed through tall carved stone pillars and rounded the gravel driveway and stopped in front of The Clemens Maria Children's Home.

Gerhardt drove passed the entrance and parked on the verge and walked back to the entrance. In front of him, at the end of the gravelled driveway stood and imposing white painted L shaped late 19th century manor house. Huge windows punctuated the whole of the façade including the third storey where some windows had been inset in the red tiled roof. He stood watching as Naomi and Schatzi walked up the front door and entered. A few teenage children ran in to see who the new arrivals were.

Gerhardt could not go any further and sat down with his camera and took some shots of the exterior and gardens, then read the plaque on the wall. This house was founded in 1916 by the priest Clemens Maria Hofbauer to take care of war orphans. 'Now it should read from both wars or all wars,' thought Gerhardt.

Inside, after Schatzi and Naomi explained that they had met here in 1945, they were allowed to tour the outside and the cloisters on their own. The supervisor went to check the historic records. The structure was very familiar to both of them as they entered the cloistered area overlooking a sunken play area that now housed modern children's play-things, a far cry from a ball and tag that Schatzi watched from inside his world all those years ago.

'This is where we met, Mum,' said Schatzi sitting on his hands leaning against the stone pillar. You remember?'

'I'll never forget, my love. Wow!' she joked.

'Wow. What is 'Wow'?' Schatzi asked with a contrived innocent look on his middle-aged face. They laughed hysterically, so much so that the supervisor came back to see what was so funny. They explained the joke. She too laughed with them.

'Funny,' said the supervisor. 'I cannot find your name in the records. I know there are some gaps, but the British and Americans had to be very meticulous because of missing persons and it's somewhat rare for someone to fall through the net, so to speak.'

'It was all very confused, as I recall. My husband, Captain Stuart Campbell, arranged it all. He was here in the Intelligence Section of the British Army in 1945.'

'If he was in Intelligence, maybe that could explain the oversight.'

'Can I see where I used to sleep?' asked Schatzi, treading air with impatience.

Do you know where, things have changed over the last years since you were here. Schatzi led the way, never doubting his memory.

'This is my room. Did you know that, Mum?' Naomi shook her head.

'There used to bunks over there, not this lovely single bed. The guy on the top used to snore terribly. I had to throw my pillow at him regularly. He didn't give me any time to think. I tried to teach him to read but he wasn't interested. Just wanted to run around playing ball and pestering the girls from the other section over there.'

Schatzi sat on the bed and became silent, looking around slowly methodically.

'I like the pastel green colour now, used to be light brown, glossy to the touch. Easy to clean they told me. I wonder what happened to Ronald,' he said with a sadness in his eyes.

'Come on Schatzi, better not keep our taxi man waiting,' urged Naomi, not wanting a repeat of this morning's problem as Schatzi could easily turn from bright to dull in a flash.

Schatzi was unstoppable with memories as they drove back to Munich. Naomi couldn't stop him from rambling from one topic of recall to another, no thread between the recalls save the time when they took place.

They checked back into the hotel just after six that night. Both were exhausted as they entered their rooms agreeing to meet for dinner at eight.

Gerhardt entered the hotel lobby, having changed into his uniform and made his way to reception.

'Register, please?' he asked. Not an unusual request from a police officer.

'Anyone in particular, Officer?'

'No, just a random check we do now and again.' He took out his reading glasses and scanned the information of all the guests currently registered in the hotel.

'A copy of these pages please, for the records at the station.'

Back in his office, he discarded most of the copied pages, retaining the one with Naomi and Schatzi Campbell's information, full UK address and telephone numbers, exactly what Johann may need. He parcelled them together with the best images he taken and addressed them to Johann. After speaking to the Supervisor of the Clemens Maria Children's Home, he wrote a small note and added it to the parcel, beckoning his secretary, he told her to post them immediately.

Chapter 46

Johann Bron opened the small parcel and took out the contents, placing the photographs side by side on his desk. His hands trembled a little as he sorted them. One particularly caught his attention. Gerhardt had captured Schatzi with his hands and arms over his head as if trying to block out the present. He remembered this pose as if it was yesterday despite looking at a grown man. He held the photograph to his cheek recalling the comfort he'd given back in those days.

Gerhardt had checked with the Children's Home supervisor after he got back to the office. He was able to confirm that their records did not show that Schatzi was sent to The Clemens Maria. There was no record of his stay there. And yet the supervisor had listened to most of the conversations between Naomi and Schatzi and was certain beyond doubt that he had lived there during the latter part of the war. All those who worked there during those times would be impossible to trace as most were volunteers from the Allied Army staff. He concluded that the records had been tampered with. Schatzi's name had been expunged, but by whom and why.

He took another photograph and looked deep into the eyes of Schatzi. Yes, this was definitely, his grandson. 'What am I going to do about it after all these years?' He said to himself under his breath.

230

That night Johann slept badly. Names, places, hidden memories came to the surface, he suppressed for years. Nightmares of fire, blinding light, shivering with fear. Faces melting in and out of focus, grotesque images of the dead, all with faces he recognised, all smiling like loved ones then pleading with him to help them, then the faces turned to anguish. His arms held out, beckoning for them to come to him as they melted away consumed by the night. He fought to touch them, yet his own feeble body didn't have the strength of youth to help.

'Captain, what's wrong. You all right. I heard the screams and came.'

Johann looked up blankly at the night sister, blinking away the horrible images and wiping the perspiration from his face and hands.

'Had a bad nightmare. Memories of years gone by,' he murmured quietly. 'I'm all right now.'

'I'll get you some tea and take these, they'll relax you. It's one o'clock in the morning and you need to rest.'

Morning came later than usual. He felt rested despite the trauma of the night. He had lain awake for about an hour mulling over what he should do. He had made his decision and needed to make a few telephone calls.

Chapter 47

The rain incessantly washed against the panes of glass as Stuart Campbell looked out, holding a cup of tea in one hand. It had been raining for days and the garden was sodden, and the array of flowers planted this spring looked forlorn. Out of the corner of his eye he saw a taxi approaching up the gravelled driveway coming to a halt by the front doorsteps. He wasn't expecting any visitors and watched as a stranger, someone he'd never seen before, slowly got out of the rear seat. He was carpeted in a long green raincoat and slowly mounted the steps to the front door. The bell rang. Annie, the housekeeper opened the door.

'Is Mr Campbell in?'

'Which Mr Campbell, older or younger?' she asked curtly.

'Older.'

'Who shall I say wants him?'

'An old acquaintance. I've come all the way from Munich, will do, I think.'

'Wait here, I'll see whether he's in.'

Stuart Campbell who had overheard the conversation, came to the door.

'How can I help you?'

'May I come in out of this awful rain?'

Stuart Campbell stood aside and let the stranger inside and watched the taxi disappear into the rain.

'I'm afraid I haven't had to courtesy to introduce myself. My name is Johann Bron, Captain Johann Bron.'

Campbell's face flickered with disguised horror as he ushered him into his study and closed the door as Campbell took the wet raincoat and hung it on the array of pegs on the inside of the door.

'Do sit down and tell me why you're here and…' Campbell never finished the sentence as he started to put names and year together.

Bron sat opposite Campbell and crossed his legs with a painful sigh. Bron opened his briefcase and laid the unopened file on Campbell's desk.

'We are all much older now and I hesitated the make the journey unannounced particularly at my age. I kept asking myself whether it would be better to write beforehand to explain who I am and what I am here for, but now that I am here, I feel I made the right decision. He consulted the file that Gerhardt Steiner had helped compile then lifted his head and looked directly into Campbell's eyes.

'Your wife, Nadine, and your son, Schatzi, visited Munich a few weeks ago. Is that correct?

Campbell nodded, still thinking in the back of his mind about 1945 and since.

'I am a resourceful man, Captain Campbell. I see you are beginning to realise that I did not die in my escape from Stalingrad. You have my grandson actually here. I came to meet him with his and your permission, of course.'

Campbell sank back into his chair, head in his hands, never, for one instance, believing this could ever have happened, but it now had. Bron handed over the photographs of Nadine and Schatzi showing them in Brienner Strasse and Clemens Maria and the most telling of Schatzi in the carpark where he survived the bombing in their apartment's former garden shelter. Campbell looked at each one with gathering emotion, as Bron watched his face.

'He is the son of my late daughter, Roberta.'

Campbell leaned forward with his head in his hands. Falteringly, he said. 'You were never found. We had no record of you from the battlefields of Stalingrad. You went missing in action according to the Wehrmacht unit you served in. I did all I could to ensure, like all the other orphans, that there were no relatives alive. I assure you of that, Captain Bron.'

'I am sure you did. I returned from the Soviet gulags in 1956. It had been transit camp after transit camp. The journey took months and first brought me to Moscow, then westward. In the December cold the train reached Frankfurt an der Oder. I was on my way to Munich but as that station was a designated meeting point for us, ex-prisoners. I still felt like a prisoner. I was issued new clothes by the Red Cross and given my release papers and 50 marks. I arrived back home in Munich after six days of arduous travel. No one showed any interest in the home comers. We were greeted as unceremoniously as we were captured, without a word, nothing. No one wanted to give me work. My CV was almost empty and even in some cases threatening. It was only when I found the Steiners, my friend Helmut Steiner from army days had been killed in the war, that Gerhardt, his son, took me in and I started slowly getting a life. Captain Campbell if you hadn't hidden Schatzi's records, my life would have been very different. Why did you do it? Please explain to me why you removed the records from the Children's Home.'

Johann Bron held his hands in the air and then placed them on the desktop, pleading for an answer with his eyes.

'Captain. Schatzi was not an ordinary child, you must have known that. He was at an age when he needed a great deal of help to recover from losing his entire family and his mental condition was very unstable. My wife fell in love with him on sight. We couldn't have children. She was warned that fostering a child with Aspergers, as it is now known, would require a lifetime of commitment but she was willing to try.

'In Germany, in the aftermath of the Nazi regime where any form of disablement, was viewed with... What shall I say, distaste at best, ridicule and horror at worse? If we hadn't rescued him, I am certain no-one else would have and I dread to think what life he would have had. Rather than let him be institutionalised, I took the decision, after no relatives could be traced, to expunge his time in Munich and start all over again.

'Furthermore you must understand that when I was in Germany trying to locate Nazi war criminals, there were a series of trials held in connection with the Nazi euthanasia in Dresden, Frankfurt, Graz, Nuremberg and Tübingen.

In December 1946, an American military tribunal prosecuted twenty three doctors and administrators for their roles in war crimes and crimes under your 'AktionT4' regime. These crimes included the

235

systematic killing of those deemed 'unworthy of life', including the mentally disabled, the institutionalized mentally ill, and the physically impaired. I cannot now remember the exact details, but I can tell you that the courts pronounced over ten of those charged defendants as guilty.of crimes of murder. They were executed following year. You must realise, Captain, that your grandson, Schatzi would, in all likelihood, have been one of those chosen to die even in later stages of the war and its immediate aftermath.

'Captain Bron, this is the background, we were living in. In fact, I was with part of a team that visited the children's ward of Kaufbeuren-Irsee hospital, state run, in Bavaria with some American troops in July 1945. They told us that the last child to be killed under Aktion T4 was Richard Jenne on 29 May 1945. Can you believe that?'

Captain Bron started to cry and through the tears said that he'd known Schatzi was unusually intense, very intelligent and at times uncontrollable and inconsolable and that is one of the reasons they originally lied to the authorities about the birth because of Aktion T4, but also the scandal that would have ensued if it was known that his daughter had given birth to an illegitimate child.

'I am so sorry to accuse you. I had no idea what was happening thousands of miles away in Russia for all those years. I should have thought more. Forgive me, Captain. I was not a Nazi and never would have been, but times were treacherous for everyone in Germany.'

Bron started to rise and offered Campbell his hand conciliation. Campbell hesitated as there was a knock on the door. Naomi appeared. She saw Bron standing at the desk and noticed the photographs of her and Schatzi laid out.

'What on earth is this?' she said accusingly as she looked at herself and her son on the steps of the Clemens Maria.

'Darling, let me introduce you to Captain Johann Bron from Munich. He's Schatzi's grandfather.'

Naomi dropped the photograph and gasped. She dropped onto the sofa by the window.

'Why! Why, did you follow us?' she shouted uncontrollably.

Campbell took her hand and sat by her side. He explained the conversations that had passed between them. Cautiously, she regained her composure and looked at Bron.

'We thought you been killed, Captain Bron.'

'I know. Sometimes I wish I were. Surviving the Stalingrad battle and the walk back to our lines only to be taken to Siberia. There were many times I thought that death would be a familiar friend I could rely on. All those I loved had been lost to me. Only Schatzi is left in my twilight years.'

Campbell started to say something but held himself, trying to consider what to do next.

Chapter 48

Hampshire England

Naomi went to speak to Schatzi in his quarters on the ground floor about the arrival of his grandfather. They had decided amongst themselves that this was the best way to avoid a meltdown. Surprisingly, Schatzi took the intrusion in his stride and came running towards the study and threw his arms around a very surprised grandfather who didn't know quite what to do with his arms until he gently embraced Schatzi whose head rested firmly on the old man's chest.

Stuart and Naomi looked on at the reunion after decades of absence, there was a sadness in Naomi's eyes that she couldn't hide. Stuart put his arms around her in comfort as she had taken a step back in a confusion of emotions. Nobody moved for several moments until Schatzi finally disentangled himself from his grandfather and came over to Naomi and gave her a huge hug.

'Mummy, this is wonderful. My two families together for the first time,' he said. There was a long pause before he continued. 'My two other mothers died while you were away in Russia. I found that very sad that you didn't know what happened. Why did they send you away, grandpapa?'

'After gathering his thoughts, Bron turned to look at them one by one and finally said, 'Some things went badly, Schatzi. Someone, I have never found out who,

238

told the local Gestapo at 45 Brienner Strasse, the Nazi Headquarters near where we lived, that you were not our child and that you were the son of our daughter who had been pregnant outside marriage. In those days such a scandal was unacceptable for a ranking officer and we paid the consequences.'

'So being forced to move from our apartment and you been sent to Russia would not have happened if I hadn't been born.'

Silence pervaded the study. The statement was true enough on the face of it, but an innocent child could not be blamed for being conceived during an act of love. Voices in Schatzi's head were telling him all sorts of things, confusing his mind. He held his hands over his ears. He'd not done that for years at home, but now the sounds were back with a vengeance, exploding in his head. Naomi saw the signs that she hadn't seen for years, save the one time recently in Munich. She rushed to his side cradling his head in her arms and soothed his hair.

'My poor boy, this has been too much.'

Bron stood rigid looking aghast at his grandson, quite unable to take in what he'd seen. Campbell took his arm and guided him out of the study into the hall, gently closing the door on Schatzi and Naomi and began to explain to Bron that this was what his life had been like in the beginning, but gradually Naomi had taught him to cope and brought stability to what otherwise would have been a chaotic institutionalised existence with no purpose. Campbell knew that Naomi would be in the study for some time and took Bron into Schatzi's domain. The first thing Bron noticed was that it was sparse. No paintings, posters or artwork of any kind, no mementos, no reminders that people keep in case they forget.

'He keeps it all in his head. Has a most remarkable ability to recall places, scenes, facts and figures that you and I would struggle with. As you said earlier, he is intelligent, in fact he has been described by his scientific peers as a genius.'

At that point, Bron noticed three framed pieces hidden behind the door. He took put on his glasses and took a closer look.

'That is an amazing achievement, a Doctorate from London University at his age.' He then worked out that Schatzi was 19 years old at the time. By the time he received his Nobel prize he was 28 years old as Bron looked proudly at the framed letter of recommendation.

'What's this third one all about?' he said holding the frame in all directions trying to make some sense of what he was looking at.

'That, my dear Bron, is the photograph of the first double helix that Schatzi helped to discover for his research team. His theories on DNA structure. It took him from obscurity to worldwide scientific celebrity. That was something he definitely didn't relish at all. That is where Naomi took control of his exposure to the outside world. She spent hours with him, guiding him, travelling to lectures, keeping him from metaphorically exploding.'

Bron was silent for a minute contemplating what was now and what may have been.

'You Brits and Yanks were way ahead of us in Germany in child psychology and treatment of paediatric trauma. May I call you, Stuart? Your wife obviously undertook a great and difficult task in bringing up Schatzi. I admire what she has done and you for that matter, Stuart.'

'Johann, thank you. Shall we go back and fetch the others and have some tea. Now that the rain has stopped, maybe a stroll around the garden beforehand. I find the peace and quiet is a good time to reflect and talk.'

'That would be nice. Thank you. In fact, why don't we go now, there's something I want to tell you.'

'Naomi, Schatzi. All OK now? Johann and I are going for a stroll around the garden. We need to talk. Can you ask Annie for a little tea, perhaps?'

Stuart took Johann by the arm and guided him towards the small patio with a table and chairs. They stood silently admiring the gently curves of the manicured lawn to the stream beyond, swollen by the rain of the past few days as it babbled and splashed over the rocks beneath.

He continued, 'My friend, please sit. Let me begin when I was in Germany in 1945. As you will now know, the Holocaust had taken a lot of us by surprise. Not the fact that it was happening, we knew that a few years earlier, but the scale of the slaughter. I was seconded into the Intelligence units and had the task of tracing those involved. My first experience was with those who had survived Birkenau-Auschwitz. One of those survivors, was a remarkable man named Solomon Isaacs.

Stuart continued, 'He had survived two years in the camp along with his mother and father. He was a brilliant scientist, with an incredible mind that was capable of storing the minutest detail and with absolute clarity. He had worked in the hospital with Mengele. They had similar scientific goals in mind, but Solomon's future had been stifled by the regime as he was a Jew. Genetics was his field and he'd worked alongside Mengele at university in Munich albeit when Solomon was a first-year research graduate and Mengele was studying for a Doctorate. By working in the hospital block in Auschwitz, Solomon managed to save his family.

Johann had listened with interest but wondered what this had to do with him, apart from the nagging in his mind about the name Solomon Isaac.

'Where are we going with this story, Stuart?'

'Wait, be patient, Johann. I am telling you the whole story for a very good reason. He worked in what was known as Block 10. One night about ten months before the Nazi's retreated from the horror they'd created whilst the Russians fought their way into Eastern Europe and opened the gates of Auschwitz, a young girl had entered Block 10 and been hidden there by Solomon. He found her one night and gave her a nurse's uniform. He knew from past experience that she was going to be a victim of experimentation and eventual extermination if he did nothing to help her so he devised a plan which was accepted by Mengele after speaking to Dr Clauberg who was gathering information on sterilisation and when told of a healthy young woman that could raise Aryan children, Lebensborn. Solomon had a theory about artificial insemination and put it to Clauberg. He approved the experiment subject to all Solomon's notes being duplicated to him for onward despatch to Berlin under his name. To cut a long story short, a child was born to this young woman not long before the liberation of the camp.'

Do we know what happened to them all?' asked Johann, his interest peeked.

'Yes, Johann. I know all about them.

'Go on, tell me more, this is fascinating.'

'Well, I had heard of this family of four and that Solomon had been working in Block 10 by a fellow survivor. He dictated the story to one of my colleagues and this is why I asked you to sit down here away from the house.'

'You've told me about Solomon, but what has this got to do with me?'

'Johann,' he paused looking into Johann's eyes, 'the girl who gave birth to the little boy they called Stewart was named Nadine Rekova.'

'Nadine. Oh my God. She survived.' He put his head in his hands and wept uncontrollably until Stuart got up and put his hands on the old man's shoulders.

'Sorry, it must be a great shock to you, Johann. She said that if it wasn't for you and your resolve, she would never have survived Stalingrad and the Stalinist post war regime of terror and fear. You also saved her life.'

'Not entirely, Stuart. I left her alone and told her to keep going east. I had given up hope. What happened to her afterwards?'

'Yes, I know. Solomon Isaacs gave me all this evidence in 1945.She was taken in by the German's and after various interrogations was sent from camp to

243

camp and eventually to join other Russian prisoners of war in Auschwitz. She had outlived her usefulness but then what else were they to do with a lone Russian in their midst in a rapidly deteriorating situation.'

'After interviewing Solomon at length, and may I say we were, on his testimony, able to capture some serious criminals, I arranged for the family to receive visas to go to the UK.'

'So, they are all here now!'

'Well, yes and no. I resumed my work at London University and Solomon joined the University to resume his doctorate that was interrupted by the persecution of his family and his incarceration at Auschwitz. He then undertook some serious genetic research. Some of his incites were to say the least far more advanced than we had assumed at first. He had a detailed knowledge of infertility and cloning. It seemed that all his ideas worked in practise. Quite remarkable really. The time we saved in advancing research was staggering. It was if he had already undertaken tasks in a former life. No such information from the Auschwitz papers had revealed anything other than what came into the public domain very soon after the invasion of Germany.'

Stuart stopped when he realised that Johann had stopped listening. He could see that the old man was assimilating all that he had heard.

'Anyway. Nadine. I only met her a few times. She was enthralled at bringing up young Stewart, Solomon's son as it transpired. Another very able, some say brilliant, scientist. He's the head of some department at Cambridge University, now. Lives in Cambridge. I have to say I am not sure where Nadine lives but I may be able to find out for you.'

There was a wave from the front of the house. Tea was ready. They slowly made their way to the house. The sun was now encasing the old Barn in warm yellow light reflecting off the window glass at different angles. Stuart had his arms around Johann's shoulders as he eased him into the hallway.

'Schatzi. You all right?'

'Yes, I am now. Mum's been great as usual, I now know I cannot be responsible for all those bad things that happened to my family.' He turned, that part was over dead and buried in his mind. 'How are you dear Grandpapa?'

Not expecting such an effusive response, Johann was momentarily lost for words.

'Fine. Just Fine.'

'Johann's feeling a little confused, Schatzi. I told him the story about Nadine Rekova who married Solomon Isaac. Well, Johann thought she had died up until now.

'Grandpapa, you saved her life all those years ago. You should be proud.'

Schatzi approached his grandfather and hugged him, whispering in his ear, 'I love you.'

Johann hugged him back but there was a lingering question that remained hidden in the past about Solomon Isaac that wouldn't stay away. What was it that nagged him so much now?

Chapter 49

Hampshire England

'Why? What happened?' asked Jonny.

'Jonny, I won't bore you with the details suffice it to say that Captain Johann Bron knocked on our door not long after Naomi and Schatzi returned from Munich. Apparently, he had arranged for them to be followed after Schatzi started asking questions at the Town Hall on the first day. He then told us about getting our address from the Hotel through a police connection and just arrived here.'

'What? That must have been a shock. A hell of a shock, I'd say.'

Jonny was silent for a moment lost in thought. Jonny knew that Bron had lied about going to Caen, he'd been to see the Campbell's here at their house. Why hadn't he said anything to Jonny. Wait till you get home, Jonny said to himself. Jonny looked at Captain Campbell.

'You're certainly right about that. Schatzi had one of his bad turns to begin with thinking he'd been responsible for everything bad that had happened to the Bron family after his birth. Naomi managed to calm him down then he took to his Grandfather in a big way. Naomi was quite overwhelmed by his reaction. Well, we all were. '

'How did he know for certain that he had the right person, Schatzi, I mean?'

246

'Several details. Schatzi's request for the Bron family at the Town Hall, the addresses they visited, the photographs and the Hotel registration.'

'Pretty convincing evidence for him then.'

'Oh yes. He'd been through hell and back, poor fellow and survived. I told him about Nadine Rekova and how she survived.'

'What was his reaction?'

'Stunned at first, then joy in his eyes. I didn't know where she was now, but said I'd try to find here for him. Not so sure now whether that was such a good idea, in the circumstances.'

Jonny didn't know what to say, again Johann Bron hadn't said anything.

'What happened after he left?'

'Schatzi was fine. I think he felt he gained a relative, a Grandpapa, as he called him. It was Naomi that took things badly. She didn't show it outwardly so that Schatzi didn't suffer, but I could see she wasn't well after that. She became depressed. Locked herself away for hours on end. I heard her crying at night in her room. Our local doctor came a few times. He gave her some pills to cope. Said they'd take some time to take effect, but we needed to be patient. I suggested she saw someone to talk it through.' He paused to take another sip of whiskey.

'Did she take your advice about seeing someone, Stuart?'

'No. Said she'd be OK with the pills. After a few weeks, she brightened up, but she wasn't the same Naomi. I tried to get her to talk but she didn't want to.

'I will in time, Stuart.' She'd say, so I decide to take matters into my own hands.'

'How?'

'I rang a colleague of mine at the University. He recommended a therapist who specialised in cognitive behaviour. I spoke to the chap on the telephone and he agreed to see her.'

'Stuart, sorry to be ignorant, but what do these people do that could help Naomi?'

'I had to check it out myself. In short, Jonny, what my colleague in London said is that Cognitive Behavioral Therapy (CBT) is now recognised as an effective treatment for depression. At the heart of CBT is an assumption that Naomi's mood is directly related to her patterns of thought. The negative, dysfunctional thinking, after Bron's appearance in our life affected her mood, her sense of self, her behaviour, and even physical state.'

'So how is it supposed to work?'

'Naomi had to learn to recognize her negative patterns of thought, she was taught to evaluate their validity, and then replace them with healthier ways of thinking.'

'Did it work?'

'Their aim was to help Naomi change her patterns of behaviour that come from dysfunctional thinking. All the jumble of thoughts inspired by Bron's visit and Schatzi's reaction to him. She could only think of the bad aspects, negative thoughts that created her depression. If I hadn't got involved when I did, I was told that she may have made it nearly impossible to escape a downward spiral. It was noticeable when her patterns of thought started to change so did her mood.'

'So, Stuart, what happened? She started to improve, getting back to her normal self and then?'

'That, I will never know, Jonny. Nothing untoward happened. I have tried to think about it many, many times but I cannot tell you. She just seemed to slip backwards at an alarming rate. Stopped eating, became irritable, refused to continue the sessions with the therapist.

'In the last few days before she died, she took on a grey gaunt look. Whenever Schatzi appeared she rallied and was her usual self, but I could see beneath the fabric. She was just fading away, as if she didn't want anything to do with life anymore. It was heartbreaking.

'Annie and I found her sitting over there outside by the stream leaning against the old willow tree. Thought she'd fallen asleep, her eyes were shut and there was a kind of serenity of peace that comes over some when they die. Her face was cold to the touch. There was no pulse and her body was cold. The post-mortem revealed no unusual findings. Her heart had just stopped.

—

Chapter 50

Munich Germany

Johann settled into his chair back home. It was early evening and he had telephone Stuart Campbell to tell him he was safely back. He took out a tumbler and poured himself a whiskey topped up gingerale and ice. He sipped it slowly reflecting on the past few days at the Campbell's house that were bound to change what was left of Campbell's life and his own.

The next morning, he telephoned Gerhardt Steiner and told all that had happened in England.

'She survived the war, Gerhardt. Isn't that amazing?'

'Where is she now, Johann?' You going to get in touch?'

'No idea where she is now. Find her, can you do that for me, Gerhardt?'

'Yes, of course. What's her full name and where was she last living? That's a minimum to start with.'

'She married Solomon Isaacs. First name, as you well know is Nadine. Campbell said that she always, to his knowledge, lived in London.'

'Big place, London, Johann, I'll do my best.'

Gerhardt put down the telephone and rang records in Berlin. Their Interpol connection was better than his and Reinhart Schreiber, his colleague from long ago at college, was his first point of contact.

'Old friend of my father's has asked me to trace a woman in London, he thought had died in the war, but has now discovered, survived. They were very close at one time. Any chance of a favour?'

'Fax through the details, I see what I can do, Gerhardt. Give my love to Munich.'

'Thanks, Reinhart.'

Two weeks later, as Gerhardt was sitting at his desk pondering a list of unsolved house burglaries that was upsetting his boss, the telephone rang. His private line.

'Gerhardt, I don't know what you are getting into but there's some shit coming out of your request. This guy, Solomon Isaac, in a high security prison, the highest, in London. Breach of Official Secrets Act, thirty-five-year term with no remission.'

'What/ Oh my god, Reinhart. Look don't do anything. I'll call you back after I've checked with my father's friend.'

'Johann, why didn't you tell me about Solomon Isaacs?' said Gerhardt.

'What do you mean? I told you all I know, Gerhardt.'

'The guy's in Belmarsh, a high security prison in London. Messing with Official Secrets or something. You didn't know?' sighed Gerhardt irritably.

'No. I'm sorry, has this got you into trouble?'

'No. Not yet anyway. Look, Johann, I may be able to get an address now and will kill this enquiry in Berlin. That should do it.'

'Thanks, Gerhardt.'

He replaced the receiver ending the call then looked at his watch and immediately the picked it up again.

'Reinhart, I've spoken to my chap. Didn't know anything about it. All I need is last known address of the wife so I can start my trace. You can drop your end. Is that OK?'

'Yep. Last known address coming up.'

'Thanks, Reinhart. See you my friend.'

Chapter 51

Jonny returned to his flat upset and deflated by his time with Stuart Campbell. He stood in front of the board willing someone's face to talk to him. `Come to me!', he urged to himself silently.

Campbell's eyes shone out of his enlarged photograph. He had had reason to feel very aggrieved at Solomon over the Porton Down affairs and as his mentor he had been saddened by Solomon's inability to talk to him before taking matters into his own hand. Campbell had never said too much about his feelings towards Solomon over this matter and Jonny knew his University tenure, life and work had been eventually devastated by the events of Solomon's whistle blowing at Porton Down, but he had attended Solomon's funeral. Jonny couldn't help, at this stage, allowing Campbell to remain in the frame.

Next, he looked at Johann Bron. Bron had stalked Naomi and Schatzi around Munich and then confronted the whole family in Kent. Campbell had been very upset at the aftermath of the Munich affair. He'd said so on many occasions to Jonny. It seemed that Bron nursed a deep-seated emotional turmoil borne of incarceration for years in Russia, being ostracised by the war and the regime for his daughter's pregnancy and then on his return finding that all his past had been eliminated in his absence. He had not accepted his loneliness and had sought to be advised of anything that might rekindle his past. That had come with the telephone call from Town Hall. Now, he stood in the forefront of Jonny's board. He'd lied about Nadine and being at the Campbell's house, but why?

Jonny sat at his desk and put his feet over the edge and closed his eyes. The light was fading outside as evening gave way to darker thoughts in Jonny's mind. Cascading pictures from the board swung backwards and forwards, making no sense to him.

He must have fallen asleep. He awoke, in his mind he had a picture, the Missing Persons Poster, of a face that he couldn't see properly but a name he knew.

He fumbled to find the light switch and grabbed Solomon's papers. Leafing through the original manuscript to the markers he inserted, he found what he was looking for. He'd had overlooked something fundamental in his search for the story. Solomon's emotions. Yes, they'd erupted occasionally from the pages of 'Stealing the Staircase', but they were not those feelings from far inside oneself. The ones that you have in the pit of your stomach that have no rational explanation. Now he determined to look closer.

Chapter 52

London

Here it is, he said to himself pulling out the page. What had Solomon said?

'I have never had any interest in girls, but to my amazement I kept thinking about the sparkling brown eyes of the older girl who introduced me to the wonderful world under the microscope. Some days during those weeks we would talk together but that would be all because I was a Jew and she was not. I would think of Fraulein Roberta Bron and her long brown hair and sparking eyes an awful lot'

Jonny wanted to know if he had missed anything else in the manuscript, but Solomon had not added or subtracted words in the finished printable version. There were many hand-written loose-leaved pages of second thoughts, matters that Jonny may have wanted to add but didn't. He slowly laid them out on the table in the middle of the room. They were all dated, and Jonny laid them out chronologically. Most were not relevant as they were dated after 1944. He wanted earlier notes.

The search was proving a long shot and nothing was leaping out at him until he noticed what at first he thought was writing on the reverse side of several pages but on further examination was the impression of pen marks. He held the sheets to the light and turned them slightly to reveal the faintest of shadows. It was clearly writing but impossible to read.

'Is this the colour grey I've been looking for, Solomon' he said aloud. He made copies of the pages and put them back into the manuscript folder. Jonny put the originals in a clear plastic folder and picked up the phone and rang Rod Taskner of Photo Blending Tech Limited. There was no answer. Then he realised the office would be closed at 11.30 pm.

'Good morning, Rod. How goes it?'

'All the better for seeing you this bright and sunny day.'

'Got another job for you,' said Jonny studying the large photograph that Rod had draped over his desk. 'Interesting photo.'

'Yes, one of our archaeological client companies. Taken from one of those satellites you can rent for a fee, a big fee. They're looking for a lost city site in the Middle Sahara, actually. Cannot say any more, signed a comprehensive non-disclosure agreement with them.'

'Perhaps, I should get you to sign one, Rod,' said Jonny smiling at the thought.

'No need, mate. Most of our stuff here is very hush, hush. No-one here can talk about anything outside these walls, on pain of instant dismissal. Well, what have we this morning?'

Jonny handed Rod the plastic folder containing the sheets of paper.

'There are the impressions of some writing on these and I need to see what it is. Maybe nothing but, can you help?'

Rod carefully removed the papers holding by the corners. Holding one of them at an angle to the bright desk lamp.

'Yes, see what you mean, Jonny. Leave them with me. Shouldn't be long. I'll courier them around when their done. You in all day tomorrow?'

Chapter 53

Jonny opened the envelope and looked at the writing. There were some gaps but essentially it was complete.

'I became infatuated with her. It was a feeling that I'd never experienced before. I was young and thought about her every waking moment, even when we were close together looking into the microscopes. I felt like touching her soft skin and stroking her hair. I didn't for fear of rejection and foolishness. We spent our breaks from the lab, talking about our thoughts and aspirations. She did most of the talking. I felt I had known her for all my short life. It felt so natural to be with her, by her side. I would walk her home. At least part of the way. She was worried that her parents would start asking questions and she wanted us to be private. I'd watch her walk away towards her part of town until she was a speck in the distance and then gone until tomorrow.

'With a skip in my step, I would glide home not noticing anything around me, just lost in my own reverie. The nights would be long without her. Sleep would eventually come as I lay with my arms hugging myself imagining that I was wrapped in tenderness. One day, without apparent warning, although I know I am a little awkward, she turned to me and kissed my cheek tenderly. I responded by taking her hand in mine and looked straight into her eyes. She kissed me on the lips.

It was a sensation that I will hold dear for the rest of my life. My first lovers kiss.

'From that time onwards, my awkwardness as a lover seemed to dissipate. I felt that I could have some sort of control of my destiny. I invited her out for a day at the weekend before she and her family would be gone for their summer vacation. She gave some excuse to her parents and we met and took the train to Ammersee Lake. It took us fifty minutes by train that dropped us off in the town of Herrsching from where we walked together hand in hand to the lake, relaxed and swinging our arms together. It was too hot to walk to the Kloster Andechs monastery although we started along a well-marked path, but gave up to unpack the picnic we'd bought in Herrsching. We lay down on the warm grass watching the leaves on the trees above sway silently to and fro, listening to the shallow waves of the lake fall on the shingle shoreline. It felt as if I was transported into another world.

'I lay back, eyes closed, a shadow passed over my face. Roberta was watching me from a few inches away, her sweet breath tickling my face. She then kissed me on the lips and I wrapped my arms around her pulling her on top of me. We were both transported onto another plain as I wriggled out of my clothes and she did the same. She let me explore her body, I kissed each part delicately and she responded as if the most natural thing was for me to make love to her and for her to accept me.

'I didn't know at the time this was to be the last time we would ever have together. I tried to see her, but she left her job at the University and there was no sign of her anywhere I looked. I was distraught as weeks melted into months and gradually, I began to recover as University beckoned and a new stage of my life would begin.'

Jonny sat for a while. Was this his missing link in the chain?

Chapter 54

London

There was no doubt that Roberta gave birth to Schatzi and according to Solomon's chronology, it was likely that the dates they were at Ammersee lake coincided with the normal pregnancy unless she had a sexual liaison during the summer vacation under the watchful eyes of her parents. Jonny dismissed that as very unlikely. There were no records to substantiate that Schatzi was Solomon's child. Roberta's parents were never told who the father was.

Jonny knew that there were too many similarities between the two, Schatzi and Solomon. He got up and wandered over to the board and took down the two photographs which confirmed the physical similarities. The mental one's were the clincher, apart from Schatzi's Asperger's.

Jonny was certain that Solomon did not know that Roberta had given birth to a child after their brief liaison and that he was Schatzi's father. There was no reference directly in 'Stealing the Staircase' save for this one hidden sheaf of papers. One's that Solomon had discarded as they expressed his first brush with love. He thought they were too personal to appear in his story. Jonny's mind slid back to Solomon's reference to being a Jew and Roberta being an Aryan. That said a lot about why he maybe thought that her parents had forbidden any contact after that summer. It made sense to him, particularly as her father was a Captain in the Wehrmacht.

Had Stuart Campbell any of this knowledge? He'd had never even alluded to it whenever they spoke together. It would have inconceivable that there could be any meaningful relationship between Solomon and Campbell if either had any knowledge of the situation and yet there was a deep relationship between them from the time they met in 1945 to his death. Only interrupted by Porton Down and what Jonny suspected, Campbell was very upset about Solomon's behaviour, irrespective of the fact that he'd probably understood that Solomon would have been sickened by human experiment after his experiences in Auschwitz.

Johann Bron certainly did not know or if he did, he was very good at concealing it. This revelation would add motive to some of those on Jonny's board if it were true. Jonny decided now he had to end the speculation with some hard irrefutable facts. He picked up his diary of contacts and spoke into the telephone handset. He needed proof of his theory.

Chapter 55

'I need some help in a case I'm dealing with, Alaister?'

'Jonny, long time. How are you my friend and what's this about?'

Jonny explained that he wanted to see if two people were related. Paternity issue.

'What do you need from me?'

Jonny knew that even though we are all unique, most of our DNA is actually identical to other people's DNA.

'Body tissue or fluid. Must be uncontaminated because otherwise we cannot get to the specific regions which vary highly between people, 'polymorphisms', is the word,' said Alaister laughing at the other end of the phone.

'Polymor...what?'

'phisms. You and I inherit a unique combination of polymorphisms from our parents. DNA polymorphisms can be analysed to give a DNA profile.'

'Right, I see. So, you can tell from two profiles, with one parent's profile missing whether the two are related with a high level of accuracy?'

'Hey, Jonny. All I can say to you is 'short tandem repeats'.'

'What are short tandem repeats, Alaister?'

'I'll tell you next time we meet. Now you get the samples and I'll do the work. OK?'

Jonny put down the phone and looked at the list he'd written in his note pad of possible DNA sources. He repeated them to himself as he logically dismissed them one by one as he had two dead men to deal with, Solomon and Schatzi. White blood cells, semen, body tissue, body fluids, saliva, perspiration and hair roots.

Both Solomon Isaacs and Schatzi Campbell had been cremated. It looked like a dead-end, then he remembered that both had been the subject of post mortem examination to determine the cause of death. Who did he know who could help? Again, he consulted his 'little black book' of contacts. Flicking through the pages nothing immediately came to the fore, until he got to the word 'Undertakers' Maybe they could be his source. He picked up the telephone.

'Rachel, my right-hand lady, how are you?'

'Jonny, what's going on everybody's asking what the hell you're up to. I keep fobbing them off.'

'Hope it won't be too long now, but I need your help again. You remember a year or so ago, we managed to get some info from those Undertakers in Chester. I need to find some DNA of two bodies that cremated recently. All I can say is 'Paternity'. If I give you the names of the deceased, can you find the names of the official Undertakers?'

'Yep, shouldn't be too difficult,' replied Rachel as she wrote down the names and last known addresses of the deceased. She raised her eyebrows at the name of Isaacs.

'Is that the guy shot in a London hotel recently, Jonny?'

'The very same, Rachel. I'll tell you soon but be discreet. OK.'

'I'll do what I can. Be in touch. Discreet. Don't even mention the word, Jonny.'

Jonny wasn't convinced he was going to be lucky. He rang Alaister again.

'Sorry to bother you again but tell be about embalming. Does it destroy DNA?'

'Not necessarily. For individuals that recently passed away, within a week or so, taking samples collected by swabs from inside the cheek can still produce sufficient DNA. The embalming process will destroy DNA over time, Jonny, however, even after a body is recently embalmed, there is still a window where buccal, sorry cheek, swabs still work or alternatively, removing a patch of skin.'

'Thanks, Alaister. I'll be in touch.'

'Hey, wait a minute, Jonny. If what you tell me is true I'd say that you'd be unlikely to have uncontaminated swabs but we'll see. If I might suggest, maybe there's a chance of a sample of teeth, fingernails, hair. See what you can do, the more the better. Anyway, who's paying me?'

'The Journal, of course. Going to tell me about 'Short tandem repeats', Alaister?'

'Sit down and put your brain into gear, my friend. To obtain a profile, we examine STRs at ten, or more, genetic locations, these are usually on different chromosomes. Let me give you a simple example of non-coding DNA that contain repeats, TAGATAGA

TAGATAGATAGATA is an STR where the nucleotide sequence GATA is repeated six times. If these occur in two samples from different people, then it goes towards a match. We are usually looking at ten plus locations. Got it?'

'Not really. I'm beginning the regret the question. I better wait until you have the samples then, perhaps, it will make more sense to me. See you Alaister and thanks.'

Jonny sat waiting for Rachel to call. She didn't disappoint. Jonny listened carefully writing furiously on his pad.

Chapter 56

Pimlico London

'A flat in Pimlico, central London. Thanks Reinhart,' said Bron.

Debating with himself, he finally decided to go straight to London and make his decision about how to contact her thereafter.

As he exited Terminal 3 at Heathrow London airport, a smattering of recent snow lay trodden into the pavement that led to the taxi rank. Hang the cost, he wasn't in the mood to travel by train. The taxi pulled up outside the entrance to the Strand Palace hotel in central London and Bron slowly walked up the entrance steps and entered the revolving door. He was travelling light and shook his head when a porter arrived by his side to assist with his bag. Registration took a minute or two before he made his way across to the bank of lifts.

He opened the bedroom door and sat by the window before opening the fridge to help himself to a generous glass of scotch. He opened his case and took out a map of London looking at the circle he'd put indicating Nadine's address. A short taxi ride away. Tomorrow, he'd arrive quite early to make sure she was in.

He dressed in his newly pressed medium grey suit with blue tie and white shirt. woollen scarf wrapped loosely around his shoulders and heavy navy blue

267

overcoat, Bron stepped into the back seat of the London taxicab.

'They don't have any lifts here these old houses, which floor do you have to get to.' Bron studied the address.

'That will be top floor, mate,' said the cabbie as Bron paid the fare.

He stood on the pavement and studied the building. It was going to be quite an effort. The entrance was guarded by a porter in maroon livery.

'May I help, sir?'

'I'm visiting Nadine Isaacs. It's a surprise. We have seen each other since 1943.'

'Gracious, that is a long time. Have you come far?'

'Not really, arrived from Munich yesterday.'

'Well, sorry to say you've just missed her. She went for her morning walk about ten minutes ago. Usually takes half an hour.'

'Where does she walk to?'

'Usually, in fact always, she turns left out of the front and then arrives back from the right. Not sure where she goes in the middle,' he laughed. 'There's a nice sheltered seat in the park, there on the right, unless you want to wait here in the warm?' he said pointing through the front door. Usually, a coffee van parked there till after lunch time. 'Sorry, we don't stretch to refreshments here,' he laughed again.

Bron lowered himself onto the bench seat and cradled the warm coffee in his hands. He had a view of the building and the pavements and paths that led in all directions. He felt nervous for the first time since he heard from Campbell that Nadine was alive. What were his first words going to be? Would he recognise her? Would she recognise him? All these uncertainties crossed his mind as he sipped the hot liquid. The air was cold but bright and each hot breath was caught in the light breeze and wafted away. Pigeons gather nearby hoping for some food but eventually flew off to some more probable gift zone.

He hadn't been sitting there very long when Nadine appeared walking across the small park in the long shadows of the bare trees. She looked a lot younger than he did and carried herself upright as opposed to his slight stoop of age. Bron's heart began top beat rapidly. When should he stand? She walked towards where he was sitting without a glance left or right lost in her own thoughts. He'd practised the words carefully and with slight amusement.

'Calculating,' he said in precise German.

Nadine stopped immediately and looked at Bron studying the face in front of her closely. A flash of recognition leapt into her face.

'Oh my god, is it you Johann?' she said stumbling towards him. He held out his arms for her to fall into.

'Yes, it's me,' he said quietly.

She pulled away to look at him carefully.

'Oh my God, you're alive.' She stroked his face gently with her gloved hands. 'Come, let's get out of this cold. I live just over there.'

'I know. That's where I met your porter.'

'How did you know where to find me?'

'Long story.'

Nadine took his arm and guided him across the road and into the building. Inside, he slowly climbed the stairs holding onto the bannister, catching his breath every now and again. Nadine opened the door to her apartment and waited as he finally made it to the top.

'Too much for me these days, Nadine.'

'Well, you're here now. Please sit and let me look at you.' She cupped her hands around his face not wishing to let go. 'I'll get us some coffee.'

Soon the aroma of freshly ground beans pervaded the air and she handed him the coffee and he wrapped his fingers around the warm mug. She sat staring at him and held his hand when he put the cup down.

'You first or me?'

'I know what happened to you. Captain Campbell told me all about your capture and that Solomon Isaacs saved you. What actually happened after that he was a little hazy about. So, I want you to fill in the missing pieces after you were given passage to England, then I will bore you with my travels,' he smiled that smile she remembered from the dark days of 1943.

'It was a long time ago, Johann. Memories fade a little. Times change. Captain Campbell was in charge. I had no desire to remain in Germany and Solomon certainly didn't. He blamed his parents for not trying to emigrate. They left it too late not appreciating the dire straits they were in until the opportunity passed when all the world closed their doors to the plight of the German Jews. It was Solomon's intellect that Campbell saw and wanted. Also, his incredible recall memory helped find and capture many war criminals. I know this is not the Germany you want to hear about, but you did ask.'

'I know my leaders committed huge crimes, Nadine. In fact, my time in Russia was based on Soviet retribution of the basest kind. Most of my contemporaries didn't survive.'

'When we stumbled out of the barbed wire compound at the end of our time in Auschwitz, all we wanted was to get away from the European continent and settle somewhere where the birds sang and people smiled. I know now that my own people were being persecuted and slaughtered in their millions by Stalin. Maybe you experienced that first-hand but let me continue.

'I remember Captain Campbell sitting us down after we decided to go to Britain. He told us that the Anglo-Jewish community had exhausted their ability to pay for Jews settling in England and that now it was up to the Government to pay. The good thing was there was no quota system like the Americans had introduced. We were assured by Captain Campbell that our case would be dealt with on an individual basis and that being so, he had not doubt we would be accepted. He had already paved the way for Solomon to continue his studies.

'On the 12 June 1946, we boarded a train to Calais in France and across the English Channel then made our way to London. I have this abiding memory of the train full of people gabbling away in different languages, German, French, Polish, Hungarian, English, Russian. It was very strange.

'Captain Campbell had arranged for us to live in a small apartment near the University in Euston Road Bloomsbury London. It was like a palace to us. Privacy, a door that would close and we could lock. Three rooms, we could call our own. Solomon's parents had one bedroom and we shared ours with Stewart. Soon life returned to normal as both Solomon's parents got jobs and Solomon took a Government research job.

'Things started to go badly wrong a few years later.' Nadine started to cry, and Johann leaned forward to hold her hand.

'I thought I had got over this, Johann. Clearly, I haven't. I am sorry, this is meant to be a happy time.'

'Look, Nadine. Let me get you something a little stronger. Do you stock brandy here? I could do with one, myself.' Nadine pointed to the cabinet behind the settee.

He sat down again next to her and handed one glass. Cradling his glass, he swilled the contents around the glass smelling the aroma. Nothing was said for a few moments then Johann broke the silence.

'Can you tell me what happened?'

'Solomon was working on highly classified research into genetics and cloning at a government research establishment in Wiltshire called Porton Down. Captain Campbell had set it all up. It was very prestigious. I only saw Solomon for long weekends when he came back to London. One day, I can't remember the dates now, but it was early 1950s, he came home. Something was troubling him, but he wouldn't say what. He didn't want me to get involved. Better that I didn't know anything so I couldn't say anything.'

Nadine hesitated, clearing her head. She looked at Johann.

'I haven't seen him since he was sent to prison for thirty-five years. He insisted that Stewart and I did not visit him. He wrote a long letter explaining that he felt so wretched that he'd put us through the whole mess and that there was little likelihood of any time reduction because of the gravity of the accusations and in all likelihood he'd die in prison. We should start a new life with the savings he had and try to make the best of things. He refused to see his parents, literally all visitors. I received one letter just after he had been transferred to Belmarsh High Security prison in London. He wanted to see Stewart one last time. Apparently, he was quite ill at the time but as we have heard nothing, we both assumed he had recovered.'

'So, what did you do?'

'Well, he had been very frugal and also received a little money from his parents' estate. Must have been the war years. There was enough. I sold the house, with his solicitor's cooperation and bought this flat. Invested the rest and educated Stewart, mostly with scholarships.'

'You never considered divorcing and remarrying?'

'Solomon wanted me to if I met someone, but no that never happened. Although the memories have faded and sometimes I have trouble imagining what he looks like. I have no feelings as a wife anymore,' said Nadine with a slight sadness that Bron noted.

'Did Stewart say anything about meeting his father?'

'Just that he was sorry for doing what he thought was his duty and, in consequence, ruining our lives.'

'That was all?'

273

'That's all. I suppose he just wanted to make sure we understood and could forgive him.'

'Could you, forgive him.'

The front door closed with a bang.

There stood Stewart. He'd heard the latter part of the conversation. His face was thunder as he looked at Nadine then at Bron ignoring his outstretched hand and shouted

'No, never, mother.'

Chapter 57

Jonny flicked through his telephone pad and dialled the number drumming his fingers on his desk.

'Inspector Rainham, please,' he asked the switchboard, waiting nervously.

'Graham, it's Jonny Wightman. Have you got a moment? And by the way, how are you?'

'Great actually. Have I got a moment? Maybe, Jonny, depends on what you want.'

'Excellent, my dear friend. Simple. A sample for DNA analysis, preferably several from each if possible.'

'Whose DNA are you looking for and why?'

'Two deceaseds, I'm afraid. Paternity suit question.' He hated not telling the whole truth, but needs must be.

'Big money dispute, I suppose.'

'No. No money involved, at least very little, so it isn't anything to do with big lawyers and court cases.'

'Well, I glad to hear that. I know I owe you so give me the details, names, addresses, coroners, if any, undertakers. I see what I can do.'

'Thanks, Graham.'

Chapter 58

London

Two weeks later, Jonny was sitting in the cramped office of Alaister Simmons at Kensington Research Limited just off the High Street in Chelsea London.

'Well, Jonny, most of what you gave us was unusable, but…'

He lined up in front of Jonny, photographic images of lines of dark spots.

'When the strands of DNA decay and give off light, they leave dark spots on the film. The DNA bands of a person. What make up the fingerprint are the unique patterns of bands, we are all different and unique (other than identical twins). What you now see, once the filter is exposed to the x-ray film, are the radioactive DNA sequences. This creates a banding pattern.'

'Well, that's great but what am I looking for?' said Jonny.

'Here,' said Alaister pointing to the sequences. 'These STRs match here, here, here, and in other places too.'

'We have a match. These two people's DNA show they are closely related. Father and son?'

'Yep, without a doubt, my dear Jonny.'

The revelation now did not surprise Jonny. He knew he was on to something. Now the real question arose. Who knew about this? He doubted Solomon knew. He never mentioned the pregnancy or the birth

276

of a son. Roberta just disappeared from his life after the summer vacation. Roberta knew that Solomon was the father, but she never told anyone.

Jonny knew now why Roberta had keep this secret. At the annual party rally held in Nuremberg in 1935, the Nazis announced new laws which institutionalized many of the racial theories prevalent in Nazi ideology. The laws excluded German Jews from Reich citizenship and prohibited them from marrying or having sexual relations with persons of German or related blood. Ancillary ordinances to the laws disenfranchised Jews and deprived them of most political rights.

The consequences for Solomon, if Roberta revealed that he was the father, were dire. Punishment for race defilement for men was the death penalty and for women it was being sent to a concentration camp. Roberta would have heard from her father the implications of the new law and probably read about the situation. The propaganda press had made it plain when they quoted Hitler on the question of women breaching the Nuremberg Laws when he said, 'having her hair shorn and being sent to a concentration camp'.

Chapter 59

Johann Bron looked at Stewart and stood up slowly.

'Perhaps I should introduce myself,' putting out his hand again.

'I know who you are, Captain Bron. Why are you here, is more to the point?'

'I came to see your mother after visiting Stuart Campbell. I had no idea that your mother was alive and wanted to see her again. Is that so wrong? You seem upset.'

'I am upset. Not because of you being here. The concierge told me you had a visitor and I have been listening to you from the hallway. No, I'm upset because they are releasing Dad next week. The prison thought it best that I should know first, as I was the only one on their call list.'

'Oh, my god. What's going to happen to him? Where's he going to live?'

'They wouldn't tell me, except that he has accommodation already arranged. That's all I know.'

'Why did you shout 'no, never, never' when you came in. We were talking about forgiveness, Johann and I,' reprimanded Nadine.

'I need to tell you something that I never thought I'd have to. I don't want to say anything in front of......'

278

'Look, Stewart, the past has a way of coming up on you unawares when you least expect it, Johann, for example. I had never expected to see him again. He was so helpless when I left him. No, if there's something to be said, let have it out in the open. Johann saved my life once a long time ago,' said Nadine. 'You and I wouldn't now be here if it wasn't for him and Solomon.'

'Mother, this is very difficult for me to say. I have kept this secret for many years. Dad knew because he was responsible.'

'Knew what?'

'He was responsible for you not being able to have any more children. The reports from the medics after you had those tests years ago. I didn't tell you the whole truth because Dad would have been finished if the truth were known. I know he finished his own life when he tried to stop those experiments in Porton Down, but the truth is he had done experiments on you, Mother.'

'What do you mean? I don't understand.'

'I am the first human clone, Mother.'

Stewart let the words sink in. Nadine looked uncomprehendingly at him then at Johann. There was a long silence. Stewart knelt in front of his mother and looked into her eyes.

'Mother, you know Dad was a brilliant scientist. He had worked out theories long before anyone else, but he had the chance to put them into practice without the constraints of ethics and approval, apart from those Nazi's at Auschwitz. He manipulated the system to save you but also to further his theories. I say this as a scientist not as your son, but what he did was absolutely brilliant. The only thing that went wrong was during the

279

impregnation of the fertilised egg. He was in a hurry and I suspect and that cost you the possibility of bearing more children.'

'You mean, he experimented on Nadine just as they would have done,' said Bron, aghast at what he'd heard.

'You could say that. Yes.'

'But….' Nadine stopped and held Stewart's hand.

'I know, Mother, but in doing so, he saved your life as well. You would have been dead by now if he hadn't come up with a story of perpetuating the Aryan race by perfecting artificial insemination procedures using the highest echelons of the Nazi regime as providers.'

'Why then are you so set against forgiveness, Stewart?'

'Because of this.'

He reached into his pocket and pulled out two sheets of paper. I don't feel real. My DNA is an exact fit. Look. I've known for a long time and when he asked to see him in Belmarsh, I confronted him. He told me the truth of what happened in Block 10. I feel that part of me is a dead woman's ova, part of me is your nourishment and part his sperm. All mixed up. Can you understand?'

Stewart wept in his mother's arms. A grown man with grey flecks spouting from his black hair resting on her lap, shaking gently seeking comfort from the only one who could give it to him. Johann Bron remained impassive. His thoughts milling around looking for a home to comfort him as well. Too many to put in boxes on their own, Roberta, his wife, Schatzi, Nadine and now Stewart. Was their one link to tie them all together and let him rest?

'Johann, you know where the kitchen is, can you put on the coffee machine for us all? Oh, and get the brandy bottle for the second cupboard on the left, top shelf. We could all do with something.'

Little was said as they drank coffee and sipped brandy, finally, Bron leaned forward and touched Stewart on the arm.

'Forgive me for asking but can I see those DNA profiles, Stewart. I never seen one before.' He studied them closely including the name of the company that did the profiling. Stewart had obviously tried to keep this matter private away from his life at Cambridge.

As Bron looked at them, a strange thought flew in and out of his unconscious, so quickly it didn't register until after he had returned to the hotel that night.

Talk of the consequences of Solomon Isaacs' imminent release he would leave for another time.

Chapter 60

London

The next morning, Bron dialled the number.

'Professor Isaacs, please.'

'Who shall I say is calling?'

'Stewart, I need your help. Are you willing to give me a rundown on how to obtain samples for DNA analysis?'

'What are you up to?'

'Please. I will tell you when I think you need to know. Please trust me, Stewart. You know I'd do nothing to hurt Nadine or you. Enough hurt has already been done. I just need finality on something.'

Professor Stewart ran Johann Bron through the procedure. Bron kept asking him to slow down as he wrote furiously on the hotel note pad.

'One more thing, Stewart. Can you authorise me to look at your DNA results?'

Johann Bron took a taxi to Chelsea. He uncrumpled the note paper from the hotel and looked at the address. It was an unassuming office beyond the glass partition, Bron could see several lab technicians coming and going. He waited patiently as the receptionist paged Alaister Simmons.

'Hello, my name is Simmons,' Alaister held out his hand.

'Johann Bron,' as he shook the outstretched hand.

'Please, follow me.'

They sat at a clear glass topped desk with a carefully stacked in-tray containing one file. Alaister ordered coffee.

'Well, what can I do for you?'

'Ah, yes. We had a call from Professor Solomon earlier this morning followed by a special delivery letter authorising me to talk to you. Said you'd be calling in. We keep our records for many years, just in case. Like now, for example. You enjoy the coffee I'll be back. Didn't have time to get the originals from archives before you arrived, I'll go myself. Probably be quicker.'

'I'm in no hurry,' said Bron.

Previously he'd spoken at length to Stewart Isaacs and decided to extend his stay in London for a few days and advised his Care Home where he was and that he was fine. He'd been really happy to see Schatzi again and spend the day with him. During the course of the day he'd taken several samples of what he hoped would be acceptable for analysis.

Alaister sat down and took notes to accompany each sample Bron handed to him.

'I'm going home back to Munich in a couple of days. I assume your report will follow. I need to know if these two samples make a match,' pointing to Stewart's DNA profile and that of the samples.

Back in Germany, Bron waited for the results.

Chapter 61

London

'Jonny, It's Alaister Simmons. You know those DNA results. Well, something strange, occurred to me the other day, so I thought I'd check back in my records.' he said excitedly. 'I thought for a minute that there had been some mix up, your sequences, the ones of the deceased, looked so familiar in retrospect, so I checked.'

He picked up the other file that Bron had previously left.

'I think you should come in. I don't like talking on the phone and in any case, I shouldn't be telling you all this. You know the rules. Can you come now?'

'This will be going nowhere, Alaister. You know me well enough. I'll be there within the hour,' said Jonny snapping down the phone and catching his raincoat as he ran through the door.

'Well, here I am.

'Jonny, remember the paternity question? Well, I have found something strange. There's a third match, but this only came to my attention by chance. A German man came to see me and asked me to sequence some DNA. I had forgotten about it until yesterday and checked his request and yours. They were identical, so someone knew what you now know.'

Jonny described the man and gave his name, Johann Bron. Alaister was taken by surprise. You know him?

'Not personally, but I know of him. He's part of the paternity suit,' lied Jonny. 'Hey, but thanks that's very helpful. You have no idea how helpful. They shook hands and Jonny left.

When Jonny returned to his apartment, he looked at the board. Against Johann Bron he wrote in the column 'motive', changing 'possible' to 'probable'. He knew Schatzi was his grandson and now he would know soon who the father was. There were still Nadine, Schatzi, Stuart Campbell and Stewart Isaacs. They all had possible access to the killer's gun, the Walther P38, including Bron. Jonny was now at a dead end. As much as he threw the possibilities around in his mind, nothing came to him until......

He reached for Solomon's 'Stealing the Staircase'. Had Solomon passed over Stuart Campbell's comments on the resemblance between his adopted son Schatzi and himself? He had certainly done so when they discussed his own son, Stewart. Campbell must have noticed a resemblance to Schatzi, but then again everyone has a doppelganger somewhere.

'Am I clutching at straws,' muttered Jonny to himself, peering at the board again.

Chapter 62

Munich Germany

Johann Bron opened the envelope he'd just signed for and took out the two profiles and looked at them and read Alaister Simmons letter. So, Solomon Isaacs was the father of Schatzi. He hadn't wanted to believe it but there it was in irrefutable black and white. No wonder poor old Roberta had hidden the paternity. Had Solomon Isaacs forced himself upon her? Got her drunk? Why else would she…? He didn't want to believe anything else. It was bad enough that she had brought shame on the family by being pregnant outside marriage, that they coped with but the consequences of bearing a Jewish child would have spelled disaster for all of them.

Bron sat back and considered what to do next. He'd said to Professor Stewart Isaacs that he'd tell him what he was up to at the appropriate time. What a mess Solomon Isaacs had created.

'I need to see you about that profile. Are you in London any time soon?'

'Johann, I am seeing mother this weekend. We're going to a concert at Covent Garden. Actually, I have an extra ticket I was going to give to a colleague. You'd be very welcome to join us. Mother would be delighted.'

'That's very kind.'

'Come and stay at the flat. Mother would love it. Oh, by the way, it's Wagner. Right up your street, I expect.'

'Let's say it's interesting. Are you sure about staying at the flat, because if so, I'd be delighted?'

'Of course. I'll be there from Thursday evening. Get a flight over and I'll meet you Paddington station from the Heathrow Express. It's very convenient, you know.'

Nadine, flanked by Stewart on her left and Johann on her right, settled into her seat. The men waited and then sat beside her. The curtain rose to the sound of clapping as the audience surveyed to scene. The music began, Johann was transported back in Munich before being ostracized by the Nazi's, stepping down the stone steps, opening the door of the black Mercedes for his wife. He'd always been aware that Hitler reinterpreted the story of Wagner's final opera 'Parsifal', the one they were now watching, to fit his own ideological vision. The programme hinted that the story carries elements of Buddhist renunciation suggested by Wagner's readings of Schopenhauer. Johann remembered what Hitler had written about it. He muttered the words to himself, 'What is celebrated is but pure and noble blood, blood whose purity the brotherhood of initiates has come together to guard. His thoughts are intimately familiar to me, at every stage of my life I come back to him.'

Johann had learned these lines by heart when Roberta had to recite them as part of Hitler's teaching in school.

'What did you say, Johann?'

Turning to Nadine, he shook his head and whispered. 'Nothing. Just a few words I remembered from long ago.'

Despite his misgivings about Wagner, Johann enjoyed the spectacle and the dinner afterwards. Shifting uncomfortably in his chair, warming the bandy that Stewart had poured, Nadine and Stewart looked expectantly at Johann.

'Well. Come on tell us what you're here about. Sing for the supper you have just had.'

Johann took a long breath.

'I had a hunch, as they say in the detective novels I sometimes read. The hunch proved to be correct. You have a brother, Stewart.'

Nadine and Stewart looked at Bron unbelievingly.

'What do you mean? What brother?'

'My grandson is your brother. Schatzi is your brother. Just as I had suspected after meeting my grandson, Schatzi and then you. The physical resemblance had been uncanny, not to mention certain mannerisms, I noticed. You are brothers in a peculiar manner, of that I am sure. You showed me your DNA profile and after I met with my grandson. I took a sample for Alaister Simmons to compare. It was a match. Didn't you guess?'

'No. I have never met Schatzi Campbell. I don't know what he looks like. I've read his scientific papers, of course. Everyone in the field does.'

'But you must have seen his picture. He won a Nobel Prize in your field and yet you never met?'

Stewart's denial left the thought hanging in the air. Was he lying? It is true that Schatzi didn't court

288

publicity and did most of his research hidden from view as would be expected from someone who needed his mother's social support most of the time and remained a recluse, and yet Stewart Isaacs didn't know or suspect. Bron was sceptical. There was something about Stewart, he couldn't put his finger on. He liked the man and they got on well, but he was unusually agitated the other day about forgiveness. Maybe he hadn't told the whole truth and he knew already what Bron had told him.

Chapter 63

Jonny decided it was time to talk to Inspector Graham Rainham again. It was his turn to pay back a debt.

'Graham, Jonny Wightman. I need to speak to you, off the record. Any chance of you coming to my apartment. I have all the papers here and it would be very convenient for me not to have to cart them elsewhere.'

'What's this about, Jonny?'

'I'll tell you when you come. Not over the phone. It'll take too long. OK. Not in uniform, please. Must think of the neighbours. And one more thing, Graham, I know I am asking a lot, but can you familiarise yourself with the death of Solomon Isaacs.'

'What! You can't be serious. It's not my case. Vernon Smith's is the senior officer in charge. Asking me to divulge details of an ongoing investigation to an investigative journalist like yourself, Jonny. No, that's a step too far.'

'Graham, I am not asking you to divulge anything. I asked you to familiarise yourself. It may help you to understand more when you see me. Of course, I love to see the investigation file, but that's not what I'm asking. Just for me, please. I have never let you down over the years. I am not about to do so now. When can we meet?'

Jonny marked his diary, not that he would forget but this was habit.

Just before 5pm the next afternoon, he tidied the sitting room and laid out the loose leaved copy of 'Stealing the Staircase' on the dining table in front of the two chairs he arranged side by side. The board could be seen easily as it hung on the wall in front of the chairs. The entry phone buzzed, and he admitted Inspector Graham Rainham. Rainham entered the sitting room glancing all around him.

Looks like you've been busy, Jonny,' he said shedding his coat. He walked over to the board and studied the array of photographs and the names and the headings of the columns.

'Just like our control room. I already feel at home,' he joked. 'What's this?'

'We're off the record, right.' Rainham nodded. 'This. It's where it all started. Landed on my desk one day. Couldn't stop reading it. It's a fascinating story of one man, Solomon Isaacs.'

'When did you get hold of it?'

'Weeks after he was released from Belmarsh, we were about to launch the publication of the book when Solomon askcd to meet me.'

'So, were you with him when he was shot? asked Rainham.

'Yes, Graham. I was there.'

'I never saw a witness statement,' said Rainham who had clearly read the file in the meantime.

'No, only what I'd said at the Coroner's hearing. There were a considerable number of witnesses as you know now I see you've read the file. I would have said what they said. I was at the inquest. There was nothing I could have added, Graham. Honestly.'

'Did you see the shooter?'

'Of course, as did everyone else. There was panic and chaos, as you'd expect. People running everywhere thinking the whole place was under attack. He or she just disappeared into the street and vanished. You know all that. Off the record, I did hear something. Remember, I was there to discuss the future with the writer. What happened was a shock to me. More so as I felt I knew this man better than most. I knelt beside him. He'd recognised me and started to say "Jonny, I recognized the ...." I have pondered the words so often and yet there are so many possibilities of who he was referring to. He obviously recognised the shooter from somewhere.'

Chapter 64

'Solomon gave you an incredible insight into life in Auschwitz, Stuart.' Said Jonny.

He'd invited Campbell to his London apartment after Rainham's unhelpful visit. All that Rainham had said was that when he looked at the police file it was surprisingly sparse for a murder investigation. All he could suggest, after listening to Jonny and scanning the wall board, was that somewhere in the past life of Solomon, maybe amongst the evidence he produced to help round up of war criminals, he may find the answer. Jonny had so far concentrated on everything in `Stealing the Staircase'.

Jonny wasn't surprised that Stuart accepted the invitation after he'd explained he had a room full of exhibits and files that they could look at together. Stuart had wandered around the wall board closely examining everybody's photograph, old and new.

His first word was `remarkable'. He turned to Jonny.

'Am I still one of your suspects, my dear boy?'

'Not anymore, Stuart,' said Jonny removing his name from the `possible' column.

'Glad to hear it and you can wipe Schatzi's name off the list as well. Neither of us would ever do such a thing even assuming there was a motive.'

293

'May I sit down? Little too old for standing too long,' he said lowering himself into plush leather settee putting his own battered file of papers from 1946/7 on his lap.

'This must never see the light of day. I have reread it over the last few days since you rang me. Strange how it all comes back so immediately once you start prodding into the dim memories of those awful months. Anyway, I have marked a few pages that were traumatic for me because Solomon's attitude, according to the stenographer's side note, became very animated as he dictated his recollections. To my knowledge, this was the only time he became emotionally.... How shall I say, `vengeful'. Yes, that's the right word.

Jonny took the papers and read the case. 'Did the Tribunal prosecute?'

'Yes. I believe the death sentence was carried out immediately.'

Chapter 65

An impossible theory was beginning to form in Jonny' mind. He'd taken time to closely cross examine Stuart Campbell on the case he'd suggested and had asked Johann Bron for help in Munich through police contact. Bit by bit everything started to fit into place. Why hadn't Jonny taken Solomon seriously when he said he was being tailed?

'Graham, I haven't had the chance to thank you.'

'What for, breaking my oath as a policeman?'

'No. You set me thinking outside the manuscript.'

'And....'

'Well, I am now in some difficulty. I don't know where to turn next.'

'I assume you want some police guidance?'

'Yes.'

O.K. What sort of guidance, Jonny.'

Can you give me an hour or so, but beforehand, I think you should read the evidence I have compiled. Can you come to the flat? Oh, one more thing.' Jonny explained what he needed.

Carrying his shopping bags through into the hall, Jonny left Graham Rainham reading the new evidence, pen already poised to make notes.

'My God, Jonny, I think we have the murderer.'

'So, what I asked you over the phone is not a problem?'

'No, it isn't. The problem is what do we do now?'

'Yes, I know. You're the policeman, so over to you.'

Chapter 66

'Ladies and Gentlemen,' said Sir Martin Grevelle, prosecuting for the Crown, 'as he walked towards the jury members, 'We have a very strange situation in this case.'

'It is the Crown's contention that the Accused deliberately set out to ensure that this crime was never solved and would eventually become a cold case that the conspiracy theorists could have a field day. My learned friend, Sir David Thornfield, will tell you that his client is innocent of the charges and that all the evidence that I will put forward is circumstantial and could point the other possible culprits. I intend to show you that beyond a reasonable doubt that the Accused is guilty as charged. I ask you to be very careful not to become confused by other theories put forward by the defence in their contention that Accused is not guilty.

'First of all, we need to establish motive. Ladies and Gentlemen of the jury, what I am about to describe may at first not seem to bear directly on the Accused but you need to appreciate what festered in the accused's mind all the years before his fatal shooting of Solomon Isaacs.

'Let me take you back to the concentration camp at Auschwitz. The deceased was a Jew working in the camp hospital, his training at University was stopped by the Nazi regime and he and his mother and father were arrested as part of the `Final Solution'. Their ultimate fate was to be gassed in one of the chambers. They survived.

'Solomon Isaacs witnessed some of the most horrific excesses that humans can perpetrate on other humans. You may not be aware of the term *Funktionshaftling*. It is the name given to prisoners who collaborated with the Nazis in order to serve over others interned in the concentration camps. Others used to call them *kapos* or bosses. The camp system would not work without these men or women because of the sheer numbers involved. In return, these people received more rations and better treatment hoping they'd survive. However, some took their new found power into the same realms as their SS guards treating their fellow Jews like sub-humans.

'I have here the records taken by Captain Stuart Campbell from evidence provided by the deceased in this case, Solomon Isaacs. Let me read this to you. Captain Campbell is present in court but will not be giving evidence as the Defence have agreed the authenticity of these papers.'

With that opening, Sir Martin Grevelle, Prosecuting for the Crown looked at the bundle of evidence.

He started with the killing of the little boy who had survived the mass gassing but had been suffocated in the autopsy room when Solomon Isaacs was present.

'I was walking to the hospital in Block 10, when I saw Gurt Heidmann, the Accused's father, explained Counsel, *standing over a small girl, no more than twelve or thirteen, he was beating her with his baton. She was covered in blood and curled into a ball, shouting and screaming for him to stop. My father*

tried to stop him but he was too strong and threw him to the ground and beat his legs savagely. Abruptly, he stopped and walked away as if nothing had happened. My father managed to make back to our hut and I took the little girl to the hospital and we tried to do what we could. She told me that he had raped her and she had wriggled free and run away and he had chased her. That small child died in my arms as I cradled her. Later, I bandaged my father leg and put a splint above his left ankle. I had no idea whether there was a broken bone but acted as if there was just in case. He was in great pain for several days thereafter but feared to show it.

Picking up another large sheaf of papers, Prosecuting Counsel, started to read from another record.

Elsie Heidmann, Sir Martin Grevelle told the jury she was the Accused's mother, *was a good looking woman but I feared she was not confident in herself for she chose systematically to disfigure or humiliate any of the prisoners she felt were a threat. She relied on her husband, Gurt, to fight for her if needed. All the prisoners were aware of his sadistic temper. In one instance, a young girl had been caught by her talking through the wire enclosure of one compound to a friend and she horse whipped that girl's face until it was unrecognisable. I did the best I could for her as she told me the story. She died of blood poisoning several days later. Many inmates told me that Elsie Heidmann stood alongside Mengele on the arrivals platform pointing to healthy women who would normally be useful but suggesting they were unsuitable despite Mengele's decision to keep them. When I asked why, each related their opinion that those chosen were pretty.*

Prosecuting Counsel then confirmed that the extracts he had read were just a small part of the evidence against the Accused's parents, Gurt and Elsie

299

Heidmann. He then walked to the Judge, Mr Justice Hugh Davey, and handed him the two sets of papers. He then gathered copies and handed one each to member of the jury.

'You have before you in those papers the complete evidence that the deceased, Solomon Isaacs, gave to the War Crimes Tribunal in 1945 with corroboration from others. I want you to read that evidence very carefully before I continue.'

He then turned to Mr Justice Davey and asked for the jury to be given time to read the papers before he continued. The Judge turned to the jury and ordered lunch for them and dismissed them until the following morning at ten am. As Captain Campbell rose with Stewart and Nadine Solomon to leave the court room, he did not envy the members of the jury having to read the horrors within those papers.

**

'I hope you have now seen that motive is clearly established. Now let me turn to the actual shooting.'

Sir Martin Grevelle took a bundle of papers from the desk in front of him and passed one copy to the Judge and further copies to members of the jury. He then started to read from the detailed resume of the Report of Proceedings that took place on the 17 April 2006 at the Southwark Coroner's Court into Solomon Isaacs' murder pointing out the murder scene in the hotel, the weapon used, a Walther P38, a vague description of fleeing gunman. Surprisingly, he then admitted that none of this evidence, in itself, pointed to the Accused as the murderer but then he produced a copy of the murder investigation file that the Defence had tried to suppress.

'I am in serious difficulty here, members of the jury, when I read this and that will become apparent when the accused tells you his story. So, let me call our first witness, Mr Jonny Wightman.'

'Jonny Wightman, you were one of the last people to see Mr Isaacs alive. Did he say anything to you before he died.'

'Yes. He started to whisper in my ear, "I recognise the......".'

'Do you know who he may have recognised?'

'To begin with I had no idea but under my breath I promised Solomon, Dr Isaacs, I would find out.'

'You knew Solomon well, didn't you?'

'Yes. During the time we spent together getting the manuscript ready for publication, I found out a great deal about the man and his life.'

'Did he tell you anything about what happened immediately after his release from Belmarsh?

'Objection, Your Honour, this is pure hearsay. The Defence cannot possibly ask the Deceased in cross-examination if this is true or not.'

Mr Justice Davey asked both barristers to approach the bench. After a huddled argument, he agreed to allow a continuation of this evidence as the Crown were prepared to call corroborative evidence from members of the police involved.

'After Solomon was released, he began to write his memoirs but became aware that he was under surveillance. He was being followed everywhere he went. I told him it was probably just standard procedure after being released from Belmarsh but he was certain it was more than that.'

'After his death, did you investigate this further?'

'No. Not at first. We, Solomon and I, knew there were loose ends in his book, so I tried to fill in the gaps. I had nothing concrete to tell the police, so I didn't advise them of what I was doing.

'Did you find the Accused in those with possible grudges?'

'No. I eliminated all of my possible suspects, one by one. I then came to a dead-end until a colleague I have known for years in the police force came to see me, at my request, and I showed him 'my incident room' as I had come to call the sitting room in my apartment.'

'What transpired from that meeting?'

'We concluded that somewhere hidden in Solomon's manuscript was a new suspect that I had overlooked. Someone who didn't have a place in the manuscript but may have a motive and the means. I met with Captain Campbell and he gave me his notebook and I suddenly noticed his comment when Solomon was recalling some of his evidence. He'd written something to the effect that Solomon had become very agitated at this point.'

'In itself, it wasn't startling, but I started to look into all matters relating the Accused's life. I discovered that the Accused had as a baby been smuggled out of Germany at his parents requested before they arrested and sent to Auschwitz.'

Jonny then went on to describe all he'd discovered.

The police investigation was not being rigorously pursued. He was also able to find out that the Accused had at some stage owned a Walther P38 similar to the murder weapon which was never found.

Chapter 67

Defence Counsel, Sir David Thornfield, rose.

'I call Mrs Olga Davies.'

Olga walked to the witness stand. The jury watched her intently as she cast her eyes over them and then turned her attention to Mr Justice Davy. At 81 she stood dressed in a plain light grey two piece with silk scarf wrapped loosely around her shoulders. Her hair was snow white and cut short. Her blue eyes sparkled despite that gravity of the evidence she was about to give. The Judge invited her to sit after she gave her oath. The jury watched as she carefully lowered herself into the chair and took a sip of water and glanced at her husband, Rees, for support. He smiled at her.

'Mrs Davies, what is your relationship with the accused?'

'I am his mother.'

'That's not strictly true. Is it, Mrs Davies?'

Olga looked at her son in the prisoner's dock and then at the Jury.

'No, I'm sorry. It is complicated.' Olga then related in great detail, as she was instructed to do by Sir David Thornfield, the events of escaping Nazi Germany and then finding her family here in Britain where she had come to escape had been killed by those she had run away from. Whenever she missed something out, he reminded her. The whole courtroom was silent, hanging

304

on the description every dreadful event. Every now and again, she'd stop and wipe a tear from her eyes as the memories flooded back. It was clear to every member of the jury that this woman had endured as much as anyone else in the courtroom and survived.

Prosecuting Counsel tried to curtail her evidence with various interruptions as to relevance in this murder case, but Mr Justice Davy would have nothing of it after it was put to him by Sir David Thornfield that his client's best interests were served by a full disclosure of his background history and in any case when he gave evidence in his defence, the Court would know him better.

When Olga stood down and walked to the back of the Court, she saw her son smiling at her as if to say, *thank for everything, Mum.*

Sir David Thornfield then called the Accused.

'Your former name was Avyar Smit?'

'Yes. I anglicised it by Deed Poll as soon as I was 18 and entering University. I am Vernon Smith.'

'You have heard your mother's evidence. I assume there was nothing new in what you heard.'

'That is correct.'

'When did you start actively looking for your real parents.'

'I started to ask questions as soon as I entered the London School of Economics. I was studying law and that opened up new lines of enquiry.'

'Can you tell the jury in detail how and what you discovered?'

'As you have heard from my mother, my real parents, Gurt and Elsie Heidmann, were taken by the regime and transported to Auschwitz. That was the last record I had of them. For years, I accepted that they must be dead. They must have known that we had escaped and I reasoned that if they were alive they would have found a way to contact me.'

'So, what happened to make you start looking again?'

'After University, I joined the Metropolitan police force. It was here that I learned how to carry out proper painstaking thorough investigations always looking for clues that may have been overlooked or dismissed as not being relevant. I became quite a good lateral thinker.'

'Is this why your rise through the ranks was swift, do think?'

'I'm sure it helped.'

'Look at the document that the Usher has handed to you. Do you recognise it?' Vernon Smith nodded.

Sir David Thornfield started to read the document directing the power of the contents to the jury.

Inspector Vernon Smith on the 26 June 1973 displayed outstanding courage and a complete regard for his own safety when faced with a dangerous armed man who did not hesitate to use his weapon. Inspector Smith approached the man who fired and hit him in the shoulder. He drew his weapon and fired a warning shot and continued to advance towards the gunman and wrestled him to the ground before he was able to fire again.

'Were you rewarded for this act of bravery and am I right that this award is only given where the risk of death is deemed extremely high?

'Yes, to both questions. I received the George Cross, Sir.'

Sir David started to read from another document, this was dated December 1982.

Inspector Vernon Smith entered the building ordering his colleagues to remain outside. He was in the entrance hall and about to summon support when he was confronted by a man who produced an automatic machine pistol. Despite the circumstances Inspector Smith had the presence of mind to advise his assailant that the gun was still in a locket position, in the time it took the gunman to glance down, Inspector Smith was able to take the upper hand as a spray of bullets ripped into the ceiling and shattered the glass screen behind them. His colleagues were then able to enter and overpower the gunman.

'Were you rewarded on this occasion?'

'I received the George Medal, Sir.'

'Now turning to your family, you said you started to make enquiries whilst studying law at the LSE, did these produce any results?'

'Not really. What they did do was eliminate certain lines of enquiry, such as missing persons and those released from Russian camps in the 1950s, so that later I knew where not to look.

'So, am I to assume that your eventual position in the Metropolitan police gave you access to files that would otherwise be forbidden for, say members of the jury, to see?'

'Yes, that is correct.'

'Can you tell the court about your research.'

'It may come as a surprise to this court that there are still many aspects of activities today relating to the immediate aftermath of World War II that remain classified. It very soon became apparent to me that I would have to delve into the Allies' intelligence network to discover, if I could, to see what happened to my mother and father. Britain, the US and Russia raced to bring secure Nazi scientists for themselves and that allowed war criminals to escape justice and all these activities remain classified even though the majority of the participants are now deceased.

'Auschwitz was deep in the Russian held territory as they fought their way to Berlin. Whilst the British and American had access to pursue war criminals, most sought refuge in the West not wanting to be caught and summarily executed by the Red Army. My problem was very simple, most of the Soviet era archives are still classified or simply cannot be accessed. Also, much of the intelligence community's work with the Nazis before, during and after the war is still classified.'

'Inspector Smith, so what did you have to do to get behind this curtain of secrecy?'

'To begin with, I had to find the names of those British Intelligence officers who interviewed camp survivors and potential war criminals. That wasn't difficult in my position.'

'Why wasn't that difficult?'

'When a telephone call comes from an Inspector in the Metropolitan police, doors tend to open.' He looked towards the members of the Jury to seeing nodding heads of understanding.

'And you opened quite a few doors, I believe. Tell the Court what you discovered.'

'All were dead ends until one day, sometime during the night at home, I received a series of copy papers that were dated 1945 and 1946. I had them examined privately. I didn't want my personal life to become an embarrassing subject of the Met. No forensics, no finger prints, no postal details were found after examination. Nothing. Someone had been very careful to conceal their own identity.'

Sir David delved into his bundle and produced copies. He handed one to his client and another to Mr Justice Davy and the Court Usher handed copies to each member of the Jury.

'Inspector Smith would you tell the court what is the significance of these papers, please.'

'First of all, they were copies in English, German and Russian and I had experts ensure that all three copies were exact translations. They were. The first few pages contain the names of a few inmates who escaped from Auschwitz.'

'Do you recognise any of those names, Inspector?'

'Yes, my father, Gurt Heidmann and my mother, Elsie Heidmann.'

Sir David turned to papers again.

'What else do these pages contain?'

'On the right-hand side, there is a column headed *"recommended action taken".*'

'Please read to the court the manuscript words against your parents' names in that column.'

'Execution by firing squad.'

There an audible intake of breath as they realised that Inspector Vernon Smith was holding his head in his hands and crying. He pulled a white handkerchief from his pocket and dabbed his face.

'Do you want some time, Inspector?' asked Mr Justice Davy.

'No. I'm fine now.'

'Is there any evidence in those papers to confirm that the recommendation was carried out?' asked Sir David.

'No.'

'So, what did you do next?'

'I had heard of Simon Wiesenthal and decided to visit his Documentation Centre of the Association of Jewish Victims of the Nazi Regime in Vienna in Austria in 1961. As you know he managed to survive the Janowska concentration camp and the Kraków-Płaszów concentration camp. This labour camp was near Auschwitz. I believed that he may have some records that I could inspect. I had been told that he had been active in helping refugees in their search for lost relatives.'

'So, you arranged to visit the Documentation Centre?'

'Yes. I was allowed to inspect some of their records.'

'What did you discover?'

'The records show that the largest and the most notorious of the death marches took place in January 1945 when the Soviet army advanced on occupied Poland. Nine days before the Soviets arrived at the death camp at Auschwitz, the SS marched nearly 60,000 prisoners out of the camp toward Loslau, thirty nine miles away, where they were put on freight trains to other camps. Wiesenthal's records show that approximately 15,000 prisoners died on the way in sub-zero temperatures. Some residents of Upper Silesia tried to help the prisoners, and many prisoners also escaped and regained freedom between Auschwitz and Loslau.'

'Was there any record of your parents reaching Loslau?'

'No and there was no mention of them being liberated by the Russians in Auschwitz either.'

'So, Inspector Smith, at this point, they had disappeared altogether.'

'Yes, completely, but….'

'I am sorry to interrupt this evidence but aren't we getting off the point with this elaborate journey of Inspector Smith's, your Honour?' said Sir Martin Grevelle rising to his feet and tucking his hands under his gown behind his back. 'I have listened very patiently for some time now and I am sure your Honour would like to move on.

Mr Justice Davy lowered his glasses and looked expectantly at Sir David Thornfield.

'Sir David, we already know that the Accused's parents were eventually captured. Why is this journey of search necessary?'

'Your Honour, it is necessary to show that the Accused's parents where not part of the Nazi regime and were never anything other than pawns caught up in a vicious circle of degradation and despair as were thousands of other. However, I ask that you indulge me a little further as I am sure you will agree that I should nullify the Prosecution's assertion of motive and witou that, their case falls.'

Sir David picked up two pieces of paper, with the Wiesenthal Documentation logo at the top of each page, from his table and approached his client.

'Inspector Smith will you read to the Court and the members of the Jury the content of this document.'

This is the Testament of Ifran Klein made this 24 day of March 1945. I have tried to recall accurately all the events that took place on my journey from Auschwitz to the Displaced Persons Camp. If you are reading this I am probably no longer of this world and cannot answer any of your questions but what I say is a true account of my last days in my journey to freedom. One can never forget, such experiences stay with you in detail all the days of your life.

As darkness fell on the first night all those who had survived the march so far huddled together by the roadside just outside a small village. I remember even our guards were beginning to realise that the end was near. I had noticed during the day that some of the SS officers exchanged their clothes for Wehrmacht uniforms and were gradually disappearing into the night. I have no idea what the time was, it was still very dark, when two German inmates I recognised as Kapos Gurt and Elsie Heidmann woke me and those immediately around me. They pointed to the place where the other guards were meant to be watching over us. There was no-one there. Gurt slowly crawled away from us towards the road. No-one stirred. When he returned, he beckoned us to follow. Gurt was still very strong and carried my friend, Tobias Greenbaum, who I had been helping along. Fearful that if we stopped that would be the end for both of us. Quietly and slowly all eight of us disappeared into the darkness away from the village into open countryside. When we were far enough away from the Germans, we settled into forest of pines. I remember the smell was beautiful. Gurt and Elsie left us alone for several hours and to our delight returned with food and water. Nobody asked where it came from, nobody cared, it was our first sustenance for a day and a half, and we were just so grateful.

When darkness fell the next night, Gurt and Elsie led us through the forest. I could tell we were heading west as the sun had

312

set and there remained a red glow on the horizon. After several hours, Gurt could see that Tobias was getting weak again and hoisted my friend onto his back and we continued until dawn. We were trying to avoid roads and rail lines, following cart tracks. One led to a small clearing surrounded by farm building. Gurt ordered us to remain hidden while he approached the main house. What we didn't know then was that a majority of the German-speaking population of Upper Silesia had fled leaving us with coats and boots to wear and food stocks.

Over the next week we began to recover our self-esteem and gain some strength. Later that night, Elsie shook me awake and put her hand over my mouth. Somewhere below us we heard the movement of an intruder. Elsie pulled on her coat and was followed by Gurt. I watched from the landing as the torch beam from kitchen flickered through the open door. Elsie straightened her coat and put her hands through her hair and approached the kitchen. Gurt remained in the shadows and followed her to the door. She pushed it open and stood there momentarily. A cry of horror echoed in the still night air and she ran back into the next room, tripping over the rug saved her life as a gunshot tore through the air splintering the panelling behind her head. I then heard a thud and saw an SS officer fall to the ground motionless. Gurt had hit the man with something. Blood from a head wound glistened on the stone floor by the rug. Another shot rang out and then another as the second SS officer stumbled and fell. By now all of us were awake and clambering out of curiosity down the stairs. We watched as Gurt checked both men. They were dead.

In the darkness that covered the courtyard, we dragged both corpses into the car that had woken Elsie earlier. Gurt got into the driver's seat and disappeared into the night. He never talked about what he done but on his return several hours later, I could smell petrol on him. Well before dawn, we packed our rations and *moved further west passing deserted houses and farm buildings along the way. Just as the sun started to cast its yellow beams across the earth, we stopped to rest in a barn.*

The roar of the jeep's engine as it sped into the farmyard, woke us all at the same time. It was followed by a covered wagon out of which four armed soldiers jumped. We had no idea at first who they were, but we all recognised the small British Union flag flapping in the breeze on the jeep and there was a tangible air of relief as Gurt opened the front door.

Four machine guns were trained on him as he raised his arms high above his head.

'Wer bist du?' shouted the officer.

Gurt pointed to his left arm and pulled down the sleeve of his jacket. The officer immediately relaxed.

'Es gibt andere in,' said Gurt pointing inside and holding up his fingers to indicate seven.

'Kommen, es ist OK,' shouted the officer. 'Englisch sprechen.'

I nodded and stepped forward.

'I am Captain Stuart Campbell, from the Supreme Headquarters Allied Expeditionary Force.'

There was a gasp of surprise that echoed around the Court at the mention of the Captain's name at this point. Inspector Smith continued the narrative, unmoved by the noise.

'Are you all from Auschwitz?'

'Yes.' I rolled up my left sleeve and gestured to the others to do.

'We found the burnt-out wreck of a German car not far from here. SS, I believe. Know anything about it?'

Silence, no-one said a word.

'Right. You better come with us.'

We were asked to get in the lorry and driven several miles west to a makeshift camp. The British officer explained to us that combat operations, ethnic cleansing, and the fear of genocide had uprooted millions of people from their homes all over Europe. The army estimated that between 11 million and 20 million people were displaced. The many, like us, were inmates of Nazi concentration camps, Labour camps and prisoner-of-war camps that were freed by the Allied armies. We were the lucky ones to be picked up by his men, as in portions of Eastern Europe, both civilians and military personnel fled their home countries in fear of the advancing Soviet armies, who were preceded by widespread reports of mass rape, pillaging, looting, and murder.

It was clear to all eight of us that we were now facing an uncertain future. Allied military and civilian authorities faced considerable challenges resettling us. He explained that DPs (Displaced Persons) like us would be sent to their original homes. As we were all German citizens before the war, our situation was simpler than most, but for some Germans where the border was splitting our homeland into East and West, their future was very uncertain and often dangerous.

I and Tobias Greenbaum remained at the camp until in 1949 we were given passage to the newly formed State of Israel. Captain Campbell interrogated all of us. He seemed interested in Gurt and Elsie Heidmann and I told him that without their protection, help and encouragement in the last days,none of us would be alive now. I don't know what happened to them, as they left the camp well before we did.

Signed Ifran Klein.

'Thank you, Inspector.'

In cross-examination, Sir Martin Grevelle, approached Inspector Smith with the police investigation file.

'Forgive me for being a little skeptical, but I have been privy to many such murder cases such as this and I would have expected to see a great deal more evidence gathering, Inspector. What do you have to say?

'Sir, can I say that the substantial evidence from the Coroner's court led me to the conclude very early on that as there was no description of the assailant, no murder weapon, no ballistics to match, no finger prints, no DNA available, so we were at a dead end almost immediately.'

'A perfect murder then?'

'Yes, I suppose you could say so.'

'But for the fact of all the circumstantial evidence point to you. You had motive, opportunity, no alibi, owned a Walther P38 at some point, had Dr Solomon under surveillance and, I my view, didn't investigate the case thoroughly.'

'I didn't murder Dr Isaacs, Sir.'

With that, Sir Martin Grevelle sat down.

Sir David turned to Mr Justice Davey.

'Your Honour, I would like to call Captain Campbell to the stand, with your leave.'

The Jury looked towards where Captain Campbell was seated and watched him rise and walk to the witness box.

'You have heard the written evidence recited by my client from Ifran Klein. This document comes from an impeccable source and I am sure you would not want to question the Wiesenthal Centre's authority in these matters. Do you agree?'

'No. I wouldn't presume to do so.'

'Good. So, your notes make no mention of conversations with Mr Klein concerning the exploits of Gurt and Elsie Heidmann. Why is that?'

'Well, my instructions were to gather evidence for the War Crimes Commission. As you will already appreciate from what you have heard in this courtroom, the situation that confronted the British and Americans was chaotic. We were dealing with millions of displaced persons and those Germans who fought against us trying to return to their homeland, some disguised other not.

'I was fortunate to meet with the late Solomon Isaacs. Solomon was a remarkable man with a prodigious capacity for total recall of events. The evidence he gave us relating to events in Auschwitz including detailed descriptions of the Commandant, SS officers and staff resulted in the apprehension of men who were directly responsible for many atrocities there. Many others corroborated his evidence. I had no doubt that he was telling the truth.

'That said, I also have no doubt that what happened to Ifran Klein and the others took place in their immediate escape from certain death on that march and the Gurt and Elsie Heidmann did all they could to remain alive. However, you have not considered the important point here.'

Sir David stood and approached the dock and looked Campbell straight in the eye.

'And what important point am I and my client missing?'

Captain Campbell looked away from the stare and fixed his eyes on the Jury.

'Like many camps in Eastern Poland, instructions came to destroy them and remove the prisoners that had survived. It was a hopeless task in Auschwitz. There were too many bodies dead and alive. It was at this point that Kapos Gurt and Elsie Heidmann were again afraid for their lives. They no longer had the protection of the SS and German camp guards. You have to remember they were *Lagerpolizist* (camp police) with armbands to identify their station within the camp. When I interviewed them, they were dressed in their camp clothes. Gone were their armbands but they were better nourished than the others. I found this suspicious. I had previously interviewed a woman who told me that it was tempting to become a Kapo but to push around their mates, to spy on them, to denounce them for extra rations and other perquisites, was not something her conscience would allow. She'd rather die than live without integrity. It was at this time that I realised that whatever Mr Klein told me in 1945 confirmed my suspicion that again Gurt and Elsie Heidmann had made another pact with themselves.'

'And what pact was that, Captain Campbell?'

'To survive at any cost. They were now just Jewish prisoners once again. None of the other six men, we captured at the farmhouse, knew the Heidmann until the march. They were under the control of other Kapos not Mr Heidmann. They never witnessed their criminal behaviour in the camp.'

'So, you did not consider any mitigating circumstances in passing sentence?'

'You think it was I who passed sentence. I am sorry but you are sadly mistaken. I was accountable to a

318

tribunal of senior officers from the American and British Armies of Occupation. Do you mind showing me those copies that your client said he received mysteriously through his letterbox?'

Captain Campbell examined the manuscript part carefully under the heading "recommended action".

'Is that your handwriting, Captain?'

'Yes, it is.'

'So, based on your submission of the evidence of Mr Solomon Isaacs alone and no other information, the tribunal sentenced my client's parents to death.'

'There was other collaborative evidence as I have said so as the interrogating officer, I merely wrote down the tribunal's final recommendation. In any event, may I remind you that it is your client, not me, who is on trial for murder,' said Campbell with vehemence in his voice directed at Defence Counsel.

The Jury appeared to have some sympathy with Captain Campbell and after he had recovered his composure and taken a sip of water, he noticed a new face appear through the court entrance door and wave a piece of papers at him. Captain Campbell turned to the Judge.

'I appreciate that this may be unusual, but last evening I took advantage of the time and telephoned my old intelligence section, now part of MI5. I do believe that my request for information has just arrived by messenger. I have no idea of the results, your Honour but ask that you read these papers?' he beckoned the messenger forward and two sets of papers were handed to Mr Justice Davy before anyone could object. Both barristers were on their feet ready to object to this strange turn of events.

Chapter 68

Mr Justice Davey asked Prosecuting and Defence Counsel to approach the bench. He handed a copy each to them. The silence around the Courtroom was tangible whilst the next move was anticipated.

Sir David Thornfield walked to his client and showed him the new evidence. A whispered conversation took place. If anyone was close enough, they would have heard Sir David advise his client that the Judge would insist that the papers were a vital part of the case and there would be no point in objecting. They would also have heard that Sir David, if his client was convicted, would appeal and call for a mistrial. Their attack on motive was bearing fruit by pure chance. Inspector Vernon Smith tried hard to conceal a faint smile that passed over his face.

Turning to Prosecuting Counsel, 'If you have no objection, Sir Martin, I propose that we let Sir David read this to the Court for the Defence.' Knowing that the Prosecution case could not be prejudiced, Sir Martin Grevelle concurred with a nod of the head and sat down.

'Captain Campbell, can you remain in the witness box but please be seated.'

The jury now focussed attention on Sir David as he stood facing them, his half-moon glasses perched precariously on the bridge of his nose. He began to read slowly and deliberately pausing now and again to ensure that none of this evidence was missed.

This is the transcript of an unofficial Report written by the Allied Forces Intelligence Agency (AFIA) in Munich on the 26 July 1946. It has been collated by members of the Agency who were employed to oversee that the International Committee of the Red Cross were assisted in documenting the treatment of German citizens and prisoners of war. By far the greatest number who have died in captivity were held by the Soviets. We are unable to give an exact figure, but the numbers indicate many hundreds of thousands. It is not without regret that some of those were handed over by the British and American armies whilst in their care.

Sir David read the addendum before continuing with the transcript. There was a note attached to the papers explaining that of the thousands of names that were recorded as handed over to the Soviet Army of Occupation, they have been edited out for the sake of brevity.

For example, two German Jews, Gurt and Elsie Heidmann were held by the British pending execution for the part in crimes at Auschwitz. On the 29 September 1945 a small delegation from the NKVD (State Security Police) submitted to the AFIA a demand for the release to them of several hundred prisoners. Each name had a resume of charges against it. Their request was accepted and two days later a convoy of lorries arrived at the camp and took the prisoners away.

Sir David returned to his desk and picked up the papers to continue to examine Captain Campbell's evidence.

'Captain Campbell, did you know that the death sentence was never carried out by the British?'

'No. I was unaware, until now, that your client's parents became Soviet prisoners. I had assumed that the sentence was carried out.'

As Captain Campbell walked away from the witness box. Mr Justice Davy suggested that the court adjourn until Monday morning.

Chapter 69

Sir Martin Grevelle and Sir David Thornfield entered Mr Justice Davy's chamber at 9 am on the Monday morning. Sir Martin had requested the conference.

'Martin what is going on?' said Jeffrey Davey. In the privacy of the Judge's chambers, it was first name terms, all formality forgotten.

'Well, Jeffrey, I have been discussing this case with David over lunch yesterday. I received a telephone call from the Prosecution Service late on Friday evening after we adjourned. It seems that we have a new witness who to date had been reluctant to come forward for personal reasons and ill health. I have given a copy of the evidence taken by the police to David.

'David, what do you have to say?'

'Too say the least, Jeffrey, it doesn't help my client's case and initially I was going to ask you to deny Martin's application to call this new witness. However, on reflection and after yesterday's discussion with Martin, we both think that justice will be best served by further disclosure and that it will bring closure to this very sorry matter.'

'On that basis, gentlemen, I will read the new papers and will make up my own decision bearing in mind your joint views. I assume Martin that you will ask the usual permission once we are in open court and that you will object, David.'

They both nodded and left Mr Justice Davy to relax in his armchair with the bundle of new evidence.

Chapter 70

The main court door opened, and the Usher assisted an old man with walking stick, immaculately dressed in dark grey suit with white shirt and blue tie, as he made his was slowly to the witness box.

Nadine gasped aloud as she saw Captain Bron take the stand and held Stewart's hand in a vice-like grip.

After swearing to tell the truth, the whole truth and stating his name clearly for all to hear, the witness asked if he could be seated.

'Why, may I ask, did you feel obliged at this late stage to come forward and talk to the police?'

'I have been following the case closely. You may not have noticed me, but I have been in court since the start of evidence, not as you see me now but much more modestly dressed. I did not want anyone to recognise me as he fumbled to put on some heavy rimmed glasses.'

'Why was that?'

'I know of all the main witnesses, the deceased and of your client and I know of matters first-hand that no-one here is aware of.

'Can you tell us what those are?'

'It was 1946, I had been imprisoned since 1942 and was moved from one Gulag to another. We were treated harshly by the Soviets as many of the camps were run by convicted criminals. The camps included

326

others from the war in Yugoslavia and Poland. We were prisoners and toiled as slave labour for years.'

The witness described harrowing stories of life in Soviet Russia. Counsel for both sides allowed the witness to ramble, but the Sir Martin interrupted.

'Sorry and I know this must bring back terrible memories, but can you now direct your mind to the events of 15 April 1952.'

'I was moved to Vyatlag was one of the largest prison camps in the GULAG system when I arrived there were more than 20,000 prisoners. Political prisoners were sent there for counter-revolutionary or other subversive activities, treason, spying or terrorism, and there were the criminals as well as hundreds of German POWs. The work they did was building a railway and logging.

'I was assigned to settlement no 11 in the very north, nearer to Syktyvkar, capital of the Komi Republic. I was in a group of about eighty prisoners and we were force marched from the station. It was night-time when we arrived, but there was light shining all around and I thought to myself that, thank heavens, the village didn't look too bad but as I was being taken to a wooden hut I began to realise it wasn't a village but a camp with watchtowers, guards with guns and dogs. The hut was small with four trestle beds in it, on one of which a woman in a red coat was asleep. I said, "There must be some mistake here, surely men and women live separately?" but was told that, no, everyone lives together here. The woman, it turned out, had come here with her husband, a fellow prisoner. That woman's name was Elsie Heidmann and later that first night I met Gurt Heidmann.

'Let us be clear. You are telling us that the accused parents were alive and well in 1953.'

'Yes, Sir. Let's just say they were alive. None of us were well.'

'Are you able tell us what happened after that first meeting?'

'We were assigned to the same work group, felling trees in the forest. They found out that I was a Captain in the German army and assumed I was also a Nazi. We got into some vicious arguments. They couldn't accept that I was a Wehrmacht officer not a member of the SS. They accused me of being responsible for their plight. The Russian guards took great pleasure in seeing German prisoners at each other's throats.'

Bron took a sip of water as he looked at the rapped attention the jury were giving him, he then continued to explain the continued goading and threats he received daily from Gurt and Elsie Heidmann then his voice faltered, and he stopped. An eerie silence hung over the court. Finally, he turned to Inspector Smith sitting between two police officers and shouted at him.

'You killed the wrong man, Inspector. I killed your parents. It was either them or me. Do you understand?'

Uproar burst out in the courtroom as Captain Bron held his head in his hands, cried and slumped to the floor holding his chest. Nadine ran to him shouting his name. Stewart Isaacs started CPR and managed to restarted Bron's heart.

Chapter 71

The Boar's Head Inn London

'I don't think there was much doubt about the guilty verdict. Campbell's evidence was a pretty good clincher giving the evidence about Solomon's recollections as you did yourself, Jonny.'

Graham Rainham held his pint of beer aloft and nodded at Jonny in a gesture of well done. 'Not quite what we expected. *Too many loose ends,* that's what you said about the manuscript, Jonny.'

'Bron's evidence seemed to be one of personal closure. Sitting in that courtroom, he could have pulled that stunt much earlier.'

'Why didn't he?'

"I am going to see him now he's recovered from his heart attack, but that's not a question I'm going to ask, Graham. It just seems not to matter anymore and in any case Nadine has asked to go with me.

'I'm no match maker but something tells me they'll make each other happy for the first time in years,' said Rainham with a twinkle in his eye.

Johann Bron looked better than either Nadine or Jonny had hoped. He seemed to have had a new lease of life. They sat outside under the shade of large umbrella. Johann's face shielded under an ancient panama hat. Nadine sat beside him and put her hand on his arm, he covered it with his and smiled into her eyes, she turned to Jonny.

'Are you going to publish?'

'Yes, but only if you agree. You're his heir. It's your decision, of course, I'd like to if only to bring finality.' Nadine nodded her approval.

Chapter 72

October 21 had arrived all too quickly. Despite the early autumn chill in the air, the sun at midday day illuminated the exterior of what the designers, Captain Francis Fowke and Major-General Henry Scott, had hoped would be a modern version of an ancient amphitheatre as the foundation stone was laid in 1867. It certainly felt like that as the Rufus Alroyd, Jonny and Nadine Solomon walked towards the elevated stage. Behind them as they faced what would be an audience of several hundred, hung a collage of images representing important points in Solomon's narrative.

Grange House Publications had received a generous sum for the film rights to *Stealing the Staircase* and so such an auspicious and expensive event was now beginning to make sense.

Nadine sat down and leaned her arms on the table dais in front of him. She held her head in her hands looking at the Royal Crest in the distance, deep in thought. Her mind wandered back in time. Had she done the right thing? She had not read Queen Victoria's speech when she opened the Hall in 1871 as a practical memorial to her late husband Albert who died six years earlier. She must have had her doubts about the occasion and how it was going to be received, just like her. Stewart, her son, had reluctantly agreed to support

331

her and sat in the front row with Johann Bron and Captain Campbell.

The three retired, in silence, to the back-stage area. Each was tense in their own way. Rufus knew the book was going to be a monumental success. The feed-back from the ARCs, all two hundred of them, was incredibly encouraging. Advance orders were pouring in and Grange House would be hard pressed to meet the worldwide distribution dates.

He could not help himself from peering into the auditorium as the guests took their seats. As befits such a venue, everyone despite the afternoon timing, had dressed appropriately. As two o'clock arrived he shook Nadine's hand and patted Jonny on the shoulder.

'And, so to battle,' he whispered as the curtain opened and the three walked purposefully amid rapturous applause onto the stage and took their seats.

Rufus introduced Jonny and Nadine, but it was quite unnecessary. He covered the usual pleasantries and then launched into why Grange House had such pleasure in offering *Stealing the Staircase* to a worldwide audience. Not many were listening too intently, it was Nadine they'd come to hear, but they'd have to wait. Jonny recalled the Osborne case and the unusual way the manuscript came into his hands. Mrs Green, at Jonny's insistence, had been invited and when Jonny pointed her out at the back of the Hall, she burst into tears she couldn't control, as all eyes swivelled to see who the mystery lady was. They clapped generously. Jonny sat down.

Rufus then turned to Nadine. Her time had come. She stood and gave a deep bow. Everyone stood in unison and eventually once the hoots and clapping had finished, she sat down again. Time hung perilously in the air. Rufus and Jonny began to worry as they looked at each other. The audience was just about to wonder what was happening when she began to speak.

'You will have to forgive me, but years ago Solomon asked an old man, many years older than he at the time, to what do you attribute your great age. "Simple the man said, when I'm standing and I can sit down, I sit and when I sitting, and I can lie down, I lie down". Nadine got up and stepped to the front of the dais and lay down and for the next few minutes remained there, she seemed to be mesmerized, looking at the backdrop behind as she faced away from the audience, with the picture of a young Solomon Isaacs gazing out from the collage of his life. Another uproar cascaded around the auditorium as she slowly rose to her feet.

Nadine's speech started with the work of code that Solomon produced in Belmarsh. No-one in the audience had any idea that he had smuggled his book out of prison and were now silent as she gave them examples of the code he formulated. She then turned to Rufus. None of this was in the carefully prepared script from Grange House, but what the hell, she had this audience in her hand just as he'd hoped.

'Have you a copy of the seating arrangement, Rufus. I only know where Wendy, Mrs Green, is sitting?'

Rufus shook his head. Back-stage, the Manager beckoned and within a few seconds a large plan appeared. She scanned it and handed it back.

She then started to rattle off all the names and who they represented in order along the front row. Each one looked at their neighbour, as she ventured along the line.

'It's easy when to how,' she chuckled. She was no Solomon with his photographic memory but she'd practised this quietly behind everyone's back just to give life to his intellectual ability.

Rufus whispered in Jonny's ear, 'that's another million copies!'

It was now that she started on the real script. It was based primarily on the collage behind the dais. At one stage, tears streamed done her face as she recalled the suffering in Auschwitz.

'Forgive me, even now I think of those poor little ones who never had a chance to live as long as me and for those who have suffered, may we not forget your torment'

She dabbed her eyes but was unable to continue and mumbled, 'I am sorry, I thought this was all over,' as she sat down to complete silence. Then as one, everyone rose and clapped.

The End

KEEP IN TOUCH

Thank you for taking the time to journey through my fictional account of some harrowing times during the C20th century with Solomon Isaacs and Jonny Wightman in **Prisoner 441**. Auschwitz is real. What happened there and in all other concentration camps was appalling. Porton Down is real but only glimpses when things go wrong are documented for us to read. I hope you felt that the different threads of secrecy can be dangerous depending on where they occur or who the lawmakers are. If you would like to contact me with your thoughts, visit geoff@geoffleather.com or my website; www.geoffleather.com

Get your free no-obligation download today. Visit geoffleather.com

Mike Randell, Economic Attaché to the British Embassy in Cairo, is not all he seems. His secret life is hidden from his colleagues and contacts until he is summoned to investigate the disappearance of a British National, Jason Eldridge.

Colonel Ragia Nassar of the Egyptian Police Force, who has known Mike since their days at University in London and has also been investigating the disappearance.

Working together they uncover a ritual murder in the backstreets of Cairo, a scene that poses more questions than answers, leading Mike into the dangerous world of Egyptian nationalism with murders stretching back to 1906.

When Mike and his Australian girlfriend realise that their lives may be threatened, how far will Mike's boss at MI6 override his clearance and divulge secret files?

How far will Colonel Ragia Nassar go without jeopardising his own position to help them?

SEE BELOW FOR DETAILS

337

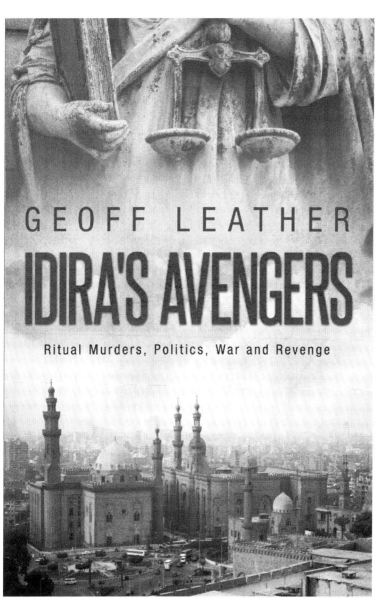

GEOFF LEATHER

IDIRA'S AVENGERS

Ritual Murders, Politics, War and Revenge

visit my website www.geoffleather.com

ACKNOWLEDGEMENTS

Thanks to David at d.ology Ltd for guiding me through the pitfalls of computing with his vast knowledge of the science and explaining to me in simple terms how to connect lose ends and to May for her additional incisive input.

Thanks to Warren Design for juggling my ideas and thoughts into great covers.

To Chris and Cliff Freeman who struggled through some early efforts with encouraging words.

To my children, Rachel, Sophie and David, who were never bored with at my constant questioning.

To those at Jericho Writers for their invaluable advice.

But most of all to my wife, Judy, who read the drafts, suggested better ways of expression and wording and kept up my spirits when they were flagging.

COMING SOON

A DEADLY PRICE TO PAY

Hidden away in a Tea Plantation in Sri Lanka the scientists make a sensational discovery in their search for revenge. News of their work on coca plant leaks out and puts their lives and those closest in danger. They need protection and help from abroad.

Surviving an attempt on their lives they arrive in Britain and a covert operation is put together with a former SAS officer, the American Drugs Enforcement Agency and the Columbian police.

Two deaths and one murder are personal. Three grieving families and only one suspect. Can two research scientists, one British Police Superintendent and a Columbian Drug Squad officer take on a powerful Cartel boss and win?

GEOFF LEATHER

A DEADLY
PRICE TO PAY

MURDER, DRUGS AND POTENT REVENGE

Printed in Great Britain
by Amazon